W9-BYI-496

"**I should have known,**" Michael said quietly, desire deepening his voice.

The moonlight glowed on Cassidy's pale skin and tousled hair as she stood by the window. The sight of her took his breath away and fired his imagination.

"You should have known what?" she asked.

"You're supposed to stay off that foot, remember?" he said.

"Is that why you're here, to yell at me one more time before you go to bed?" Cassidy trembled slightly as Michael moved close and cupped her face in his hand.

"I couldn't sleep until I had the answer to a question that's been driving me nuts," he murmured.

She didn't push him away. "You think I might have the answer?"

"I'm sure of it." His gaze slid down to her mouth. "I can't wait any longer to find out how you taste. . . ."

WHAT ARE *LOVESWEPT* ROMANCES?

They are stories of true romance and touching emotion. We believe those two very important ingredients are constants in our highly sensual and very believable stories in the *LOVESWEPT* line. Our goal is to give you, the reader, stories of consistently high quality that may sometimes make you laugh, sometimes make you cry, but are always fresh and creative and contain many delightful surprises within their pages.

Most romance fans read an enormous number of books. Those they truly love, they keep. Others may be traded with friends and soon forgotten. We hope that each *LOVESWEPT* romance will be a treasure—a "keeper." We will always try to publish

LOVE STORIES YOU'LL NEVER FORGET
BY AUTHORS YOU'LL ALWAYS REMEMBER

The Editors

Loveswept ® 586

Patt Bucheister
Struck by Lightning

BANTAM BOOKS
NEW YORK · TORONTO · LONDON · SYDNEY · AUCKLAND

STRUCK BY LIGHTNING

A Bantam Book / December 1992

LOVESWEPT® *and the wave design are registered*
trademarks of Bantam Books, a division of
Bantam Doubleday Dell Publishing Group, Inc.
Registered in U.S. Patent
and Trademark Office and elsewhere.

All rights reserved.
Copyright © 1992 by Patt Bucheister.
Cover art copyright © 1992 by Ed Tadiello.
No part of this book may be reproduced or transmitted
in any form or by any means, electronic or mechanical,
including photocopying, recording, or by any
information storage and retrieval system, without
permission in writing from the publisher.
For information address: Bantam Books.

If you purchased this book without a cover you should be
aware that this book is stolen property. It was reported as
"unsold and destroyed" to the publisher and neither the
author nor the publisher has received any payment for this
"stripped book."

If you would be interested in receiving protective vinyl
covers for your Loveswept books, please write to this address
for information:

Loveswept
Bantam Books
P.O. Box 985
Hicksville, NY 11802

ISBN 0-553-44315-1

Published simultaneously in the United States and Canada

Bantam Books are published by Bantam Books, a division of
Bantam Doubleday Dell Publishing Group, Inc. Its trademark,
consisting of the words "Bantam Books" and the portrayal of
a rooster, is Registered in U.S. Patent and Trademark Office
and in other countries. Marca Registrada. Bantam Books, 666
Fifth Avenue, New York, New York 10103.

PRINTED IN THE UNITED STATES OF AMERICA

OPM   0 9 8 7 6 5 4 3 2 1

Preface

The rhythmic tapping of long, artistic fingers on the polished surface of the desk was the only sound in the room, and it drew the housekeeper's attention from the view outside the window.

"You'd think after all these years you would have learned patience," she said in her broad English speech that betrayed her cockney origins.

King Knight's American accent was the same as it had been a decade ago when he'd come to live in England. "And you'd think after all these years you would have learned respect for your employer." He smiled when she gave him a look that could sour milk.

Alvilda Gump's usual amiable expression had been replaced by frown lines across her forehead and around her mouth. Though decorously clothed in a flowered dress with a white lace collar, she was not the type of person to stand on ceremony, and she spoke to King with the familiarity of long acquaintance.

She shook her head slowly in exasperation. "At your age, I thought you were through doing dumb things, King Knight. It seems I was wrong."

The leather chair squeaked as the large, gray-haired man leaned back in it, his gaze amused rather than offended. "Why is it dumb to want my children settled and happy, Alvilda?"

"They are settled," she argued. "Michael has his ranch in Montana. Turner's a fancy corporate lawyer. Ryder's digging his oil wells, and Silver is turning Wall Street on its ear. They are all content and happy with their lives. You saw that for yourself when they were here for your birthday last month."

"My seventieth birthday," he muttered, his disgusted tone making it clear what he thought of that particular number. "My birthday made me realize I have to do something about their single status before another year passes. If I wait for them to find someone, I'll either be too old to enjoy their children or dead."

"You're too old now to be playing patty cake with children."

He gave her an affronted look. "You're fired."

"Again?"

"Damn right again. The day I'm too old to play patty cake or any other game with my grandchildren is the day I take my last breath."

"You don't have any grandchildren."

"That's why I'm going ahead with my plans," he said, exasperation in each word. "Those kids of mine need a good shaking up."

"All four of your children are adults now, King. You can't move them around like pieces on your precious chessboard."

"I'm not moving them around. I'd call it giving them a little push in the right direction."

The elderly housekeeper made a rude sound as she turned away from the window. She walked over to the glass display case built into one wall of the study, rising nearly to the ceiling. Ignoring the many awards, plaques, swords, and antique guns that hung against the red tapestry background, she stood in front of a specially built glass case placed within the larger one. She stared at the gold chess pieces and the game board, which resembled a stone and mortar castle.

Alvilda ran her forefinger over one of the five indentations in the frame of the glass case, each shaped in the form of a knight's shield. Only when all the shields were put into place could the case be opened. Each of the five lock mechanisms was different, requiring the correct counterpart in place to release the intricate security system. King and each of his four children possessed one of the shields apiece.

"Aren't they going to wonder," she asked. "why you didn't ask them to bring their shields with them when they came for your birthday?"

"I'm telling them I didn't have an offer to buy the set then." He grinned at her shocked look. Holding up his hand, he warded off the protest he could see bubbling to the surface. "There has been an offer, but I turned it down just like I've turned down every other offer I've ever received. I wouldn't sell the set for any amount of money. You know that and I know that. I'm relying on my sons and daughter being unsure whether I will or not. They need to be shaken up, to realize there is more to life than horses, court cases, oil wells, and stocks and bonds."

"I don't suppose there is any way I can talk you out of this ridiculous scheme?"

His mouth twisted into a rueful smile. "Isn't that what you've been doing for the last hour when all I wanted was my afternoon tea?"

When he saw his teasing didn't get the result he'd hoped for, he became serious. Leaning his arms on the desk, he sat forward in his chair.

"I've achieved everything I wanted as an artist. I couldn't ask for four finer children. I wish Myrna could have been by my side longer than the thirty years we had together, but her memory will always be with me. I've had an exciting, satisfying life that isn't by any means over, yet I find I'm greedy. I want grandchildren before it's too late to enjoy them. Several months ago, just before he died, Robert Harrold told me that one of the deepest regrets he had was that he probably wouldn't be around to see his daughter's children. I don't want to have the same regret when it's my time to go. I want to know Knight blood will flow in the veins of another generation. I want the sound of children laughing in this house again. Is that so wrong?"

"It's not wrong to want grandchildren," Alvilda said gently. "It's the way you plan to manipulate your children I'm objecting to, King. Manipulating your adult children, might I add. You and Myrna raised them to be independent, free-thinking people with minds of their own. Now you're saying you're going to trick them into meeting the people you think they should marry. When they find out you've hired investigators, pried into their personal lives, they aren't going to like it one bit."

"They aren't going to find out. I'm certainly not going to tell them, and I don't think you will either even though you don't approve. Myrna and I could always count on your loyalty, Alvilda."

"I give up." She threw up her hands in a gesture of defeat. "Do whatever you want. You will anyway. I just hope this whole thing doesn't backfire on you."

He rubbed his hands together with obvious relish. "I've got it all worked out. Timing is everything."

"So who's your first victim?"

Unabashed by her disapproving tone, King grinned. "The first demand for the shield went out this morning. To Michael."

One

The tall man wearing cowboy boots, a sheepskin jacket, and a western hat looked as though he had wandered onto the wrong movie set. He would have looked more at home stalking over a hard-packed Texas corral than strolling across the heather-covered moors of Somerset County in Great Britain.

His hands were shoved deep into the pockets of his fleece-lined jacket, the collar turned up around his neck, and his hat pulled down low to keep his black hair from being whipped around by the wind. His smoky blue eyes were directed upward as he assessed how soon the heavy clouds over-head would dump rain on him. He'd spent enough time in his father's adopted country to know rain wasn't all that unusual for March in England. Or for any other month.

The somber sky matched Michael Knight's mood

perfectly, dark and gloomy with a more than even chance of a storm.

He was also impatient, frustrated, and near enough to being cranky that he'd taken his lousy attitude outside rather than alienate his father's housekeeper completely.

It wasn't Alvilda's fault that King had suddenly gone on a research jaunt the day before Michael arrived. When King went on one of his searches for background material, he visited stables and various landscapes, filling up a sketchbook with details that would later appear in the portraits he painted of horses. Since King rarely knew where he would end up, he didn't leave any address or phone number where he could be reached. Sometimes he would be gone only a few hours, sometimes several days, and occasionally a couple of weeks.

Michael hadn't called his father from Montana before he left or from London Heathrow Airport after he arrived. He hadn't wanted to give King any warning that he was coming. Obviously, it wouldn't have made any difference. According to Alvilda, his father had left Knight's Keep the day after he'd sent the fax to Michael, demanding that he bring his shield to England immediately.

Michael bent down to break off a sprig of heather and rolled the stem between his fingers. It wasn't like his father to run away from a fight, but that's what it looked like King had done. And that was one of the things that had Michael worried. King was unpredictable and somewhat eccentric, but not when it came to standing his ground when he felt he was right.

Michael brushed aside the low-hanging branch of a birch tree with more force than was necessary, but the gesture did nothing to diminish the frustration tensing his muscles. He was accustomed to activity, to dealing with either his strength or his mind with whatever stood in his way. This feeling of impotence wasn't something he was used to, and he hated not being in control.

The heels of his brown leather boots dug into the soft earth beneath the coarse grass and patches of heather as his thoughts drifted back to the Quarter K. Snow had been falling at the ranch when he'd left, and there had been a forecast of more to come. This wasn't a good time for him to be away, not when there was so much work to be done. Not that any other time would have been better, he conceded. In early spring, though, the weather was especially unpredictable and could create a lot of problems. He should be there, not here in merry old England waiting for King to return so he could find out why his father was considering selling a part of their family history. Michael couldn't wait indefinitely. He would hang around for another day, maybe two, then leave if King didn't show up.

If his father wanted his shield, he could come to Montana to get it. And bring a damn good reason along with him.

Shoving his hands back into the pockets of his coat, Michael glared at the threatening sky. What was his father up to? he wondered again. That question had turned over and over in his mind since he'd read the latest fax from his father.

When he'd first seen the familiar letterhead—an

artist's rendering of Knight's Keep—Michael had expected another not so subtle hint from his father about getting married. Ever since his brother Turner had given King a fax machine for his birthday, Michael and his brothers and sister had been bombarded almost daily with dispatches extolling the many virtues of marriage and parenthood. Michael's personal favorite was the list of medical statistics suggesting married men live longer than single men. His brother Ryder, who had received the same bulletin, had sent copies to Michael and Turner of his reply to King. In large block letters, Ryder had printed: IT ONLY SEEMS LONGER!

Michael hadn't been able to get in touch with his brothers or sister before leaving for England. He'd left too quickly and hadn't wanted to wait until he could talk to them. He knew Turner, Ryder, and Silver wouldn't allow their shields to be used either, and King needed all four of them plus his own to open the specially built glass case. Michael had always considered that security measure excessive, but now he was glad it was in place. His father couldn't open the case, and thereby sell the chess set, unless the rest of the family agreed. And Michael certainly wasn't going to agree unless King could come up with a damn good explanation for wanting to sell a family heirloom.

As he stepped out of the woods behind his father's large William and Mary country house, he heard the sound of hoofbeats. Glancing around, he couldn't see any sign of a horse and rider, but the sound was unmistakable to a man who had been around horses most of his life.

His long strides covered the ground swiftly as he climbed to the top of a hill to get a better view of the countryside. Even though his father had a stable of horses, there wasn't anyone at Knight's Keep who would be riding them at this time of day. The stable lads exercised the horses early in the morning, and it was nearly noon.

Maybe King had returned.

The sound came closer. Michael turned to see a chestnut mare sail over a three-foot-high hedge. The rider was bent low over the neck of the horse, hands clasping the reins against the horse's dark mane.

Michael sucked in his breath.

He had heard the phrase "poetry in motion," but this was the first time he'd ever seen it quite so breathtakingly portrayed.

As the horse and rider came closer, he could tell that the person riding the horse was definitely not his father, or even a man. Tight white breeches clung to slender thighs, black riding boots encased her calves. As the woman and horse soared over another hedgerow, he caught a glimpse of an ivory turtleneck sweater under her brown and tan tweed jacket. A black English-style riding cap hid her hair.

Michael knew every horse in his father's stables, and this Morgan mare was not one of them. Even from a distance he could tell the horse was not young, which would explain why the rider wasn't forcing her over higher jumps. The rider wasn't any of the stable hands King had hired either. Michael would certainly have remembered if he had ever seen her before.

He couldn't take his gaze off her, and he wondered who she was. She rode as though she and the horse were one entity. He wondered, too, about the athletic body under her riding clothes. Experienced horsewomen had strong thighs, and he found himself pondering how her legs would feel clasped around him.

Shoving his hands deeper into his pockets, he tried to force his body to cool down. It wasn't like him to get turned on by the familiar sight of a woman riding a horse.

He didn't look away, though. The woman rode with a hint of recklessness, even though her experience was obvious. Michael had seen the same sort of abandon when a rider was racing against a clock or competing against other horsemen. Or was attempting to outrun a personal demon.

His curiosity grew with every passing second.

As the woman directed the mare toward a set of thick shrubs higher and broader than any they'd already jumped, Michael started forward. She'd set the horse too far back for the jump; they'd never clear it.

Michael was ten yards away when she tumbled out of the saddle. The horse had suddenly stiffened its front legs, stopping rather than attempting the jump. The woman didn't make a sound when she hit the ground. She also didn't move.

The mare was nuzzling the unconscious woman's shoulder as Michael ran up. He slowed his pace when the horse jerked her head up, protesting his presence by shaking her head back and forth.

"Easy girl," he murmured. "I only want to make sure she's okay."

The bridle jangled as the mare again shook her head, but she took several steps back to allow Michael closer to the fallen rider.

Kneeling on one knee, Michael took a few seconds to look at the woman's face. Her cap had fallen off and long, wavy strands of hair the color of burnished straw were spread out on the coarse heather under her head. Light brown lashes lay on porcelain skin and her lips were slightly parted. The bottom one was full and sensuous, a temptation to any man to taste and savor.

Michael gave himself a mental shake and tore his gaze away from the woman's mouth. Unbuttoning her tweed riding jacket, he gently pressed his hands against her slender rib cage to check for breaks, returning his gaze to her face to catch any reaction to his probing. When he didn't see any sign of distress, he ran his fingers over her slim waist, her hips, and each shapely leg, then moved up to her shoulders, searching for any signs of injury to her arms and then her wrists and hands.

A slow liquid heat burned into the pit of his stomach, and his callused fingers tingled from the feel of her strong body. His clinical exam was changing to something entirely different, entirely personal.

He didn't know her name, but he felt as though he'd been struck by lightning, singed to the bone with desire. His hands lingered on her rib cage just under her breast, no longer concentrating on anything but the feel of her.

When he suddenly heard her speak, he jerked

his hands away from her body. Sitting back on his heels, he stared down at her. Her eyes were still closed as she cursed with a remarkable versatility in a clipped English accent. The bulk of her tirade was directed at herself and her ability as a rider.

Over the years Michael had heard a wide variety of responses from riders who had taken a spill off a horse. His own usually consisted of a short, blunt oath or two before he dusted himself off and got back into the saddle. Hers was definitely in a class all its own.

When she paused to take a breath, he interjected, "Where I come from, you'd get your mouth washed out with soap for using language like that."

Her lashes rose instantly, and clear green eyes met his. "Who the bloody hell are you?"

"I was just going to ask you the same question." His smile softened his accusation. "You're trespassing."

Her gaze shifted briefly to take in his western-style hat, then returned to meet his eyes. "Ah," she murmured. "The cowboy from Montana."

He raised a brow. "How do you know I'm from Montana?"

"King has mentioned his four offspring in glowing detail. Your western attire gave you away. You have to be the one who's a rancher in Montana, or else I've died and gone to cowboy heaven."

"I'm the furthest thing from an angel here or in Montana," he said with amusement.

"Then that leaves my original theory."

"I have a name."

"I have one too. Isn't that a coincidence?"

Michael fought against a feeling of being lost in a foggy maze as he struggled to follow her conversation.

"Mine is Michael Knight," he said. "Since you're obviously acquainted with my father, you must know you're on his land."

She patted the ground she was lying on. "I certainly am. Is Nougat all right?"

"Who's Nougat?"

"My horse."

The sound of a hoof scraping the ground drew her head around. Relief softened her features when she saw the animal standing several feet away, apparently unharmed.

"Just be glad your horse had more sense than you did. You could have broken your neck and possibly hers if she'd tried to jump that hedge. Your mare isn't a young horse."

She plucked a sprig of heather out of the dirt and held it up. "This has more sense than I do at the moment."

He couldn't argue with that. "Why don't you try getting up? I don't think you've damaged anything, but we'll never know until you try to stand."

"If you don't mind," she muttered, "I'd like to commune with nature a little longer."

He grinned. Damned if he didn't like that tart note in her voice. He'd always preferred spirit over passivity in his horses. Now he realized he liked it in a woman as well. Especially this woman.

He straightened to his full height, towering over her supine figure. "Since you're obviously an experienced rider, this wouldn't be the first time

you've fallen off a horse. You know the proce-
dure."

She moved her legs and took a deep breath to
test her ribs, then flexed her arms and wrists.
When everything worked to her satisfaction, she
ignored his outstretched hand and pushed herself
up.

Michael felt his blood heat as she brushed her
hands across her taut bottom several times. He
knew she was only removing any debris from her
fall, but the casual gesture sent a jolt of intense
desire through him.

As a horseman, he approved of her instincts to
check her horse next. As a man, he reacted to the
gentle yet firm way she glided her hands over the
mare's legs. How would it feel, he wondered, to
have those hands skimming over his body?

He also noticed she was favoring her left leg,
although she was trying very hard not to let him
see it.

Assured that the horse hadn't suffered any ill
effects, the woman twisted her long hair into a
rope, then coiled it on top of her head. She picked
up her cap but wasn't able to put it on. Michael's
fingers had closed around her wrist.

"Leave it," he said.

Her eyes became cool, her tone haughty as she
lifted her chin and stared at him. "I beg your
pardon'?"

"It's a shame to cover your hair."

"How far the apple has fallen from the tree, Mr.
Knight," she said crisply, then ignored his order
and replaced her cap on her head.

He stared at her, momentarily lost again. Amusement won out over confusion, and he grinned. "What the hell does that mean?"

"During the occasions when I've been with your father, I've always found him to be a perfect gentleman. You are not."

"I didn't attend one of your fancy boarding schools," he said congenially, "so my manners might be a little rough around the edges compared to what you're accustomed to from your English gentlemen. I do know which fork to use, though, and have even opened a door or two for a woman. I'm not a total loss."

She pursed her lips as she considered what he said, and that little pout sent his blood pressure soaring. He wondered what she would do if he covered that sassy mouth with his. Probably slap his face. He had no doubt, however, that kissing her would be worth a sock in the jaw.

Without giving her a chance to comment, he added, "I've been more of a gentleman than you might think. I could have given you a more thorough examination while you were lying unconscious on the ground. Believe me, it was quite a temptation."

"Oscar Wilde once said he could resist everything but temptation," she murmured. "I suppose I should thank you for refraining from groping me."

"Why don't you tell me who you are instead."

Running the reins idly through her hands, she gave him a direct look. "My name is Cassidy Harrold. Robert Harrold of Chartridge Manor was my father."

Chartridge Manor was the property next to his

father's land. Over the years Michael had seen his King's close friend and neighbor a number of times. Robert Harrold shared his father's love of horses, his passion for chess, and a similar dry sense of humor. Michael had last seen the gravelly voiced Englishman at King's seventieth birthday party the previous month. Though Robert had often talked about his daughter as a fine horsewoman—high praise from a horse breeder and a father—Michael had never given Robert's daughter much thought. At that moment he couldn't think of anything else.

"Was?" he asked quietly, seeing a shadow of sadness in her eyes.

"My father had a fatal heart attack a week ago."

"I'm sorry." Thinking of his mother, he added, "It's not easy losing someone you love."

"Thank you," she said, a note of surprise in her voice.

"For what?"

"For not saying all those trite things people usually say, like time heals all wounds or at least he didn't suffer. I know they mean well, but none of their advice made me feel better."

"Everyone has to find their own way of dealing with grief. My father called me late at night to tell me my mother had passed away in her sleep. I saddled my horse and rode for hours. At dawn I stood on the edge of a bluff and shouted obscenities at the sun as it rose over the horizon. It didn't seem right that the sun should be coming up in a world that no longer contained my mother. Some people might think screaming at the heavens is an odd thing to do, but it helped me."

He knew already to expect her to say the unexpected, and he wasn't disappointed.

"Damn," she muttered.

"Now what?"

"I'm going to have to retract my statement about you not being a gentleman, and I really had my heart set on disliking you."

Her explanation didn't help one bit. "What does one have to do with the other?"

She didn't choose to give him a direct answer. Instead, she said, "After my father's funeral, King whisked me away from the manor and drove me to Knight's Keep, where he proceeded to get me royally sloshed. He kept pouring champagne and making toasts to what he called my father's uncanny luck at chess, his bad taste in smelly cigars, and the dilapidated trilby my father always wore. The last thing I thought I would be able to do the day we buried my father was laugh."

After a brief pause Michael asked tightly, "You drank champagne with King?"

She gave him an odd look. "It wasn't a drunken orgy, if that's what you're implying, Mr. Knight. As I said, King is a gentleman."

"You consider a man who sets out to get you drunk a gentleman?"

"It was his way of comforting me. Isn't that why you told me how you reacted to your mother's death?"

He shrugged, uncomfortable with the gentle tone of her voice. "Maybe."

She smiled. "I rest my case. Your method might be different from your father's, but the intention is the same."

He didn't want to talk about his motivations. What he would have liked to discuss was King's reaction to losing a close friend. It might explain why his father was behaving so strangely.

Still, he couldn't quell his curiosity about Cassidy. "Why did you want to dislike me?" he asked.

"I've had a secret yen for cowboys ever since I saw my first John Wayne film. It would be easy to be attracted to you. You're a handsome man, you know, and you fill out a pair of jeans better than any man I've known."

For the first time in memory Michael Knight blushed.

Then he scowled at her. "I thought English-women were supposed to be repressed and timid."

Her smile broadened. "It seems we have both jumped to incorrect conclusions."

Michael took the reins from her hands. "Your horse needs to be cooled down." And so did he.

He turned toward his father's house, not waiting to see if she was going to walk with him. He almost hoped she didn't. A little distance between them would be a good idea at the moment. Otherwise he might be tempted to do a really dumb thing, like take her into his arms and drag her down to the ground.

Comforting her had nothing to do with it.

He didn't get his wish. Cassidy walked along with him, although she stayed a pace behind him, trying to conceal her limp. He noticed, though. He was aware of everything about her. Any other time he might have admired her proud attitude, but at the moment it made him angry that she was in pain.

Stopping abruptly, he didn't bother asking her whether she wanted to ride rather than walk. He knew a stubborn woman when he saw one. So he dropped the reins, clamped his hands around her waist, and hoisted her into the saddle.

"Since you're too pig-headed to admit you hurt your ankle," he said, "you probably don't have sense enough to get in out of the rain either. Perhaps you haven't noticed, but those clouds overhead look like they're about to dump a lot of rain on us."

"But we're going the wrong way," she said, and jerked her thumb in the other direction. "Chartridge Manor is over there."

"My father's stables are closer. You might not care about yourself, but your horse doesn't deserve to get drenched."

A drop of water hit the top of her hand; another struck her cheek. "I see your point."

Michael managed not to sound smug. "I thought you might."

The wind became stronger as the rain started to pour down. She blinked away drops that gathered on her lashes and ordered, "Give me the reins."

Michael glanced at her over his shoulder. He was about to tell her to hang on while they made a dash for the stables, when he saw her kick her foot out of the left stirrup.

Accepting her silent invitation, he handed the reins to her and swung onto the horse behind her. The mare danced sideways in protest of the extra weight, but Cassidy patted Nougat's neck and spoke soothingly. Once the horse was calmer, she touched her heels to the mare's flanks.

Michael slipped his arms around her waist and was aware of the shudder that ran through her. He would have liked to think she was reacting to his closeness, but she was probably simply chilled. His wide-brimmed hat and sheepskin jacket protected him from the pelting cold rain, but her riding outfit wasn't designed for inclement weather. He opened the front of his coat and wrapped each side around her, and lowered his head to partially shield her with his hat.

His actions had been purely out of consideration for her comfort. He hadn't stopped to think how he would react to feeling her slender body pressed against his chest.

He wished she would stop shivering. The shuddering movements were having an electrifying effect on his already overstimulated libido. It wouldn't take much more to short-circuit his control.

The rain continued steadily all the way to the stables. Michael was both relieved and irritated to see that the wide doors were open.

The two stable boys must have left the doors unlatched when they left, and the wind had blown them open. Whatever the cause, at least they were able to ride directly into the stable. As soon as they were inside, Michael slid off the horse. Before Cassidy had a chance to dismount, he lifted her from the saddle.

Instead of setting her on her feet, he sat her down on a bale of straw. "Stay."

"I am not a dog, Mr. Knight," she said indignantly. "I need to return to Chartridge. My stepbrother will be wondering where I am."

"You can phone him from the house."

She tried again when she saw him loosen the girth of Nougat's saddle. "I can take care of my own horse."

"I'm sure you can. You just don't have to do it right now. Stay off that ankle."

He began to wipe down her horse, and smiled to himself when he heard her muttering behind his back. It was a toss-up whether he enjoyed it more when she was angry or when she smiled.

Cassidy glared at the man who was calmly brushing Nougat's hindquarters, though her re-action was wasted on him since he had his back to her. She told herself it was unreasonable to be angry with him for taking care of Nougat. He couldn't possibly know she was jealous of anyone who touched the mare that had been hers since the moment she'd been born.

Nor did he know that her stepbrother was going to sell her horse, along with all the other posses-sions she'd known and loved all her life.

She would never be able to understand why her father had left everything but the manor house to Derek. She knew her father had always believed a man was better able to take care of property, of business, than a woman. Robert had been wrong, though, when he'd willed Chartridge Manor to his stepson. All Derek cared about was money for fancy cars, expensive women, and gambling. The only horses Derek liked were the ones that ran on racetracks.

It was inconceivable to her that her father hadn't seen through Derek's affable behavior to the cruel, selfish man underneath. Her stepbrother wouldn't be able to sell the house, but he could sell the furnishings, the land, and all the horses.

Just that morning Derek had again turned down her offer to buy her own horse, and she had taken her anger and frustration to the stables for what might possibly be the last time. Sentiment meant nothing to Derek. Cold hard cash did.

The sound of Nougat blowing through her nose in appreciation of the attention she was receiving brought Cassidy's gaze back to her horse. Michael was leading her into an empty stall.

"That's not necessary, Mr. Knight," she said in a tight voice. "I won't be here long."

He gave her a look that could have boiled ice, then closed the bottom half of the stall's Dutch door.

"You aren't going anywhere until I take a look at your ankle."

"That isn't necessary either," she said, quickly scooting over when she realized he intended to sit beside her. "I twisted my foot a little when I fell, that's all."

"Then you won't mind if I take a look."

She made it obvious she did mind, but a scathing look had no effect at all. He laid her leg across his thighs and carefully eased off her riding boot. His fingers were gentle as he probed and manipulated her ankle through the cotton stocking, his gaze remaining on her face to catch any indication of pain.

When she showed no reaction, he lowered her foot to the brick-tiled floor. "Try walking on it."

She sucked in her breath when she took her

first step. Michael started to reach for her, but she held him off.

"It's not my ankle," she said. "The floor is cold."

Exaggerating her footsteps to disguise her limp, she walked away from him for five paces, turned around, and walked back. She compressed her lips as the tendons in her ankle protested and the chill from the floor seeped through her stocking. The foot wasn't broken, but she had wrenched it.

Standing in front of him, she put her hands on her hips. "As you can see, my ankle is fine, although I might have a problem with frostbite if I have to keep walking around like this."

Chuckling, he pulled her down beside him. Her hip pressed against his, but she didn't move away, even though she could feel a searing heat where their bodies touched.

"Okay," he said cheerfully as he handed her boot to her. "Here."

Cassidy took the riding boot but didn't immediately slip it on. Damn him, she cursed silently. His clever, experienced hands had thoroughly examined her from her toes to midcalf. He knew darn well her ankle was swollen.

When she hesitated, he said. "That's what I thought."

"It doesn't matter," she said defensively. "I can still ride without my boot."

"You could, but you aren't going to."

She lifted her chin. "Why do you think you have anything to say about what I do and where I go?"

"Because I'm bigger than you and get mean when I don't get my way. If you weren't so busy being a stubborn idiot, you would remember you were also unconscious for a little while and could have a concussion." When that reasoning had no effect, Michael tried again. "My father would skin me alive if I allowed you to leave in the shape you're in."

"There's nothing wrong with my shape," she said.

He let his gaze roam over her slowly. "I can't argue with that. I meant your ankle and the fact that you're cold and wet. Alvilda will make one of her numerous pots of tea while your clothes are drying. We'll put some ice on that ankle and set you in front of a warm fire. Does that sound so bad?"

She pursed her lips again, and he made a sound deep in his throat. "I wish you wouldn't do that."

She frowned in confusion. "Do what?"

"Never mind." She was already as skittish as an unbroken colt. This wasn't the time to tell her she was arousing some rather primitive urges in him. "Since you've proven you can walk unaided, would you like to hop over to the house on one foot or would you allow me to carry you? I know which would be my choice."

She crossed her arms and gave him a look intended to peel wallpaper off a wall. "I'm going to have to change my mind about disliking you after all, Mr. Knight."

She'd taken another detour and had lost him again. He pushed his hat to the back of his head. "All right, I'll bite. Why?"

"I've had my fill of men who think they know what's best for a woman. Why don't you try something really bizarre and ask me what I would like to do?"

He swept off his hat with an exaggerated flourish, then stood and bowed to her. "Miss Harrold, would you please accompany me to my father's house for a cup of tea and take off all your clothes?"

She laughed, startling him again with her unpredictable reaction. "That isn't quite what I had in mind," she said as she slipped her hand around his arm. "But it's a start."

Two

Tea was not Michael's favorite choice of beverage, yet he didn't hesitate to hand Cassidy his cup when she asked if he'd like a refill.

After changing into dry clothes, he'd joined her in the morning room on instructions from Alvilda. Few people got away with bossing him around, but his father's housekeeper was one person it was wiser to obey. Alvilda had her own notions of proper conduct, and one of them was to be hospitable to a guest, even a partially clad one.

His sudden interest in England's national drink had something to do with the woman holding the Meissenware teapot. The fact that Cassidy was wearing one of his sister's robes didn't hurt. He'd been aware that Silver had grown up, at least in age. However, he hadn't realized until then how petite his sister was compared to the woman wearing her robe.

His cup rattled on the saucer when Cassidy

leaned forward to set the teapot down. The robe gaped open, and he caught a glimpse of her breast. When he felt her cool hand on his, steadying the cup, he raised his gaze to meet hers.

"This was your idea," she reminded him, clasping the front of the robe together.

Leaning back in the chair, he smiled. "And it was a darn good one from where I'm sitting."

"Hasn't your father ever told you it isn't polite to stare?"

"Not that I remember."

"Did you realize your sister was considerably smaller than I am when you asked Alvilda to fetch one of her dressing gowns?"

"It was a more acceptable suggestion than having Alvilda supply you with *my* robe. She wouldn't have thought that was proper."

Cassidy glanced down at her legs, a generous portion of which were exposed. "And you consider this proper?"

"That's not the word I would use." *Tantalizing, sensual,* and *arousing* were much more appropriate. He wasn't about to use any of them yet. "There really wasn't any other choice. You saw Alvilda's face when she saw me carrying you into the house. She wasn't too pleased at my taking such liberties with a female guest. I wasn't going to push my luck by giving you an article of my clothing."

"How considerate of you," she said dryly.

"I try." To attempt to get his mind off the enticing picture she made in the snug robe, he looked around the room. Like most of the rest of the house, it had seventeenth-century plasterwork ceilings, elaborate moldings, and antique furnishings.

"Every time I come in here," he said, "I remember Silver's comment when my grandmother referred to this as the morning room."

As she poured tea into her own cup, Cassidy asked, "What did Silver say?"

"She asked who'd died. She thought Gram had said mourning with a 'u'."

"I'd forgotten Knight's Keep had belonged to your mother's family. King has made such an impression on this place, it seems as though he's always been here."

"The fact that it's always been called Knight's Keep might have something to do with it. My mother's family has always had a thing about King Arthur, Camelot, the whole crew. The Arthurian legends are one of the many things my parents had in common. One of my ancestors even believed he was descended from one of the knights of the Round Table."

"Which knight?"

"Lucan. According to my father, his great-grandfather spent the better part of his life researching the family tree. When he died, he'd only managed to trace the family as far back as the seventeenth century."

"And no one else took it up?"

He shook his head. "The later generations were more interested in the present than the past."

She grinned, a teasing light in her eyes. "Is that why none of you have Arthurian names? With both parents interested in the legends, I would have thought you'd have been named Balan or Gawaine or Galahad."

His smile was rueful. "Close enough," he muttered. "We all use our middle names rather than our first names."

Her eyes widened with surprise. "Which of the knights are you named after?" she asked with avid curiosity.

He shook his head, refusing to divulge that information. "The only people who know that are King, my brothers and sister, and the person who typed my driver's license when I renewed it. We were talking about Knight's Keep and how my father ended up living here."

"I'll find out your Christian name," she said, a look of determination in her eyes. "I don't know how or when, but I'll discover what it is. I have a feeling having something to hold over you would be handy for when you get arrogant and pushy."

Michael pretended not to hear her. "After my mother's parents died," he said, continuing with his family's history, "she wanted to come back here to live. By that time most of my father's painting commissions were from British horse owners. They decided to live at Knight's Keep permanently. Up until that time Dad had been running Knight Enterprises in Kentucky, but he no longer found it challenging. Did you know about the chain of department stores he inherited?"

She nodded. "I remember my father commenting that King had been bored and frustrated with the haggling over every change he wanted to make and the demands from the board to make more and more money."

"He would much rather fulfill the demands for his paintings than argue with a board of directors. Moving to Knight's Keep made my mother happy and gave King the excuse to hire a CEO to take over the business, leaving him free to paint."

"You didn't move here with them."

He shook his head. "Turner and I were in college. Ryder and Silver lived here for a couple of years before they went back to the States to attend college." He paused, then said, "Your father and mine have been friends for years. How is it you and I have never met?"

Curling her legs under her, she tucked the robe around her feet. "Fate?"

"I'd call it bad luck. I've met your stepbrother and his mother before she died, and of course your father, but I've never seen you when I've gone to Chartridge with King."

Cassidy shifted her gaze to the marble fireplace, where red coals and small, flickering flames provided more esthetic value than warmth. Michael's innocent statement reminded her of how rarely she'd been to Chartridge since her father remarried. When she had gone home, she'd spent most of the time in the stables.

The shower Michael had insisted she take had helped banish the chill from the rain, but not the feeling of loss deep inside her. She wasn't sure anything would.

She was roused from her thoughts by Michael saying her name. "Cassidy?"

She turned to meet his gaze. "Sorry. I was thinking of something else. You were saying?"

Michael had heard more flattering statements in his time. It was extremely deflating to his ego that he was so easy to forget, especially when he was in the room with her.

"I was remarking on the fact that we've never met."

"I was thirteen when I went away to a boarding school."

She didn't add that her father had married Leona Pembroke that same year. Up until that event Cassidy had planned to go to a local girls' school and live at home.

"From that point on I came home only for holidays and the occasional weekend," she finished vaguely.

Michael waited for her to continue. Her explanation had as many holes in it as Swiss cheese. When he realized she wasn't going to provide any more information, he asked, "Where do you live now?"

"London."

"Do you live alone?"

"Yes."

Her one-word answers didn't provide him with much information, but he at least liked that particular answer. It suggested she wasn't intimately involved with anyone. And if she wanted to play twenty questions, he'd just keep at her all day long.

"What do you do in London?"

"I'm a flautist."

He nearly dropped his teacup. "You're a what?"

"A flautist," she repeated, smiling. "I'm a professional musician. I play the flute."

For a man who couldn't carry a tune in a bucket or even play chopsticks on the piano, he was impressed. "What does a professional musician do?"

"Until recently I've been a member of an orchestra performing in the West End for a play called *Sing a Sixpence*. It closed a few days before my father died."

"So you're currently unemployed?"

She shrugged. "There're always other plays, concerts, recording-studio work. I'm also qualified on four other instruments and have respectable credentials. I studied at the London Academy of Music and Dramatic Arts and hold a degree from the Royal Academy of Music. Plus I have a good booking agent, so I'm rarely out of work. When I return to London this afternoon, I'll contact my agent to find out if he has anything lined up for me."

Michael frowned. "This is Friday. Why not return to London on Monday and stay the weekend at Chartridge?"

"Because there's nothing to stay for," she said, and tilted her chin upward once more, as though she expected him to debate the issue.

Michael wasn't going to argue with her. Maybe, he thought, it was better for them both if she left for London. Except he wasn't sure that out of sight would necessarily mean out of mind with Cassidy Harrold. In fact, he could practically guarantee he wouldn't forget her any time soon. Cassidy had a strange effect on him that was growing stronger and more puzzling the longer he was with her.

When he said nothing further about her staying, she changed the subject. "Miss Gump said it wouldn't take long for my clothes to dry. Would you mind checking with her to see if they're ready?"

"In a minute. There's something I want to talk to you about first."

He barely managed to repress a grin when her stubborn chin rose another quarter inch. Someone should tell her it wasn't wise to lead with her chin. A person might be tempted to take a poke. Or steal a kiss.

"What do you want to talk to me about?" she asked cautiously.

"Two days ago I received a message from my father that he was going to sell an important family possession. When I arrived I learned that King had gone off on one of his little research trips. After you told me about your father's death, it made me wonder whether losing his closest friend is behind his sudden wish to dispose of something that means a great deal to the family."

"What does that have to do with me?"

"You were with King the day of your father's funeral. You know what his state of mind was, how he took the death of his best friend."

"He was sad, naturally, yet he was able to put my feelings ahead of his own."

"By getting you drunk."

"I wasn't drunk," Cassidy said indignantly. "Just pleasantly, numb. Considering the kind of day I'd had, it was a welcome relief."

"You mentioned making toasts. Did my father have much to drink?"

She frowned. "As I told you, your father has always been a perfect gentleman with me. If you're suggesting King behaved in any other way, you couldn't be more wrong."

He held his hand up. "I'm not suggesting my father made a pass at you. I just want to know if he drank the champagne. It's an easy question to answer."

"That was several days ago," she said. "And what difference would it make whether he had a few glasses of champagne?"

"My father isn't supposed to drink alcoholic beverages, Cassidy. The medication he takes for his arthritis doesn't mix with alcohol. If he had any champagne the day of your father's funeral, it might help explain why he's behaving oddly."

Cassidy set her cup on the table in front of her. "I had no idea. If I'd known, I wouldn't have—"

He didn't let her finish. "I'm not blaming you, Cassidy. King knows what he can and cannot drink. What I want from you is whether or not he drank any of the champagne."

She rubbed her forehead as if she could physically bring forward the answer he wanted. "Let me think. I was upset, and I'm not used to drinking. Those few hours are all sort of a blur."

Michael leaned back in his chair. "Take all the time you need."

Cassidy slid her legs out from under her and stood up. She walked to the fireplace, then turned to face him.

"Miss Gump brought a bottle of champagne and

only two glasses into the study, even though King had asked her to join us in a toast to my father. Now I realize the scowling looks she directed at him were because he shouldn't be drinking."

"Did he?"

She paced in front of the fireplace. "I'm trying to remember. Give me a minute."

Another minute of watching her stroll back and forth in that too-small robe was going to do him in. With each limping step she took, the lower flap of the robe was flung aside, giving him a tantalizing glimpse of a shapely bare leg. "Maybe it would help if you reenacted that evening. You said you were in the study." He stood up. "Let's go in there. It might help you recall."

"All right," she said.

She preceded him to the door, and he closed his eyes to shut out the sight of her as she walked past him. Fighting the attraction was difficult enough from a distance. Close up, it was almost impossible. Her scent slammed into him with the force of a hurricane, leaving him badly off balance. His sensual response to her was still vibrating through him when he heard her call his name.

Turning his head slowly, he found her standing in the doorway waiting for him, a puzzled expression in her stunning green eyes.

"Did you plan on coming with me?"

"Of course." Resigned to his fate, he walked toward her. Why should he start being sensible now?

The hard heels of his boots sounded unusually loud on the polished oak floor as he followed her down the hall. Walking behind her wasn't a good idea, he realized. He should have left the room first and made her trail after him. His brain seemed to have taken a vacation since he met Cassidy Harrold. However, the rest of his body was all too active.

He stopped in the doorway of his father's study, leaning his shoulder against the door frame. Cassidy stood in the center of the room, slowly turning around as if getting her bearings.

"Alvilda carried the tray in," he said to help her along. "Where did she put it?"

"There." Cassidy pointed to the small table between two leather wing chairs that faced the fireplace. "I sat in the chair on the left. Your father poured champagne into my glass, then stepped over to the fireplace to throw in a few lumps of coal."

"He didn't pour any champagne in the other glass?"

"Not then. When he finished with the fire, he went over to the display case."

Michael walked over to the glass-enclosed case. "Then what did he do?"

Cassidy sat down in the same chair she'd used that night. She crossed one leg over the other, then yanked impatiently at the front of the robe as it flared open. Scowling, she uncrossed her legs and gave up the futile attempt to make the robe cover more than it could.

Answering Michael's question, she said, "King talked about all the chess games he and my father played over the years. He described some of the things they did together, like the time they tried to build an addition on Father's hothouse. The entire thing collapsed when they put in the last panel. King reminded me of a side of my father I hadn't seen in many years. The man who loved a challenge and who could laugh at his own mistakes, usually louder and longer than anyone else. It was a priceless gift your father gave me that night."

"Reminiscing about Robert was as good for King as it was for you."

Michael turned away from her, gazing down into the glass case. "Do you remember if King mentioned the Camelot chess set that night?"

"I don't think so," she murmured as she followed his gaze to look at the solid-gold chess pieces. "He mentioned chess only in the context of playing so many games with my father. Why?"

Michael didn't answer her question. Instead, he walked around his father's desk and sat down. "Let's get back to the champagne and whether or not King drank it."

Cassidy bit her lip as she concentrated. "The more I think about that night, I can't recall seeing King ever drinking any of the champagne. He continually topped up my glass, but mostly I remember him talking about my father. I don't believe King took even one sip of the champagne."

She was telling him what he wanted to hear, but Michael was having trouble accepting it. It would explain a lot if drinking champagne had affected King's judgment and was behind his sudden decision to sell the Camelot set. Michael wanted a reason, something tangible to grasp as an explanation. If he had to rule out a medical condition, he was back where he started.

A silver letter opener in the shape of a paintbrush lay on the desktop, and he picked it up. "Was that night the last time you saw King?"

"Yes. He drove me home and handed me over to Mrs. Tagget, our housekeeper, who poured me into bed."

His gaze left the letter opener to study her face. "Why haven't you seen him since?"

"I might have given you the wrong impression about how well I know your father. As I told you earlier, I haven't been home much. I saw King maybe once or twice a year when he came to Chartridge to see my father and I joined them for dinner."

She stood up. "My clothes should be dry by now. I should be getting back to Chartridge if I'm going to make the train to London."

Michael pushed himself out of the chair, but Cassidy left the room before he could stop her. He wasn't through talking to her, but she had evidently answered all the questions she was going to. In the silent room the raindrops hitting the window panes sounded like bullets from a machine gun. He glanced out the window and smiled.

If Cassidy thought she was going to trot her horse back to Chartridge in the pouring rain, she was going to be very disappointed.

The collar of her tweed blazer was still damp as Cassidy slipped it on over her sweater, but she didn't mention it to the woman hovering around her.

"I appreciate you taking the trouble to dry my

clothes, Miss Gump. I was going to go directly to Chartridge when I got caught in the rain, but Michael insisted I come here."

"And he was right to do so. It's still coming down quite heavily outside. Don't you think you should wait for the rain to clear before you leave?"

Cassidy laughed softly as she walked over to the stove in her stocking feet. "You know English weather, Miss Gump. I could be here for the next week if I waited for the rain to stop."

She wouldn't stay another hour if she could prevent it. She wanted to leave Knight's Keep, Chartridge, Somerset, Derek, and especially Michael Knight behind her. She had already lost more than she could deal with just then. There wasn't anything she could have done about losing her father, nor, evidently, could she do anything about her father's property being sold to strangers. She could, however, prevent any more complications in her life by leaving Knight's Keep, thereby ridding herself of Michael Knight and the unexpected attraction that had sprung up between them.

As though her thoughts had summoned him, Michael spoke from the kitchen doorway. "I'll be driving Miss Harrold home, Alvilda."

Picking up one of her riding boots, which the housekeeper had placed on the open oven door, Cassidy turned toward him. "Have you forgotten Nougat? I can't leave her here."

"Why not? Your horse is in a warm, dry stable happily munching oats. It's better than having her galloping around in mud and cold rain."

"I need to get my horse back to Derek's stables."

Crossing his arms over his chest, Michael studied her, wondering why she had referred to the stables at Chartridge as Derek's. "I'll see that your horse gets back to Chartridge once the rain stops, since you seem to be in such a hurry to leave."

The housekeeper took the riding boot out of Cassidy's hands and began to buff the leather with a cloth. "Young people are in such a rush nowadays," she announced. "It wouldn't hurt either one of you to sit down and have a bite to eat before dashing out into this foul weather. It will give me a chance to polish these boots properly."

"Don't bother with those boots, Miss Gump," Cassidy insisted. "They're just going to get wet again when I go out."

Michael saw the wary glance she sent in his direction, as though she expected him to contradict her. It would be worth his life, he knew, if he grinned at her.

"I'll pull the car around front," he said. "Don't take all day throwing yourself back together." Glancing at the housekeeper, he added, "There's a pair of Silver's moccasins in a cupboard in the mudroom, Alvilda. You might want to suggest Miss Harrold wear one on her left foot, rather than trying to stuff her swollen ankle into a tight riding boot. Perhaps she'll listen to you."

Cassidy barely resisted the impulse to throw one of her boots at Michael's back as he walked away. A chuckle from the housekeeper brought her head around.

"What's so funny? The man is rude, arrogant, and impossible."

"He's a Knight. They're all like that."

Alvilda didn't wait for Cassidy's response. She left the kitchen and returned a few seconds later, carrying a pair of beaded leather moccasins.

"You'd better put these on. I've found it easier to do as the Knights say. It saves a great deal of wear and tear on the nerves. They generally get their way in the end."

"I noticed."

Handing the left boot to Cassidy after she had squeezed her foot into the small moccasin, Alvilda added, "Michael is very concerned about his father, so perhaps you could make allowances for his rough ways."

Cassidy didn't know the housekeeper very well, yet her casual manner regarding King's disappearance seemed too calm under the circumstances.

"You don't seem to be overly concerned about King."

Alvilda found a spot on the counter that suddenly needed her attention and scrubbed it with a cloth. "King knows exactly what he's doing."

Since Cassidy couldn't see Miss Gump's expression, she decided she must have been imagining the amusement in her voice. She couldn't see anything vaguely humorous about King causing his son to worry about him.

Cassidy heard a horn honk several times and picked her riding cap up from the table. She had one more adjective to apply to King's son. He was impatient.

Before she left the kitchen she thanked Miss Gump for the tea and for taking care of her clothes.

As she walked down the hall, she ran her fingers through her hair. Realizing she was attempting to tidy her appearance, she quickly dropped her hand. Her heart was racing only because she was hurrying, she told herself.

Not because Michael Knight was waiting for her.

Three

Michael caught the glance Cassidy gave the buff-colored leather seats and burlwood interior of the late-model Jaguar as she fastened her seat belt.

"I rented this car in London," he explained even though she hadn't asked. "I like to have my own transportation."

"I wasn't going to complain. It's just that I had a different picture of the type of vehicle a rancher from Montana would drive."

Gravel crunched under the tires as he pulled away from the house. "They didn't have any horses available at the airport, so I had to settle for this."

She chuckled. "A great sacrifice." Settling back against the soft leather, she said, "Tell me about your ranch."

"What would you like to know?"

"Whatever you want to tell me. King mentioned you bought your ranch with your winnings from a rodeo. Is that true?"

Michael grinned at the way she'd mangled the word *rodeo* with her precise accent, but he didn't correct her. If she wanted it to be a "road-yo," it was all right with him.

As he leisurely drove to Chartridge, he told her about the horses he bred, raised, and trained on the Quarter K.

As Cassidy listened, she heard the contentment in his voice. And the pride. Whenever King had talked about the accomplishments of his children, he'd bragged that each had made his or her own way after finishing college. When she mentioned to Michael that King had been relieved Michael had quit the rodeo circuit, he glanced at her and shook his head.

"It's not fair that you know so much about me and I know so little about you."

"Evidently your father bragged more about you than mine did about me."

He heard the flat tone of her voice, but he didn't understand the reason for it. "Your father—"

"I'd rather not discuss my father right now if you don't mind."

"All right," he said, although he was more puzzled than ever.

As they drove through the open gates at the entrance of Chartridge Manor, Cassidy saw the tall brick chimneys of the house through the trees. She knew this was one of the last times she would see that familiar first view of her home. Since her father's death it had been difficult to stay under the same roof as her stepbrother, with his snide remarks, his jealousy, and his crude friends who'd come for the funeral and stayed. The once-peaceful house had become filled with loud music, scantily clad women, cigarette smoke, and men who thought they were God's gift to the world. The thought of enduring even one more night in their company filled her with dread.

Michael drove around the circular paved drive to the front entrance of the brick Georgian house. Stopping the car, he glanced at Cassidy. He'd been aware of the subtle changes in her with each passing mile. Tension had seeped into her voice, and her hands had restlessly rearranged the solitary riding boot on her lap too many times to count.

When she started to unclasp the seat belt, he put his hand on her arm. "Cassidy, talk to me. Tell me what's bothering you."

With anyone else she could have denied there was anything wrong. Yet she felt compelled to be honest with Michael. "There have been a number of sudden changes in my life, and I'm not adjusting all that well to them."

"I know I'm not the first person to tell you that it takes time to adjust to losing someone you care about. You don't need to be brave and noble at a time like this." He paused, then asked, "Are you serious about returning to London today?"

She could feel the heat from his hand through the fabric of her coat and sweater. "There's no reason for me to stay any longer."

"I'd like to change that."

She frowned. "I don't understand."

"You said you don't have a job to return to in London. I'd like you to stay and help me look for King. I can't wait for him to meander back in a week or so. I need to talk to him as soon as possible."

This time he hadn't made it an order, she realized. It was a request. Still, she had to give him the same answer.

"I don't see how I could help you. I don't know your father as well as you think I do. As I told you before, I don't come to Chartridge often. I'm not that familiar with King's professional life, except that I know he's much in demand. I wouldn't know the first place to look for him."

"You're familiar with this area, with the people who own horses and who've dealt with your father over the years. You could save me a lot of time by narrowing down the areas King would likely visit to get background material. I checked his appointment book, and he just finished a painting for a client. The next scheduled commission isn't for another two weeks."

"I would like to help you, but I've worn out my welcome here with my stepbrother. I think it would be best if I returned to London."

"That's not a problem. You can stay at Knight's Keep."

Her expression was skeptical. "What would Miss Gump say about that?"

Probably a lot, he conceded, but he wasn't about to tell her that. "The invitation still stands. I could wander around the countryside on my own, but I'm bound to waste a lot of time and miles and patience. England has plenty of miles, but I don't have much time or patience."

"From what King has said, you usually don't

stay longer than a couple of days when you come for a visit."

"There's nothing usual about this trip." He released her arm and cupped the back of her neck. "And you have something to do with that."

The sound she made was more of a sigh than a protest. "Michael, I don't think this is a good idea."

"It probably isn't." He stroked the soft skin beneath her ear with his thumb. "But that doesn't seem to make much difference. While we're scouting the area for King, maybe we can find out what this is between us that's making us as edgy as a cat in a thunderstorm."

Suddenly her car door was yanked open and a male hand grasped her arm. Her partially unfastened seat belt was flung aside as she was dragged from the seat.

Even before he heard Cassidy cry out, Michael had shoved open his door and climbed out. Over the top of the Jaguar he recognized the man who had ruthlessly pulled her from the car. Derek Pembroke. Though wearing only a wrinkled white shirt and tan trousers, Cassidy's stepbrother didn't appear to feel the cold. By the look of his bloodshot eyes, he evidently had enough alcohol in his system that he didn't feel much of anything.

In the open doorway of the house stood a woman dressed in a tight black leather miniskirt and an even tighter sweater. Two bleary-eyed men were beside her, drinks in their hands as they watched their host with obvious amusement.

His hands on her shoulders, Derek shook Cassidy roughly. Her riding cap fell to the ground and her hair tumbled down as she tried to push him away.

"John Edwards came by today," he said, his voice slurred, "the man I told you about who's interested in buying that nag of yours. You made me look like a bloody fool when I couldn't produce the horse."

"You don't need my help to look like a fool."

Derek's grip tightened on her shoulders, and he smiled with pleasure when she cried out in pain. Several other people spilled out of the house, their expressions curious and amused.

"Don't play games with me, Cass," Derek said as Michael strode around the front of the car. "You won't like my rules. Now, what have you done with—"

That was all Derek had time to say. The next second he was sprawled on the drive, his hand pressed to his throbbing jaw.

Surprise and pain pitched his voice higher than normal. "What the bloody hell?"

Michael towered over him, his legs spread apart, his hands clenched into fists. "You lay even one finger on her again, and there won't be enough pieces of you left over to make half a man."

He didn't wait for a response. Taking Cassidy's arm, he turned her back to the car. "Get in."

She resisted automatically. "I can handle Derek."

"You don't have to. I just did." When she still didn't move, he said, "Either you come with me, Cassidy, or I'm staying here with you. I'm not leaving you here alone."

"I'll be here only long enough enough to pack. I'll

call a taxi from town to take me to the train. There's no need for you to stay."

Michael, however, was as immovable as a brick wall. "I'm not like your stepbrother. I won't force you to do something you don't want to do. If you decide to stay here, though, you're going to have to consider me a house guest for the duration."

"This is none of your business, Michael."

"You became my business the minute you fell off your horse."

Behind him, Derek was struggling to his feet. Before her stepbrother had a chance to say anything more in front of Michael, Cassidy said, "I'll go with you for now."

She wasn't trying to protect her stepbrother from Michael. She would have liked to have been the one to slug Derek's weak chin herself. But Michael's interference had only made the situation between herself and Derek worse.

She'd taken two steps when she was suddenly swept off her feet. "Dammit, Cassidy," Michael muttered. "You hurt your ankle again, didn't you?"

He slid her onto the front passenger seat, then fastened her seat belt. The door slammed shut before she had a chance to utter a sound.

Michael didn't speak when he got behind the wheel. He simply started the car and put it in gear.

Cassidy, too, remained silent. Michael's anger was less vocal than her stepbrother's, but she sensed his controlled fury was more dangerous. A volcano didn't explode immediately, but simmered and boiled underneath the surface before erupting in a molten fury.

Instead of turning toward Knight's Keep when he reached the road, Michael drove in the opposite direction. Cassidy remained silent until he turned into a car park next to the Old Swan Pub several miles down the road from Chartridge.

Puzzled by his choice of destination, she asked, "Why are we stopping here?"

"Unless he's traded his old clunker to some poor unsuspecting boob, that battered sedan"—he pointed toward an ancient gray vehicle—"belongs to Dr. Moss. He can take a look at your ankle while we're here."

"In a pub?"

"Why not?" he said as he shut off the engine. "The doctor is here. You're here. We can get your ankle checked out and have something to eat at the same time."

"Of course," she murmured. "What could make more sense than that?"

It was just as well she didn't expect an answer, because Michael had already gotten out and was walking around the car to her side.

"How is it," she asked as he helped her out, "that a man who doesn't live in this area, much less this country, and visits only occasionally, happens to know the kind of car the local physician drives?"

He easily lifted her into his arms. "The Knights have never been known for their grace and agility. One of us has required the services of Dr. Moss at one time or another during our visits. Dr. Moss has had that same car for as long as I can remember."

She wrapped her arms around his neck. She

could become addicted to this form of transportation, she mused. "Were you one of the Knights he treated?"

"Once. I broke my wrist after a fall from the stone wall around Knight's Keep. It was during one of our visits when my grandparents still lived here. I was fourteen or fifteen at the time."

"Why were you up on the wall?"

He grinned down at her, his mouth only inches from hers. "Turner dared me to jump from the wall to one of the trees. I didn't make it."

She'd already guessed he was a man who relished a challenge. She couldn't help wondering if that was how he saw her, as a challenge, or did he really want her help? Or was he bored waiting for King to return?

Heads turned in their direction when they entered the pub. Cassidy had a challenge of her own to deal with as they became the center of attention. Appearing in public professionally rarely bothered her. She experienced the usual nerves if she had to perform a solo, but they always went away once she began to play. Being carried into a local pub was something else entirely. Rather than bury her face in his neck, she smiled and met the curious gazes of the patrons as though this were her normal mode of transportation.

Several people jumped up to offer their chairs while others stepped forward to help Cassidy get settled at a table. Michael didn't have to ask around for Dr. Moss. After being nudged by several patrons, that particular gentleman left his glass of ale on the bar and came over to see if he could be of any assistance.

The only contribution Cassidy was allowed to make was to provide her ankle. She listened to the conference between the doctor and Michael and the advice thrown in by several others. All eyes were on her bare foot as everyone bandied about opinions and argued over her injury. Michael answered the doctor's questions, watching closely as Dr. Moss examined her ankle. A short time later, a diagnosis was made. She had suffered a slight sprain. Popular opinion declared an X-ray wouldn't be necessary, and that was seconded by Dr. Moss.

A middle-aged woman peered over her half-glasses and proclaimed that her boy Neville had bunged up his foot just like hers once. The very next day he'd been up and about. The woman patted Cassidy on her shoulder and assured her she would be fine.

Cassidy's ankle was wrapped in an elastic bandage the doctor had in his much-used satchel. He recommended applying a cold compress, and the bartender quickly supplied a plastic bag full of crushed ice.

With wishes for a speedy recovery, the patrons wandered back to their tables. Michael invited Dr. Moss to join them for lunch, but the physician politely declined. As he shook Michael's hand and accepted his thanks, the doctor said to call him if there were any further problems.

Used to Englishmen's unwitting male chauvinism, Cassidy was amused that all of the doctor's comments and questions had been addressed to Michael instead of to her.

"What would you like to eat?" Michael asked as

he tugged on her stocking over the bulky bandage. He acted as though it was perfectly natural for him to dress her. "You have a choice of a plowman's lunch, fish and chips, or bangers and mash, according to the menu written on a blackboard by the door."

She wasn't hungry, but ordering lunch would delay the questions she was sure Michael wanted to ask about her stepbrother's rough treatment of her.

"I'd like a cup of tea," she said, and was surprised when he simply nodded, not arguing that she should eat.

The time it took for him to put in the order, pay for it, and deliver it to their table was all too short. She would have liked at least a day and a half. Explaining her complicated and unpleasant relationship with Derek wasn't going to be easy. She would rather not discuss her stepbrother at all.

When Michael returned, she saw why he hadn't argued with her. He'd simply gone ahead and ordered lunch for her.

After placing two paper-lined plastic baskets brimming with long strips of batter-fried fish and french fries on the scarred table, Michael sat down. He was aware of the irritation simmering in Cassidy's cool green eyes. He wished she would yell, stomp her good foot, or throw something. He would be more comfortable with any of those reactions than her silence.

Hoping she would feel better once she ate something, he said, "Dig in."

"Pardon?"

"Sorry. American slang. How about eat, drink,

and be merry? At least eat for now. The tea is on its way, then you can drink. As to the merry part, I don't suppose you feel particularly cheerful after that tussle with your stepbrother."

"That didn't take long."

This time he didn't need to ask her what she was talking about. He was rather pleased that he was beginning to follow her conversational detours.

"You really didn't expect me to ignore the way he treated you, did you? I've never been overly impressed with your stepbrother, but this was the first time I ever wanted to punch his lights out."

"Punch his lights out? That must be another one of your colorful American sayings, although I don't need this one translated." She smiled at him. "Its meaning is fairly clear."

"I'm glad something is clear. Why don't you tell me what that little scene in front of your home was all about."

A waitress chose that moment to deliver Cassidy's tea and Michael's coffee. His gaze never left Cassidy's face as he tossed some pound notes on the woman's tray.

He waited until Cassidy had poured her tea, but when she still didn't speak, he ran out of patience.

"Several years ago," he said, "one of the wells on my ranch dried up. It was an unusually dry year, and we were going to lose some stock unless we could find a new source of water. Since other ranches were having similar problems, I couldn't get a well driller out to the ranch. One company put me off by saying they could come out in a month. I couldn't wait that long. Another promised to show up in two days but didn't. I ended up driving for eight hours to pick up well-digging equipment I could lease, then drove eight hours back to the ranch. It took thirty-six hours of nonstop drilling in several locations until we located water and dug a new well."

"Fascinating," she said, meaning it. "But why are you telling me this?"

He gazed straight at her. "I've been called aggressive, stubborn, ruthless, and persistent when there's something I want. You might like to keep that in mind during our relationship."

"Our relationship?" she asked sharply, then lowered her voice when several people stared at her. "You're presuming a great deal on very short acquaintance. We aren't involved. We barely know each other."

Michael watched with amusement as she spooned three generous helpings of sugar into her cup. Interesting, he mused, considering she hadn't added any sugar to her tea back at Knight's Keep. She was trying to be cool and controlled, but he had seen the flare of sensual interest in her eyes when he'd returned to the table. Satisfaction rolled through him. She was involved. She didn't want to be, but some things were beyond a person's control.

He'd found that out when he'd first touched her.

"You can tell me," he said, "what caused that scene with your stepbrother, or I can go back and ask him. Either way I'll find out what's going on."

She made a face after taking a sip of the overly sweet tea. Setting the cup down, she glared at him as though it were his fault her tea was ruined.

"Derek was angry because I returned without Nougat."

"I already figured that out." As far as explanations went, hers was incredibly flimsy. He pressed for more answers. "What difference does it make to him what you do with your horse?"

"Legally, Nougat belongs to him. Along with the land and everything else except for the house. Dad left the manor to me with the provision that Derek be allowed to live there. He's already had prospective buyers out to look over Chartridge, but no one will make an offer unless the manor house is included. Derek has been trying to persuade me to sign over the ownership of the house to him."

Recalling how her stepbrother had grabbed her, Michael asked tightly, "Has he threatened you in any way?"

She shook her head. "He's more subtle than that. By inviting some of his friends from London to stay, he's showing me he's in control. This morning he refused my offer to buy Nougat."

"He would make you buy your own horse?"

"Haven't you been listening? My father left everything but the house to Derek. Ninety-five acres of land, three cottages, outbuildings, stables, paddocks, tennis court, the orchards, my father's Bentley. Every blade of grass belongs to my stepbrother."

Michael sat back in his chair and studied her face. He would have expected her to be bitter that her home had been turned over to someone else. Deep resentment would have been his reaction. All he could see in her eyes, though, was a resigned sadness. It was that haunted emptiness he wanted to make disappear.

"Are you going to fight the will?"

She shook her head again. "Chartridge belonged to my father and he chose Derek to take over the property."

Her flat tone told Michael a great deal. Her father's choice of heir had hurt her deeply. He felt the need to comfort her. "I saw your father's face when he talked about the ribbons you won at some kind of horse-riding contests you used to enter."

"Gymkhanas," she said absently.

"Whatever. Robert was proud of you, and he loved you, Cassidy. I hope you don't doubt that. Maybe he left Chartridge to Derek because he felt the property would be a burden to you."

"So it's better to leave his possessions to a man who cares only for money and intends to sell off everything my father loved."

"Including your horse."

"Derek won't get much money for Nougat, considering her age. Selling her is his way of getting revenge. Nougat, you see, is the last foal out of the first horse my father ever gave me."

Michael apparently didn't see, so she went on. "Derek has resented me from the first day he arrived at Chartridge after his mother married my father. To his way of thinking, I belonged at Chartridge and he was there only on sufferance. My father always treated him kindly. He gave Derek a generous allowance and offered to provide him with an education at any university he chose. But no matter what my father did to make Derek feel welcome, it was never enough."

Michael's attention was diverted from Cassidy when an elderly man at a neighboring table poked his arm with an umbrella.

"Would you be so kind, young man? I dropped one of the draughts."

Michael stared blankly at him. "Dropped what?"

Cassidy helped him out. "I believe you Americans call them checkers. There's one by your foot, and he would like you to pick it up for him."

Michael received a smile and profuse thanks when he handed the circular red piece of wood to the gentleman. Seeing Cassidy's amused gaze, he smiled.

"Now do you see why I want you to go with me to look for King? I need you to translate."

"According to the story you just told me about digging a well for water, you're a very resourceful man. I'm sure you can manage on your own. I'm going back to London."

"Do you plan on hopping onto the train with that gimpy foot? You heard Dr. Moss. He said the sprain will heal faster if you rest your ankle. I doubt if a two-hour train trip is quite what he had in mind. Since staying at Chartridge has been ruled out, come to Knight's Keep. There are seven bedrooms and both Alvilda and the day help to take care of your every wish. And I would be happy to carry you wherever you want to go. Why would you turn all that down for a long, uncomfortable trip to London?"

She glanced at her riding clothes. "For one

thing, I'd have some different clothes to wear than these. I'd even have a robe that actually fit."

He pushed back his chair. "You have clothes at Chartridge, don't you?"

"Yes, but after you embarrassed him in front of his friends, Derek will likely have thrown every stitch I own out into the drive."

Michael walked around the table and slipped one arm under her legs, the other around her back. Lifting her, he said, "After I drop you off at my father's, I'll go gather up your undies from the drive."

He hadn't lowered his voice. Cassidy heard the muffled chuckles from the people seated at nearby tables, and this time she did hide her face in Michael's neck as he carried her out of the pub. Having her bare foot examined by strangers was one thing. Having her underwear bandied about was something else again.

Michael grinned at her reaction and tightened his arms around her. She was such an intriguing combination of sophistication and innocence. She came across as a confident and independent woman, yet became embarrassed when he mentioned her lingerie.

His amusement changed when he felt her warm breath against his throat. He could get used to having her slim body in his arms. And a lot more. Wondering what it would be like to kiss her was beginning to drive him crazy, and he wasn't sure how much longer he could wait before finding out.

Outside, the rain had dwindled to a drizzle. It wasn't quite the same as a cold shower, but the cool moisture on Michael's face helped him find some control over the desire hardening his body.

No woman had ever affected him so quickly. He'd been entranced by her since the first moment he'd seen her. Instead of diminishing, his desire for her was growing stronger with every passing minute.

Once he'd settled her in the car, he took his time before joining her. He'd never considered himself an impulsive man. He normally thought out every move thoroughly before he made it. But ever since he'd seen Cassidy astride Nougat, flying over hedgerows, he'd operated on pure instinct.

Thinking was replaced with feeling when he was with her, and that had never happened to him before. He decided he liked it.

Four

The ponderous, droning chimes of a clock tolled twelve times. It was midnight. A dim white glow from the full moon fell across the end of the bed where Cassidy lay under a draped canopy. She had extinguished the lamp on the bedside table a half hour ago, but sleep evaded her.

A few minutes earlier she'd heard the distinctive sound of Michael's booted footsteps pass her door, followed by the muffled closing of another door farther down the hall. She had tensed when he'd neared her door, half expecting him to pause or knock, then had felt a ridiculous disappointment when he walked by without hesitating.

She rolled over onto her other side, thinking back over the evening.

As promised, Michael had dropped her off at Knight's Keep, then driven to Chartridge for her clothes. He'd been gone for two hours. The only reason she could come up with for his taking so much time was that he'd had another confrontation with Derek. Cassidy had phoned the housekeeper from Knight's Keep, and Mrs. Taggert had agreed to pack her clothing. Since Cassidy hadn't brought many clothes with her, the packing should have taken only a few minutes.

When he returned, Michael sidestepped her questions about why he'd been gone so long. Instead, he handed her a carved wooden cane he'd found in his father's studio. He suggested she use it, adding that he knew she was too stubborn to stay off her foot for very long. The cane was made of dark walnut, the handgrip carved into the shape of a duck's head. It was obviously an antique, but she accepted it rather than fight with Michael about it.

She probably would have lost the argument anyway. So far, she hadn't tallied up many wins against Michael Knight. Finding herself in a guest room at Knight's Keep was a good example. Thinking back, she couldn't pin down when she'd actually agreed to stay.

Because she hadn't. She'd literally been swept off her feet by him. For someone who was so independent, she was annoyed with herself for allowing Michael to take charge. Nor did she remember saying she would help him search for King. Not that there had been much of a chance for them to discuss it. The rest of the afternoon and evening had sped by quickly, with Alvilda fussing over Cassidy with ice packs for her ankle and pots of tea to comfort the rest of her. After a five-course dinner Michael unearthed a stack of maps of the area. As he was spreading several out

on the cleared dining room table, he was summoned by Alvilda, who announced his brother
Turner was on the phone.

While Michael was out of the room, Cassidy
studied the maps and wrote down several places
where King might have gone. The list wasn't very
long. It had been years since she'd spent much
time in Somerset and she hadn't visited many of
their neighbors when she'd lived at Chartridge. As
much as she would have liked to help Michael find
his father, she still doubted they'd have much
success, especially if King didn't want to be found.

When Michael returned, he started to look over
the list she'd made, but a few minutes later was
called away again by Alvilda. This time the call
was from the foreman of his ranch.

During the next hour Ryder and Silver also
phoned. Each time Michael came back, he didn't
seem preoccupied, nor did he tell Cassidy what
the calls had been about.

When Alvilda announced yet another phone
call, Michael suggested Cassidy might as well go
on up to bed. He reminded her she'd had a rough
time that day and the next day would be busy.

Because she was tired, she didn't argue. After
a good night's sleep, she told herself, she would
be back to her usual independent self. For just
one night she would lean on someone for a change.
Alvilda had prepared a welcoming fire in the guest
room and had fastened back the curtains surrounding the four-poster. It was a lovely, spacious
room with a tall leaded window overlooking the
front courtyard. A bouquet of fresh flowers, apparently from King's greenhouse, had been placed

on a vanity table, and the linen on the bed was fragrant with the scent of lavender. She was exhausted and should have fallen asleep the minute her head hit the pillow.

Like the previous nights at Chartridge, though, she couldn't sleep. At Chartridge she'd been kept awake by all the noise from the never-ending party that had been going on since her father's funeral. Derek's inviting the revelers to stay indefinitely, knowing she would dislike having them there, wouldn't be the first time he had done something for the sole purpose of irritating her.

In this case he'd succeeded. She hated all the commotion, the crude language, the drinking, and Lord knows what else that she would just as soon not know about or see. Derek was doing a good job of convincing her to sign the house over to him.

Too restless to remain in bed any longer, Cassidy turned on the bedside lamp and threw back the covers. The room was warm enough for her not to need her robe, nor did she bother with the cane as she stepped over to the window and pushed back the heavy drapes. Dr. Moss had been right. A little rest and her ankle was almost back to normal.

The rain had stopped, replaced by a thick rolling fog that enveloped the house. Moonlight added an eerie, haunted mood to the night.

Whether it was the late hour, the dismal fog, or the strange surroundings, Cassidy felt depressed and lonely. She'd been alone for a long time, but she couldn't remember feeling this void deep inside, as though something vital were missing.

She wasn't sure her restlessness was entirely

because of losing her father and her home. Even though she hadn't gone home often after her father's second marriage, she'd known the house was always there. Now she had to make a decision that could mean never returning to Chartridge. Turning her home over to Derek would mean relinquishing the last tangible tie to her family. However, along with her good memories about her childhood were the more unpleasant ones after her father's remarriage. The biting sarcasm from her stepmother when her father wasn't around. The cruel tricks Derek took pleasure in.

She was still gazing out the window when her bedroom door opened. Light from the hallway spilled into the room, falling short from where she stood.

Turning, she saw Michael standing in the doorway. The air around them changed as he stared at her, almost sizzling with the current of attraction arcing between them.

Michael couldn't have looked away if his life depended on it.

The neckline of her oversized white nightshirt had slid down one shoulder, and the hemline ended at midthigh. The moonlight shimmered and glowed on her pale skin and tousled hair. The sight of her took his breath away and fired his imagination.

"I should have known," he said, desire deepening his voice.

"You should have known what?" she asked.

He stepped into the room, leaving the door open. "You're supposed to stay off that foot, remember?"

"I think I've heard something along those lines maybe a hundred times or so today. Is that why you're here, so you can yell at me one more time before you go to bed?"

"Yelling isn't quite what I had in mind," he murmured, walking farther into the room.

"Perhaps you've come to say good-bye?"

He frowned as he kept coming toward her. "Where would I be going?"

"Home. To Montana. You had a lot of phone calls tonight."

He was finally close enough to touch her. "I'm not going anywhere. Not yet. There were a couple of things my foreman needed to talk to me about. Turner, Ryder, and Silver were all calling to find out what was going on with King. Turner received the same message I did. Only his message told him to bring his shield next week. Ryder and Silver hadn't received a request from King yet. I told them I would find out why our father is trying to shake up our otherwise peaceful lives."

"That explains why you're at Knight's Keep but not why you're in this room."

He cupped the side of her face. "I couldn't sleep until I had an answer to a question that's been driving me nuts."

She didn't push his hand away. "You think I might have the answer?"

"I'm sure of it." His gaze slid down to her mouth. "I can't wait any longer to find out how you taste."

He gave her time to protest as he slowly lowered his head. It didn't occur to her to object to something she wanted too. Excitement and anticipation shimmered through her, interfering with her breathing, quickening her heartbeat.

The first touch of his lips on hers was gentle. He wasn't tasting as much as he was teasing. He ran his tongue over her bottom lip, and she was aware of his smile when she caught her breath.

She drew back. The first step had been taken, and she understood that he was leaving it up to her whether they take the next one. For a full minute she simply looked at him. The moonlight skimmed over his chiseled features, and his eyes glowed with tamped-down heat as he waited.

She didn't make him wait long. Smiling, she placed her hands on his chest and leaned into him.

This time Michael took her mouth the way he'd wanted to for what seemed like forever. He ran his hands over her shoulders, her waist, her hips, sliding the soft cotton nightshirt over her warm flesh. He kissed her deeply, thoroughly, seeking the rich depths of her hunger, and was inordinately pleased that it matched his own.

Cassidy went up on her toes and wound her arms around his neck. It was suddenly important, imperative, to get closer to the magic that was winding its way around them. She trembled when her breasts were crushed against the rock-solid wall of his chest.

He broke away from her mouth and buried his face in her neck. Pulling badly needed air into his lungs, he held her tightly against him.

"You feel so good, Cassidy. You taste like sin and salvation."

She leaned her forehead against his chest. Her

voice was muffled, her body trembling with reaction. "Any more questions?"

A chuckle rumbled deeply in his chest. He lifted his head and smiled down at her. "Not at the moment. My resistance couldn't take another answer as powerful as that one right now."

Slowly, reluctantly, he drew his hands away from her and stepped back. When he sighed, it came from deep inside him.

"I'm probably going to hate myself for this, but I'm going to my room to spend a long, lonely night in my cold bed."

Cassidy felt chilled without his warmth. Rubbing her hands over her arms, she tried to feel relieved. And failed. Tried not to feel rejected. And failed.

She did manage to speak, though she was unsure whether she was trying to convince him or herself. "You're doing the right thing. Neither of us needs any more complications in our lives than we already have, Michael. It would be foolish to start something that has no hope of developing into anything other than a brief affair."

"I'm tempted to prove you wrong," he murmured, his gaze never leaving her face.

"But you won't," she said with an almost pleading quality in her voice.

"No." The look he gave her was tender and amused. "Not tonight."

Striving for something to lighten the mood, she said, "Miss Gump would go 'round the bend if she knew you were in my room, much less . . . anything else."

It was the "anything else" he was trying not to think about.

He took another step away from her and slid his hands into the back pockets of his jeans. "I'd like to get on the road early in the morning, if that's all right with you. I've looked over your list of places King might be, and there are several that aren't all that far from here. We can visit them tomorrow."

She tilted her head to one side. "You are aware that King could be anywhere, aren't you? My father accompanied him to Wales, Scotland, and even France on previous trips. The chances of our running King to ground tomorrow are very slim."

"At least I'll be doing something. Sitting around here waiting for him is driving me up the wall. And I'm not leaving England until I have some answers."

And not only about King's sudden desire to sell the chess set, he thought. Cassidy energized him, excited him as no woman ever had. He wasn't leaving until he'd fully explored these new sensations.

"Sometimes," she murmured, "finding the answers to questions is more painful than being left in the dark."

"I prefer daylight over darkness." He turned away and crossed the room while he still had enough self-control to leave her. "Why don't you go to sleep, Cassidy? I've asked Alvilda to bring you a pot of tea at eight. I'd like to leave around nine."

Cassidy nodded, sensing the tension she heard in his voice wasn't solely caused by his need to find his father. Her blood was still throbbing hot and thick in her veins; her skin was still sensitized from his touch. Desire radiated from his eyes as he paused in the doorway to look back at her.

"Good night, Michael."

His reply was a curt nod before he stepped into the hall, closing the door behind him.

Until she was alone in the room, Cassidy hadn't realized how stiffly she was standing. It was as though she'd been steeling herself against the feelings Michael created within her. She walked back to the bed and sank down heavily on it.

How could something that was so wrong for both of them feel so right? she asked herself without any hope of receiving an answer. At least not that night, when her body was still reacting from the rocketing pleasure she'd felt when he'd kissed her, when he'd held her in his arms. She sighed and wrapped her arms around her waist. The world had disappeared the moment their lips touched, replaced by a devastating thirst for more, a hunger that hadn't been satiated.

Just as she had feared he would, Michael had further complicated her life.

One of the places on Cassidy's list was near Glastonbury Abbey, and on impulse Michael took the road that would lead them to the ruined monastery that legend proclaimed was the burial site of King Arthur and Queen Guinevere. He'd visited the historical abbey before, yet for some reason that totally escaped him, he wanted to see the place with Cassidy.

Before he got out of the car, he asked, "Is your

ankle up to a stroll? I noticed you aren't limping at all today."

"It's fine, but I thought you were eager to search for King."

"Since we're here, we might as well look around. King often comes to Glastonbury. The chance is slim he'd be here, but I'd like to check it out."

They toured the ancient gatehouse that had been turned into a museum, lingering over the scale model of the abbey as it was supposed to have looked in 1539. They didn't climb the five-hundred-foot-high Glastonbury Tor to the tower on top, but strolled around some of the grounds surrounding the ruins. They stopped to admire the Holy Thorn tree; legend had it that the wooden staff of Joseph of Arimathea had been transformed into a tree that blossomed at Christmastime.

Holding Cassidy's hand, Michael shortened his long stride and stayed on the smoother paths in consideration of her ankle. As he walked along, he told her of how he and his brothers and sister had been raised with the legends of King Arthur and his Knights of the Round Table. One time King had even brought flowers to place on the spot where it was rumored King Arthur and his queen had been buried.

"It isn't all that unusual to be familiar with the Arthurian legends around here," Cassidy said. "Or in other parts of England for that matter. We all grew up with the fables, but I must admit your family has gone the extra mile when it comes to being a fan of King Arthur."

"You mean the Camelot chess set?"

"For starters. I was thinking more of your first names. Which knight did you say you were named after? I've forgotten."

"Nice try," he drawled.

She grinned, giving up on that pursuit for the moment. "I remember my father telling me something about one of your ancestors having made the Camelot set by carving out the figures, casting them in gold, and breaking the molds so there would be only one set in existence."

"That was Willoughby Knight. According to the family history, Willoughby started carving the set when he was sixteen. It took him the rest of his life to finish all the pieces and the board. The set has been in our family for four generations." His voice hardened. "And it's going to be around for future generations."

Cassidy let her gaze roam over the grounds. "Which is why you've come to England and why you're looking for your father. I understand why you want to preserve the family keepsake, but I'm a little confused. Since—according to King—neither you nor your brothers and sister have shown any inclination toward creating these future generations, for whom are you saving the set?"

"You sound like my father," he muttered. "He's been a broken record lately, nagging all of us to get married and breed."

She brought her gaze back to him. He hadn't answered her question, so she tried a different approach. "Getting married and having children isn't all that unusual. People have done both for quite a long time without any ill effects. Have you thought of what would happen to the chess set if none of the current generation of Knights has anyone to leave it to after they're gone?"

"I didn't say we planned on staying single and childless the rest of our lives. But we're not getting married just because King thinks we should." Defense changed to offense. "What about you? I haven't seen any husband or children clustered around you."

She'd noticed that too. "I'm not getting married just for the sake of being married either." Her smile held a trace of self-mockery. "Besides, no one has asked me. I know this is the nineties, but I'm not liberated enough to do the asking, even if there were someone I wanted to marry."

"Maybe you just haven't met the right man yet."

"Perhaps," she said, wondering if she was telling the truth. "Shouldn't we be on our way? It's obvious King isn't here."

He turned her toward the parking lot. "One of the farms on your list, Pander's Croft, is only a couple of miles from here. We'll go there next, then stop somewhere for lunch."

They didn't stay long at Pander's Croft. Michael didn't even bother attempting to open the closed wrought iron gates once he saw the FOR SALE sign. Weeds grew long and raggedly on either side of the paved lane leading up to the gate. The entrance had a neglected appearance, indicating they wouldn't have much success finding someone at home.

Chagrined at their wasted trip, Cassidy defended herself for having put Pander's Croft on the list. "I did warn you I haven't spent much time in Somerset."

"So you did." Glancing at the neglected grounds, he murmured, "By the looks of this place, the residents of Pander's Croft moved out the day after you did."

Without consulting the list, he drove another twenty miles to Sparrow Farms. Cassidy couldn't help noticing he hadn't asked her for directions. When they arrived, a middle-aged man came out of the Tudor-style house and walked over to the Jaguar. Michael introduced themselves and explained why they were there. He was astonished by the effusive welcome Mr. Sparrow gave them. He invited them to tour his stables and join him and Mrs. Sparrow for a cup of tea. When they were ushered into the front reception room, Michael understood why the gentleman was so willing to help them in any way he could. Hanging on a wall was a large portrait of a black stallion standing in front of one of the stalls of the Sparrow stables. The artist was King Knight.

As they drank their tea Mr. Sparrow, talking with Cassidy, revealed to Michael why Cassidy was so attached to Nougat. Mr. Sparrow recounted the story he had heard from her father about how Cassidy had slept in Toffee's stall for two nights awaiting Nougat's birth. Toffee had been Cassidy's horse since she was six. Mr. Sparrow's voice had deepened with sympathy when he related how Cassidy had been alone the night Toffee went into labor, and she had had to turn the foal during the difficult birth. She'd lost Toffee that night, but had taken full responsibility for the foal, nursing Nougat by bottle.

When Mr. Sparrow went on to say how proud

her father had been of her, Michael covered her hand with his, unable to bear the look of raw emotion on her face. His chest tightened painfully when she turned her hand over and squeezed his fingers.

Mrs. Sparrow changed the subject, but Michael didn't release Cassidy's hand. Nor did she let go of his.

Cassidy was mildly distressed by the time they left Sparrow Farms. She had enjoyed meeting the Sparrows. That wasn't the problem. She had enjoyed looking at their horses too. The tea had been good, the company charming, reminding her of the times when she'd visited neighbors with her father. What disturbed her was that Michael had insisted she come along with him. He really hadn't needed her.

She waited until they had driven a few miles before bringing the matter up. "Tell me again why you thought I should come with you today. You didn't need me to find Pander's Croft, Glastonbury, or Sparrow Farms. I can't see where I've been any help at all."

"I wanted you with me."

The calm statement rocked her. Turning to look at him, she struggled to keep her voice level. "I thought we'd settled that last night, Michael."

"Settled what?"

"About us getting involved."

"We did. We are."

She stared straight ahead again. "I'm going back to London tonight."

Five

"No," Michael said. "Cassidy, you are not getting on any train."

Her eyes widened at the edge of steel in his voice. "Are you offering to drive me to London?"

"No."

"If you know of any other way for me to get there than taking the train, I'm open to suggestions."

He pulled the car to the side of the road and shut off the engine. Turning toward her, he laid one arm over the steering wheel and the other across the back of the seat.

"You aren't going to run away from me too, Cassidy. I won't let you."

"I'm not running away from anything or anyone. I'm getting on with my life."

"You ran away when your father remarried, you plan on running away from Chartridge, and now you want to run away from me. You can't keep running all your life, Cassidy."

It was the first time she'd ever wanted to slap someone. "You have a helluva nerve even suggesting such a thing. You've known me for only two days."

"And that won't change if you go dashing off to London at the first hint of trouble." She turned away, and he slipped his fingers under her chin to force her to look at him. "This time you're going to stay and fight."

"Fight what?" she asked, genuinely bewildered by what he was saying. "Did you hit your head when we were in Mr. Sparrow's stables? You're talking rubbish."

Michael hadn't meant to bring all this up so soon, even though he believed he was right about her. It was his timing that was wrong. But he was known for rushing a high fence instead of taking the time to look for a lower one.

"Yesterday you told me you're between jobs right now," he said. "There's no reason you have to return to London today or even tomorrow."

"I have a very good reason. I don't want to stay."

"I told you I wasn't going back to Montana until I had some answers. At the time I meant answers about my father's odd behavior. That was part of it, but now I know there's more I need." He locked his gaze on hers. "There's you."

Shaking her head as though denying what he was saying, she unfastened her seat belt, opening the car door at the same time. In the next instant she was out of the car.

So was Michael.

She made it to the back of the car when he caught up with her. With a hand on her shoulder he whirled her around, holding her in front of him.

"You still haven't gotten the picture, have you? I'm not letting you run away from me."

Gritting her teeth, she glared at him. "You don't have any right to stop me."

"Your father let you go. I won't."

"Leave my father out of this."

He could have accepted her anger. Hell, he'd expected it, even encouraged it. He'd wanted a strong reaction from her. But not tears.

She was still glaring at him, but the moisture gathering in her eyes was not caused by anger.

Muttering a succinct curse, he brought her into his arms and held her securely against him.

He knew he was going too fast, pushing too hard with all the finesse of a bulldozer, trying to knock down the barriers she'd erected over years. A car drove by, then a truck, the driver honking several times, but Michael didn't notice. His whole attention was on Cassidy.

She held herself stiffly in his arms, neither protesting nor accepting his attempt to comfort her. She was simply there. Finally, she slid her hands between them and pushed against his chest. She wasn't strong enough to force him to let her go.

"Michael, please."

He dropped his arms and she immediately stepped back to put distance between them. "I'm sorry if I hurt you, Cassidy. That wasn't my intention. But I won't retract what I said."

She had to clear her throat before she could speak. "Why do you keep saying I've been running away? You haven't known me long enough or known me well enough to make that kind of judgment about me."

"Stay and prove me wrong." When she didn't respond, he added, "I'll do whatever I have to to make you stay, Cassidy."

"Why?" she asked in a voice hoarse with suppressed emotion. "Why are you so intent on keeping me here, Michael? I'm not interested in an affair, and that's all we could have. A very brief affair, since you'll be leaving soon. It would be extremely foolish for us to attempt to have any type of short-term relationship."

Michael couldn't be anything but honest with her, even though he was certain she didn't want to hear what he had to tell her. "I've never felt like this about anyone before, Cassidy. In a very short time you've become important to me. Necessary. Special. You're all I think about."

Cassidy closed her eyes as though to shut him out. Then it occurred to her she was doing what he'd accused her of—running away.

She raised her lashes and met his gaze. "It wouldn't do me any good to deny I'm attracted to you. With your blunt American honesty, you would probably tell me I'm lying. But getting involved with you would undoubtedly bring about a number of problems I don't want to have to deal with. I have enough on my plate at the moment. I've lost my father. I'm losing my home and my horse. I don't need to have you to lose too."

"Give me a week."

She blinked twice. "What?"

"Stay a week. Don't run away this time."

"Will you stop saying that?" she said irritably.

"Gladly. When you stop running." After a short pause he added a challenge. "Why don't you take a week to show me I'm wrong."

"I don't believe this." She brought her hand up to her forehead. "I must have hit my head harder than I thought when I fell off Nougat. I'm actually considering this."

"Why don't you give yourself a break?" he said, apparently deciding to try a different tack. "You've just lost your father, your home has been invaded by pond scum, and your stepbrother is playing games with your emotions. You haven't even had time to adjust to your father's death. Take a week to recharge your batteries. What could it hurt?"

She could easily guess what it could hurt—her heart, if her feelings for him grew any stronger. She could also imagine what would happen between them if she did agree to stay. Her experience with sensual desire might not be extensive, but she recognized it and had the sense to be wary of what it could lead to.

It wasn't easy for her to be as frank and open as he was, but she gave it a try. She needed to know exactly where she stood. "When you came to my room last night, you had to be aware of my . . . um, response when you kissed me. I hadn't known you even twenty-four hours and nearly . . . nearly . . ." She faltered and tried again. "If I stay—" Her courage gave out completely, and she couldn't finish the sentence.

He didn't have that problem. "If you stay, we'll make love. Many times."

His bald statement should have shocked her. Instead, her heart thudded and heat rose within her, hot and stifling as she remembered the way she'd ached with need when his mouth had claimed hers.

For a long moment she stared into his eyes, searching for answers to questions she couldn't ask, for a commitment she knew he couldn't make.

She would take what she could get.

"I can't promise I'll stay a week. Let's take it a day at a time."

Michael wanted more, and he would have more than one day or even two. He knew she was cautious. Hell, he even understood it. He was an unknown quality she'd met only yesterday. She simply wouldn't fall in bed with a virtual stranger. And truthfully, he wanted more from her than just that. He only hoped he could give her the time she needed.

He moved back to the car, holding open her door for her. "Unless you want to shock the people driving by, you'll get in before I follow through with the inclination to kiss you."

Her eyes darkened with swift arousal, and he almost lost the thin grasp on his control. "Get in the car, Cassidy," he ordered, his voice raw with need.

She did. He closed the door firmly and took his time walking around the front of the car, drawing in deep breaths to try to cool his blood. Nothing short of a Montana snowstorm could have accomplished that, though.

When he joined her in the car he said, "Fasten your seat belt, sweetheart. It's going to be a bumpy ride, but we'll eventually get where we're going."

"Are you talking about the drive back or the next couple of days?"

He was pleased to hear the crispness back in her voice, and tried to keep the relief out of his. "It's too early to say. But it certainly won't be boring."

Boring was the last word Cassidy would use to describe the rest of that day and the next. Occasionally, she felt as though she were speeding around a traffic circle without any chance of getting off. If it was Michael's intention to give her little opportunity to brood on her decision to stay at Knight's Keep, it was working. Between the trips around the countryside to visit various horse farms, exercising Nougat with Michael riding one of his father's horses, and attending the sumptuous breakfasts and five course dinners Alvilda prepared for them every day, she had no time to regret not taking the train to London.

Except when she was alone in the dark guest bedroom.

For the last two nights Michael had walked her to her door, kissed her with restrained passion, and ushered her into the room. Alone.

The first evening she was relieved he hadn't put any pressure on her. The second night she was more reluctant to go into the bedroom alone. They had spent the evening playing backgammon and talking about her father. Until Michael had encouraged her to share some of her memories of Robert, she hadn't realized how badly she'd wanted to talk about him. Grief still lay heavy on her heart, yet the load seemed lighter at the end of the evening.

Michael also wanted to know why she'd become a musician. It took her a minute to come up with an answer since not many people had asked her that question. "I've had two loves in my life," she finally said, "horses and music. I knew I didn't stand much chance of making a living riding horses, so I put my other talent to work."

"Your father was a wealthy man. You didn't have to work at all."

She looked straight at him. "I could say the same to you, yet you have a ranch you bought with money you earned yourself."

He smiled faintly. "I suppose I would be asking for trouble if I said it was different for a man."

"Probably."

Remembering the pleasant evening, Cassidy started drifting into sleep. A shrill, high-pitched noise jolted her upright. It lasted several seconds before stopping as abruptly as it had started. She was wondering if she should venture out of her room to see what was wrong, when she heard Michael running past her door. Yanking back the covers, she hurried to the door, opening it in time to see Michael going down the stairs two at a time.

"Michael?" she called out.

"Stay put," he ordered over his shoulder, not breaking his stride.

She didn't, but raced to the top of the stairs. Looking down into the foyer, she caught a glimpse of Michael as he went out of the house, slamming the front door behind him.

She had no idea what was happening, but she was going to find out. Hurrying back into her room, she quickly shed her nightshirt and reached for the slacks and turtleneck she'd worn that day. She didn't take the time to bother with underclothes. As she ran back out into the hall, she pulled a bulky sweater over her head and shoved her arms into the sleeves.

The hem of Alvilda's robe swirled around her ankles as she came to an abrupt stop in the foyer when she saw Cassidy racing down the stairs. Alvilda was holding one of the swords from King's collection in front of her, as though she were ready to run someone through.

"Miss Gump, what are you doing?"

"The alarm system has gone off in the stables. Michael's checking it out right now."

"He's out there alone?" Cassidy glanced at the door, fear for Michael's safety clutching painfully in her stomach. "Shouldn't you be notifying the police?"

"It could be nothing but a fox or a stray dog setting off the motion detectors. Clive wouldn't thank me if I called him out here for nothing."

"Who's Clive?"

"The chief constable of our local police department."

Frowning, Cassidy looked down at the sword. "If you think it's nothing to worry about, why do you have that?"

"I believe in being prepared."

Since Miss Gump seemed capable of taking care of herself, Cassidy's concerns shifted back to Michael. "I'm going to the stables," she said, and started toward the door.

The housekeeper didn't try to stop her. Follow-

ing her instead, Alvilda held out the sword. "Would
you feel safer if you had this?"

Cassidy shook her head. "I'd probably do more
harm to myself than any burglar."

The front entrance of the house was illuminated
by carriage lights, but the path to the stables was
unlit. It took Cassidy's eyes a minute to adjust to
the darkness. The small stones lining the drive
crunched softly under her feet as she walked
along quickly. Nearing the stables, she saw that
one of the wide doors was open and the inside
lights were on.

Stepping inside, she looked around. Everything
seemed the same. The stalls were neat and clean,
the building permeated with the scent of horses,
straw, and leather. The stall doors were closed
except for one. Nougat's stall. It was empty. After
another hasty look around, she hurried back to
the stable entrance. She stared out into the darkness, but was unable to see any sign of Michael or
Nougat. Biting her lip, she strained her eyes to try
to see something. Anything. She couldn't go looking for them, since she didn't know which way to
go.

What was going on? she wondered, trying hard
not to panic. Where was her horse, and where was
Michael? The alarm had been set off by somebody
breaking into the stables for the sole purpose of
stealing her horse. Anyone stupid enough or desperate enough to sneak around in the middle of
the night could also be dangerous. Michael evidently had gone after Nougat, and the thieves. If
Derek was behind this, she wasn't sure he would
stop at stealing Nougat. The blow Michael had

landed to Derek's jaw had bruised her stepbrother's pride as well.

She paced from one side of the stable to the other, but was still unable to see anything except dark, shadowy masses. She hated this helpless feeling. She hated not knowing what was happening to Michael and Nougat.

The sound of a horse whinnying had her running outside. Unless she was seeing things, one of the dark masses was moving.

"Michael?"

His voice came out of the darkness. "Dammit, Cassidy. I told you to stay inside."

"You might have needed some help," she said, feeling almost weak with relief when he moved out of the shadows with Nougat following close behind.

Michael had a tight hold on the lead rein as Nougat danced restlessly. They both appeared to be all right, but she wanted reassurance. Michael had just enough time to brace himself as she threw herself at him.

"Are you all right?" she asked urgently. Not waiting for an answer, she cupped his face, then ran her hands over his shoulders and chest, satisfying herself that he was unharmed.

As much as Michael was enjoying her exploration, he had to put an end to it. For now anyway. "Aside from being irritated that I didn't catch the horse thieves, I'm fine."

"Are you sure?"

He tried to conceal his smile, afraid she would misunderstand it. Her concern made him happy, but she might think he was laughing at her.

He compromised by kissing her on the forehead. "I'm sure. If it will make you feel any better, you can examine me more thoroughly when we get back to the house. In fact, I might insist on it."

Her face was in shadow, so he couldn't see her expression. The only reaction he was aware of was her tight grip on his hand. Wrapping his arm around her shoulders, he drew her to his side between him and her horse.

Cassidy smoothed a hand over the mare's neck. "Is she all right?"

"We can check her out once we get her in her stall. I think she's okay, except for being skittish over her midnight stroll."

"Did you see who took her?"

"There were three of them, all wearing long black capes with hoods, like something out of Victorian London. Evidently they weren't aware of the stable's security system and weren't expecting anyone to discover them. They were leading Nougat toward the woods when I first spotted them. The instant they saw me they dropped the lead and took off. They ran into the trees and I lost them."

Cassidy turned her head to look back at the woods. The stand of trees separated the Knights' property from Chartridge land.

She fell into step beside him as he started to lead Nougat toward the stables. Once inside, they brushed down the horse together. After Nougat was safely back in her stall, she asked, "What are you going to do about what happened tonight?"

"That depends on you."

She watched as he walked to a corner of the

stables and opened the door of a small green metal box attached to the wall. He reset the alarm, then returned to her.

"What do you mean, it depends on me?" she asked.

"It's your horse." He took her arm to draw her with him out of the stable. "Right now we'd better let Alvilda know everything's all right before she gets excited and calls for the cavalry."

"Or cuts off her foot." When he gave her a puzzled look, she explained. "She was brandishing a sword from your father's collection when I left the house."

Stopping suddenly, he pulled her around to face him, his hands on her shoulders. "Before we go in, we'd better get our stories straight."

"Our stories?" she asked, then nodded in understanding. "You mean whether we mention to Miss Gump that it was my stepbrother who was behind the break-in?"

Michael smiled. "I thought I was going to have to dance around the subject for a few minutes." He slid his hands over her shoulders to the base of her throat. His thumbs stroked the soft, cool skin above her sweater. "I should have known better. You're not only beautiful, but smart too."

"It wasn't all that difficult to figure out. Any respectable horse thief would have taken one of the more valuable, younger horses in King's stables, rather than an older mare past her prime. Trying to steal Nougat's something Derek would be dumb enough to do. He probably enlisted a couple of his house guests to help out. They could have raided the trunks of clothes in the loft for the capes."

"If you don't want Alvilda to know it was Derek, I'll come up with something else to tell her."

Thinking of the housekeeper standing guard in the foyer, she smiled. "Afraid she'll go after him with the sword?"

He shook his head, his fingers slipping behind her neck, beneath her tousled hair. "I doubt if she'd go that far, but she would want to call her old school friend, the chief constable, and report your stepbrother."

"The police can't do anything. We don't have any proof it was Derek who broke into the stables. Besides, I'd rather not involve the authorities. It would only make matters worse."

He stroked her hair, enjoying the feel of the silky strands. "He's trying to get back at you by taking something that means a great deal to you. Since that didn't work, he could try to harm you more directly."

He continued caressing her hair, and she shivered with pleasure. It wasn't easy to stick to the topic of her stepbrother when all she wanted to do was give in to the riot of sensations Michael's touch incited in her.

When she remained silent, Michael said, "I can't figure out if you're trying to protect Derek or if you're afraid of him."

She gave him a resentful look. "I don't give a damn about Derek," she said tightly. "I'm trying to find a way to keep my horse alive."

"What?"

She grabbed his wrists as his hands clenched into fists in her hair. "You're hurting me, Michael."

He dropped his hands to her shoulders. "Sorry. Hurting you is the last thing I want to do. What is this about keeping Nougat alive? Are you saying your stepbrother hates you so much, he'd kill your horse?"

"Yes," she answered bluntly. "Oh, not directly. Derek took great pleasure in telling me Friday morning, just before you and I met, that the man interested in buying Nougat is from a knacker's yard. I don't know what such a place is called in Montana, but here a knacker's yard is where they slaughter horses and sell the different parts to factories that make glue and dog food."

Michael muttered several curse words under his breath. "Why didn't you tell me this before?"

"It had nothing to do with you."

The way his eyes narrowed was an indication of how much he disliked her answer. "We haven't gotten as far as I thought if you believe that. You keep too much from me, Cassidy. We're going to have to work on that. But for now we'd better concentrate on your horse. I'll offer Derek more money than he'd get for selling your horse for dog food. Since money is so important to him, maybe he'll make a deal if I offer a large enough sum."

She shook her head. "It wouldn't do any good. You knocked him down in front of his friends, remember? He wouldn't take your money any more than he'll take mine."

He cupped her face, his fingers delving into her hair. "We'll find a way to save Nougat, Cassidy."

She didn't think Michael had moved, yet he

seemed closer. His scent surrounded her; spicy pine aftershave, a hint of horse and leather blending with warm male. A heady combination that made her heart beat faster.

Her mouth was suddenly dry, and she ran her tongue over her lips.

His gaze lowered to her lips. He gently grasped a handful of her hair, drawing her head back. He whispered her name, then kissed her, filling her with his scent and taste. Her body melted into his as she met his desire with matching hunger.

The sound of a shotgun blast tore them apart.

Six

Cassidy was right behind Michael as they ran up the front steps. She almost bumped into him when he stopped abruptly just inside the door. Peering around him, she saw Miss Gump staring down in horror at a shotgun that was lying on the floor at her feet.

Michael stepped over the gun to reach the housekeeper. "Are you all right?"

With trembling hands Alvilda patted herself down as though checking for holes and looking vastly relieved when she didn't find any. "I was holding the gun so it was pointed toward the ceiling," she said, her voice shaking. "If it didn't hit me, then where . . . ?"

Simultaneously, all three tipped their heads back to look up. Part of the fresco painted on the ceiling had been peppered with buckshot. Bits of plaster had been blasted away, leaving distinct white patches in the painting of plump cupids flying amid billowy clouds.

For several seconds they all simply stared, then Michael brought his gaze back to Alvilda. "What happened?"

"I tripped on the hem of my robe as I was walking to the front door. I was getting worried when neither of you returned. When I tried to get my balance I accidentally dropped King's gun and the wretched thing went off."

Michael bent down to pick up the shotgun. "Why did you have this? Cassidy said you had a sword."

The housekeeper made a scornful sound. "Those swords are too dangerous. I could have hurt myself."

Cassidy met Michael's amused gaze and bit her lip to keep from laughing. Taking Alvilda's arm, she could feel that the woman was still trembling. "Let's go into the kitchen, Miss Gump. A nice hot cup of tea will make you feel better."

A look of relief came over Alvilda's face. "That would be lovely." Hitching up her robe, she turned toward the kitchen. "I should never have called King," she said to Cassidy as they started down the hall. "He told me the shotgun would be more effective than the sword if the burglar got past you and Michael."

Cassidy and Michael spoke at the same time. *"What?"*

In two long strides Michael was beside Alvilda. "You talked to King tonight?"

Realizing what she'd said, Alvilda closed her eyes and rubbed her forehead with one hand. "Oh,

Lord," she said wearily. "I told King I wouldn't be very good at this."

"Wouldn't be good at what?" Michael asked, trying to keep his voice calm.

Apparently he didn't succeed, for Alvilda opened her eyes and gave him a wary look. "Please don't ask me that. I can't tell you."

Michael said nothing more as he led Alvilda through the dining room and into the kitchen. Trailing behind them, Cassidy debated whether she should leave Michael and the housekeeper alone to settle this between them. Curiosity won out over good manners.

Michael assisted Alvilda into one of the chairs at the end of the large worktable in the center of the kitchen. After propping the gun in a corner, he returned to the table, pulling out a chair and sitting down. He glanced at Cassidy.

"You were going to make some tea."

Relieved to have something to do, Cassidy did as he suggested. She poured water into the electric kettle located near the sink and turned it on, then puttered about, looking for tea, a teapot, and cups. Michael was silent again, and she looked over her shoulder at him.

He was leaning back in the chair, one booted foot crossed over the opposite knee. Cassidy knew his relaxed appearance was deceptive. All anyone had to do was look into his eyes, and they would know that underneath his laid-back slouch was a coiled spring.

Alvilda, on the other hand, sat stiffly in her chair, her fingers restlessly tracing the wood grain in the table. The longer the silence drew out, the more obviously nervous Alvilda became.

Cassidy leaned against the counter, waiting for more than the water to come to a boil.

Minutes dragged by. The only sound in the room was the ticking of a small clock and the water in the kettle beginning to simmer. When a shrill whistle signaled that the water was boiling, both Cassidy and Alvilda jumped.

Cassidy measured tea leaves into the Meissenware teapot and poured the hot water. She nearly dropped the kettle when Michael finally spoke.

"Where is he?"

"Michael, please," Alvilda said. "Don't ask me to betray King's confidence. You know I can't do that."

Sitting up straight, Michael leaned his arms on the table. "What's going on, Alvilda? If King is ill or in some kind of trouble, I have a right to know. Maybe I could help, but I can't do anything if I don't know what's wrong."

"Nothing is wrong. I can tell you that much. King is fine. As I told you when you arrived, he's sketching background material for a new painting."

"Where?"

Determination replaced the housekeeper's previous nervous expression. Lifting her chin, she faced Michael squarely. "Even though I think King is wrong in what he's doing and have told him so repeatedly, I cannot tell you what you want to know, Michael. I gave my word."

Michael nodded, respecting Alvilda's loyalty to his father. He backed off physically as well as verbally, sitting back in the chair. "You know we're all worried about him. He's acting strange, even for him, by telling us he's going to sell the Camelot chess set. I'm not going to ask you to break your word to my father, but tell me what you can about what's going on, when he's coming back, so I can talk to him."

Alvilda waited until Cassidy had set a cup of tea in front of her and Michael. Her gaze followed Cassidy as she returned to the counter where she'd left her own cup.

"I can tell you this," Alvilda said, looking at Michael again. "Everything is working out the way King has planned."

"It usually docs," Michael said dryly. His eyes narrowed as he caught Alvilda glancing at Cassidy once more. Alvilda looked . . . satisfied. "Does King's absence have anything to do with Cassidy?"

He heard Cassidy gasp but kept his attention on Alvilda. She tensed, and he knew he was right. He also knew Alvilda wasn't going to confirm that. But she'd told him more than she thought she had.

He pushed back his chair, but was stopped from rising by Alvilda's hand covering his. "King will be back in three days," she said. "He'll explain everything to you then." She paused, then asked, "That is, if you will still be here?"

"Oh, I'll definitely be here. Lately King thinks our lives are like one of the blank canvases that he can dabble with. I'm going to make sure he understands we prefer to paint our own pictures without any interference from him."

"Your father is seventy years old, Michael. He feels he is running out of time."

"I got that impression after the third fax he sent after his birthday." Michael gently squeezed the older woman's hand. "Why don't you try to get some sleep? There's still a couple of hours left of the night."

"What about the break-in at the stables? Shouldn't we call in the authorities?"

He shook his head. "That won't be necessary. They didn't take anything, and I'll see that they don't try again."

Before Alvilda could ask any more questions, he stood up and walked over to Cassidy. He took her cup out of her hand and set it on the counter.

"Let's go to bed."

Cassidy didn't protest his choice of words until they were at the bottom of the stairs, well out of Alvilda's hearing. "Do you realize how that sounded to Miss Gump?"

He slipped his arm around her waist as they started up the stairs. "About us going to bed? That's what we're going to do."

"You made it sound as though we were going to bed together."

They reached the top of the stairs, and he paused, looking down at her. His expression was serious, his eyes dark with hunger. "That's up to you."

She didn't want to have to make that decision. She wanted him to take the initiative, take her, not leave it to her to decide. As experienced as she assumed he was, he had to know she wanted him by the way she responded to him each time he kissed her. Words came so easily to him, as well as the courage to say them. She communicated her feelings through her music. Exposing her innermost thoughts and emotions any other way had never been encouraged. Her father had believed in the old adage that children should be seen and not heard. Her stepmother had agreed with him.

He waited while she struggled to find the right words. She could go into her room alone, or be with him for a magical night in his arms. It was her choice. Since she couldn't bring herself to say what she wanted, perhaps she could show him.

She placed her hands on his chest and slowly slid them upward, aware of his quick intake of breath. Cupping his head, she drew him down to her. His mouth was warm and hard, his hands firm and strong at her waist, and she was instantly propelled into a sensual tunnel of desire.

Much too soon he broke away from her mouth. "Say the words, Cassidy," he said softly, his voice as ragged as his breathing. "I need the words."

She saw the hunger in his eyes, felt the rapid thudding of his heartbeat against her breast.

"Michael," she whispered.

"The words, Cassidy. I don't want any misunderstandings between us in the morning. You're going to have to tell me what you want."

If she didn't, she knew he would withdraw from her, and she didn't think she could stand the cold or the emptiness if he left her now.

Suddenly it was very easy to say the words. "I want you to kiss me. I want your hands on me." She caressed his face. "I want you to hold me, to lie with me, to be inside me."

Michael buried his face in the curve of her neck, his body shuddering with the impact of what she was admitting to him. Her softly spoken request almost snapped his control completely.

Keeping her tightly locked to his side, he walked her down the hall to his bedroom. The light from the hall disappeared when he shut the door behind them, the room's only illumination coming from the shimmering moon outside the leaded glass windows. It was enough.

Michael leaned back against the door, still reeling from her impassioned surrender. By now, he told himself, he should be used to the unexpected from her. As badly as he wanted to accept what she was offering, he also needed to understand why she had decided to give herself to him.

He pushed away from the door. He was now close enough to touch her. "Cassidy, once we make love, there'll be no going back to the way things were before."

"I know."

"We haven't known each other very long."

"I know that too." After a brief pause she asked, "Are you trying to warn me off, Michael? Now that you've had a couple of minutes to think about it, are you afraid I'm going to ask for more than you're prepared to give?"

She didn't wait for an answer. "Never mind. I don't want to hear you confirm that I've made a fool of myself." Brushing past him, she reached for the latch on the door.

He clamped his hands around her waist and pulled her back against him. "I'm the fool." Enclosing her in his arms, he lowered his head to kiss the side of her neck. "I've wanted you so badly for what seems like forever. I just couldn't believe the waiting was over."

A rush of heat turned her bones to liquid as she felt his hard body pressed so tightly to hers. "How could you doubt I want you?" she asked, her voice trembling.

He turned her around to face him, his hands holding her hips. Leaning his lower body into hers, he pressed her back against the door, leaving her in no doubt of his arousal.

"Show me," he murmured against her lips. "Make me believe it."

She fought her insecurities, her lack of experience. It would kill her if she disappointed him.

As he rolled his hips against hers, she pressed one leg between his, and was amazed when he shuddered against her and moaned deep in his throat. Closer. She needed to be closer. She stood on her toes and pressed her mouth to his.

The world spun away along with her fears. She no longer worried about satisfying his desire. Something more powerful filled her mind, her body. Her whole being was consumed with the overwhelming need to give as much pleasure as she was receiving.

She protested with an inarticulate murmur when he loosened his hold on her. He'd let her go only in order to sweep her bulky sweater over her head. Her turtleneck followed, and she vaguely heard his long sigh when he saw she wore nothing else. She kicked off her shoes, then with shaking fingers fumbled with the buttons on his shirt.

After a few frustrating seconds she muttered,

"Is there something I don't understand about American shirts?"

An exhilaration unlike anything Michael had ever felt flooded his being. The knowledge that she was as impatient as he fueled his passion to a raging fire.

He helped her open his shirt, then shrugged it off. With his hands at her waist he slowly brought her toward him. His mouth closed over hers hungrily as her bare breasts at last pressed against his naked chest.

Cassidy became lost in the primitive pleasure of his touch, his magic. She didn't object when he lifted her off her feet and carried her to his bed. Her gaze never left him as he stripped off the rest of his clothes. She had never thought a man could be beautiful, but seeing Michael's solid, strong, aroused male body was pure delight.

He was close enough for her to touch. So she did. Stretching her hand out, she ran her fingers over his rock-hard thigh.

Michael covered her hand, groaning with both pain and pleasure. Confused, she tried to withdraw her hand, but he wouldn't let her.

"It's not that I don't want you to touch me, sweetheart. I'm trying to hang on long enough to make it to the bed."

"You want me that much?" she asked, awe and excitement in her voice.

He threaded his fingers through hers and joined her on the bed. Lying beside her, he drew their clasped hands over her head. "I've never wanted a woman this badly. I'm so hot for you, I'm about to detonate."

She lifted her free hand to his face. "Not without me."

He gazed into her eyes, which were glazed with desire. "We're going to be magic together."

Her slacks were the last barrier between them. He tugged at the fastening at her waist and lowered the zipper, then slipped his hand inside. She was so soft and warm, so ready for him. Her hips surged upward at his touch, and his mind clouded over with the need to be inside her.

With growing urgency he tugged her slacks down her legs and tossed them aside. He wanted to take the time to savor her smooth, silky skin, but his control was almost nonexistent.

Slowly sliding his aching body over hers, he settled between her legs. He brushed a strand of her hair from her cheek. "Tell me again, Cassidy," he murmured huskily. "Say it."

She could feel him poised and ready and wanting. "I need you, Michael," she whispered. "I'm aching and empty. Please don't wait any longer."

Dazed with desire, Michael was still able to rein in his hunger enough not to take her too swiftly. A fine sheen of perspiration moistened his skin as he eased into her moist warmth.

He groaned against her mouth at the exquisite feel of her sheathing him. Kissing her deeply, he gloried in her soft sounds of pleasure and the rolling shift of her hips under his. When he felt her nails scrape along his back, he fell willingly into the fire threatening to engulf them.

A spiraling tension thrust them deeper and deeper into the realms of passion, into an unknown territory where there was only the two of them. Need spurred them on as they clung to each other, bodies moving in perfect rhythm until the world shattered around them.

Michael buried his face in her tangled hair and shuddered as the aftermath of pleasure sang through his body long after his release. His heart still thundered in his chest, and he was aware of a sense of completion, a contentment he'd never experienced before.

Knowing he was too heavy for her, he rolled onto his side, bringing her with him. He brushed her damp hair from her cheek and smiled down at her.

She smiled back and whispered his name, then her eyes slowly closed. But not before Michael had seen the glow of satisfaction lighting their green depths.

Seven

A couple of sharp taps on the door roused Cassidy from a deep sleep. Barely awake, she didn't understand for several seconds what had awakened her. If Alvilda was holding to her usual schedule, it was eight in the morning and time to start another day with the cup of tea the housekeeper insisted on bringing to her room. In a few seconds Alvilda would tap again, one short knock, then she would walk in.

Cassidy made a strangled sound as the events of the night came flooding back. Sitting up as though the sheets were on fire, she quickly looked at the other side of the bed, expecting to see Michael sprawled out beside her. She collapsed back on the pillow when she realized she was alone.

And in her own room.

And naked.

She wasn't given any time to figure out how

she'd ended up in her own bed when the last thing she remembered was being in Michael's bed. Maybe it had been a dream, a wonderful, spellbinding, explosive dream. She flung her forearm across her eyes, then froze. Michael's scent was clinging to her skin. She hadn't been dreaming. That discovery, though, still didn't explain why she was in her bed.

Another tap on the door preceded the latch turning. Alvilda walked in carrying the customary tray with its tea and a plate of scones.

"Good morning, Miss Cassidy. How are you this fine morning?"

Cassidy raked her fingers through her tangled hair, then scooted up to lean against the carved headboard of the bed. She kept the sheet up over her breasts.

"I'm fine," she said weakly. Clearing her throat, she added, "You don't seem any worse for wear after last night."

In fact, wearing a neatly ironed blue chintz dress, the housekeeper was briskly efficient and irritatingly cheerful. She busied herself with setting the tray on the table in front of the window and pouring the tea.

"One of the charming benefits," she said, "about being a part of the Knight household is that life is rarely boring." She gave Cassidy a sharp look as she handed her the cup and saucer. "As I think you are discovering."

It wasn't easy to maintain a modicum of dignity under the circumstances, but Cassidy did her best. Holding the sheet to her chest, she frowned at the steaming cup of tea, wondering what she was supposed to do with it since one of her hands was occupied preserving her modesty. Sighing, she set the saucer on her thigh, then carefully lifted the cup.

She almost spilled it when it was halfway to her lips as Alvilda said, "Michael is the one most like his mother, but he has enough of his father in him to make life interesting for the woman involved with him."

Cassidy stared at Alvilda. "If you're warning me against getting involved with Michael, it isn't necessary. I know he'll be leaving England soon to go back to Montana."

Making a scoffing sound, the housekeeper shook her head. "Good Lord, child. You're misunderstanding me. You might think I should mind my own business, but as you will come to find out, I rarely do. I was only giving you the benefit of my experience with Michael's family to make you more comfortable when you meet them all."

The tea went down the wrong way, and Cassidy had to cough several times to clear her throat. As she was trying to get her breath back, she tried also to come up with a way of setting the housekeeper straight about her relationship with Michael Knight. She might have succeeded if Alvilda hadn't thumped her soundly on the back. Alvilda's help put an end to the coughing spell, but almost spilled the tea all over the bed and nearly knocked loose a couple of teeth.

Cassidy steadied the cup, then her nerves. "I'm afraid you have the wrong idea about why I'm here, Alvilda. I'm not going to be a permanent fixture in Michael's life. He's helping me by giving

me a place to stay while I decide what to do about
Chartridge. I was helping him look for King. That's
all there is to it."

"I know exactly why you're here, Miss Cassidy,"
she said, winking at Cassidy. "Now drink your tea.
Young Michael is waiting in the dining room for
you to join him, so try not to take too long or there
won't be any scones left for afternoon tea."

Cassidy didn't try to detain Alvilda so she could
more clearly explain the situation between herself
and Michael. Everyone would understand once
she returned to London.

Leaning her head against the headboard, she
sighed heavily. She'd better make a few things
clear to herself, she thought. And make some
decisions. King would be back soon and shortly
afterward Michael would be returning to his ranch.

The few hours she'd spent in Michael's arms
hadn't changed anything, except she would have
some wonderful memories to take back to London
with her.

As she showered and dressed, she decided it
was time to stop drifting and face a few facts. Her
father was gone. Chartridge belonged to her stepbrother. She couldn't change either of those facts,
but she could still do something about Nougat.
Her visit to Sparrow Farms had given her an idea.

Alvilda had been wrong. Michael wasn't waiting
for her in the dining room. He was standing at the
bottom of the stairs as she came down. She felt
her blood warm as he watched every step she
took, and she had to contain the urge to tug
self-consciously at the bottom of her sweater or
run her hand over her tweed skirt.

"It's a shame," he murmured when she reached the last step.

"What is?"

His arm snaked around her waist, and he drew her closer. His kiss was hard and hungry. All too soon he lifted his head and looked down into her eyes. "It's a shame to cover your delicious skin with clothes."

She could have said the same thing about him, although she couldn't fault the way his tight jeans and deep red shirt fit him.

Surprising them both, she rested her forearms on his shoulders and asked, "Is that why I woke up without a nightgown this morning?"

"Hmmm." He was fascinated by the teasing light in her eyes. "It took every ounce of chivalry I possess to take you back to your room when I would have rather kept you in my bed. For about the next five days. But Alvilda had the shock of her life last night when she tried to kill the ceiling with the shotgun. I thought I'd save her another one by getting you back to your room before she brought your tea and found your bed empty. She would probably think you'd been kidnapped and call the police."

He lifted her off the bottom step and set her on the floor beside him. "To show you I treat my woman right," he went on, "I'll feed you first to keep your strength up before we take off."

She nearly stumbled. "Take off? It's not necessary to be crude, Michael. I do not plan on removing my clothing in the dining room."

Damned if he didn't like that snippy tone she could get. Chuckling, he touched the tip of her nose with his finger. "I wasn't being crude, my little English dove. I meant before we leave Knight's Keep."

She rolled her eyes. "You know, it would be easier to remember your American slang if it made sense. I didn't realize you planned to . . . ah, take off this morning."

His smile widened. "*We* are going to take a little trip to Wells to see my father's lawyer."

"Why?"

Michael started to answer, but the sound of the front door knocker stopped him. Cassidy looked toward the door as Michael turned to see Alvilda enter the foyer to answer the summons.

Alvilda opened the door, but from their position by the stairs Michael and Cassidy were unable to see who'd come calling.

They could hear the surprise in Alvilda's voice.

"Clive, I didn't realize Michael had called you." The surprise turned to frost as she added, "And to what do we owe the dubious pleasure of your company at this hour, Mr. Pembroke?"

As Cassidy and Michael exchanged worried glances, the chief constable spoke, his tone professional. "I understand Mr. Pembroke's stepsister, Miss Harrold, is a guest here. Would it be possible for me to have a word with her?"

Alvilda hesitated, then opened the door farther in silent invitation. As she stepped back she sent a puzzled glance in Cassidy's direction. "Chief Constable Roan is here to see you, Miss Cassidy."

Michael slipped his arm around Cassidy's waist, halting her when she took a step forward. "Take Chief Constable Roan and Mr. Pembroke into the morning room, Alvilda. Miss Harrold will be with them in a moment."

"Very good, sir."

Cassidy's gaze followed Alvilda and the two men until they were out of sight. Then she turned to Michael. "Why didn't you want me to talk to them now?"

Taking her arm, Michael led her away from the stairs and into the dining room. He closed the door behind them.

"The chief constable is here on official business, Cassidy," he said grimly.

"What makes you think that?"

"Clive and my father's lovable housekeeper have had a thing going for several years. For him to come across like he did with Alvilda means he's not here for a social call. Considering he's accompanied by your charming stepbrother, it doesn't take a genius to figure out what that official business would be about."

Cassidy sank back against the wall. "Nougat."

Michael nodded. "If Derek has brought in the police, he probably wants Clive to enforce his legal rights regarding your horse. That means he plans to take Nougat away this morning."

Cassidy looked stricken. "Damn. If Derek had waited even one more day, Nougat wouldn't be here. I had it all worked out. I just needed some time."

"What were you going to do?"

"Remember Sparrow Farms?"

"Of course. What about it?"

"I was going to ask Mr. Sparrow if he would board Nougat."

"That is a good idea, but now . . ."

Michael heard the familiar clump of Alvilda's orthopedic shoes on the foyer's oak floor and knew he didn't have much time. He leaned close to Cassidy, his hands braced against the wall on either side of her head.

"While you're talking with Pembroke and the chief constable," he murmured, "I'm going to take Nougat out for a little exercise, with your permission. That way, even if Clive has a warrant to take Nougat back to Chartridge, it won't do him any good."

Hope shimmered in her eyes. "Where would you take him?"

"For now, into the woods until our guests are gone. Then I'll bring her back to the stables. We can call Mr. Sparrow, and if he agrees to board Nougat temporarily, we'll take her over there."

He pushed away from Cassidy just as Alvilda walked into the dining room. She was obviously not at all happy to see her friend Clive under these circumstances. "If he thinks I'm going to serve them tea and crumpets, the chief constable had best think again."

Michael winked at Cassidy before turning to the agitated housekeeper. "Don't blame Clive, Alvilda. He's only doing his job."

"Well," she said indignantly, "he needn't do it here." Turning her attention to Cassidy, she said, "He's waiting for you."

Straightening, Cassidy smiled at the housekeeper. "Don't worry, Alvilda. Everything will be all right."

• • •

Three hours later Cassidy was pacing across the brick floor of the stables. Nougat's stall was still as empty as it had been when she'd accompanied the chief constable and her stepbrother out there. Derek hadn't believed her when she'd told them Nougat wasn't at Knight's Keep, and had insisted on seeing for himself. She'd been pleased to see that Michael had ordered the stable boys to lay fresh hay in Nougat's stall and empty the feed box. It did not look like a horse had occupied that stall recently. After Derek had admitted Nougat wasn't there, the chief constable had apologized to her for wasting her time. She smiled as she recalled how he'd glared at Derek and said that his own time had been wasted as well.

Her smile disappeared as she also remembered the look of hate Derek had given her as he'd followed Clive from the stables. He'd been furious when he'd seen Nougat wasn't there, and had stomped over every inch of the entire area, even looking in the loft overhead, an impossible place to hide a horse.

Standing in the doorway of the stables, Cassidy stared in the direction of the woods. This was the second time in less than twelve hours that she'd waited for Michael to return to the stables. And she again couldn't go looking for him, since she had no idea which direction he'd gone.

She bit her lip and walked back into the stables to resume her restless pacing. Something must have gone wrong, or Michael would have returned by now. It was ridiculous to imagine he could have fallen off her horse while riding in the woods. Michael was as familiar with horses as most men were with cars. There had to be some other reason he hadn't come back yet.

There was. And she found out what it was when Michael strolled into the stables half an hour later. Walking, not riding.

She hurried over to him and hugged him tightly around his neck. "Dammit, Michael," she said with a catch in her voice. "Where have you been? I've been going out of my mind waiting."

His arms had automatically gone around her. Now he loosened his hold on her so he could see her face. "You were worried about me? Cassidy, that's the nicest thing you've ever said to me."

She didn't know whether to kiss him or shake him. She had to be satisfied with saying, "You are a very strange man."

"But you're crazy about me."

"Crazy, yes. You seem to be responsible for that condition. I was relatively sane until I met you. What have you done with Nougat?"

"She's fine," he murmured as he kissed her neck. He was more interested in sampling the succulent flavor of her skin than talking about her horse.

The way she said his name was a combination of irritation and seduction. He decided to relieve her mind. The seduction could come later. But not much later.

He raised his head, but still held her close. "I decided to take Nougat over to Mr. Sparrow's right away, just in case your charming stepbrother has someone keeping an eye on the stables and I was seen bringing Nougat back. I have trouble believing he would be that smart, but I didn't want to take the chance. I tied Nougat in the woods near the gatehouse and used the phone to call Mr. Sparrow. I had to break a window to get in, which won't make my father real happy, but I couldn't get to the phone any other way. Sparrow didn't require any explanations. Due to his admiration for my father and your beautiful face, he agreed to send a horse box to a spot on the other side of the woods to pick up his new boarder."

Relief brightened her eyes. "I'll contact him about the boarding fees as soon as I get back to London. I don't expect him to keep Nougat for free." She hugged him. "Thank you, Michael. I hated the thought of Nougat's being dragged off to end her days at the knacker's yard."

Michael didn't return her hug. Instead, he'd let his arms fall away from her, and she saw his hands curling into fists.

She slowly withdrew her arms from around his neck. He was holding himself rigid and staring down at her with dark accusing eyes.

"Michael? What is it?"

"You can still talk about going back to London after last night?"

She would have liked to step back to put a little distance between her and the force of his anger. She stayed where she was, though. This was one fight he wasn't going to accuse her of running away from.

"Are you planning on giving up your ranch to move to England after last night, Michael?"

"Of course not."

"Then why shouldn't I talk about going back to my life in London? Nothing has changed because we've gone to bed together."

"Dammit, Cassidy." He turned away from her as he raked his fingers through his hair. Whirling back, he asked, "How can you say that? Last night changed everything."

As soon as he said the words, Michael realized just how true they were. In the past he'd lightly used the phrase "making love" when referring to having sex. Last night he had made love with Cassidy. The difference had changed him beyond reckoning.

The difference was love. He was in love with her.

"Michael?" She took a hesitant step toward him, alarmed by the strange expression on his face. "What's wrong?"

He made a harsh sound. It was supposed to be a laugh but came out as a groan. Everything was wrong. Except how he felt about her. That was right and irreversible. But if he didn't do something, there would be an ocean between them.

Unable to look at her without wanting to touch her, he walked over to Nougat's empty stall and leaned his arms on the top of the half door. He'd encountered a number of difficult problems in his life, but nothing to equal falling in love with a woman who lived halfway around the world.

He needed time to adjust to being in love for the first time in his life. Hell, he needed more than time. Somehow he had to come up with a way for them to be together. And thinking clearly wasn't something he did very well when he was with her. Whenever she was near, all he could do was feel.

Lord, she made him feel.

He hadn't heard her moving toward him, but he knew she was standing close. She touched his arm, and need drummed heavily through his veins. Desire and fear, a strange combination, churned through him. He knew how to deal with the first but not the last.

"Michael?"

Fighting a smothering panic at the thought of losing her, he turned and pulled her into his arms. His mouth covered hers ruthlessly, claiming her breath and her soft, moaning response. His callused hands were merciless yet tender, and oddly desperate as they gripped her through her sweater.

With a sound of impatience, he slid his hands under the sweater's bottom. Passion shuddered through him when her silken breasts filled his hands.

Several horses stamped their hooves restlessly, but Cassidy didn't notice. She no longer worried either about whatever it was Michael had had on his mind a few moments earlier. All she could think about was the desire coiling through her. All she could think about was Michael.

She felt her head spin as he turned with her in his arms and leaned against the door of the stall. He grasped handfuls of her skirt, pulling it up, then glided his hands over her thighs. She sucked in her breath when he cupped her bottom and pressed her intimately into his hard body.

"Michael," she whispered.

He shuddered violently with the furious need slashing through him. He couldn't wait to have her, or he would explode.

As much as his mind was centered on her, he still managed to remember where they were. The last thing he wanted was to have one of the stable hands wander in at an inopportune time.

Tightening his hold on her, he said roughly, "Put your legs around my waist."

She struggled up from the dazed sensuality he'd drawn her into. "What?"

"I can't let go of you long enough to let you walk to where we need to go."

When she hesitated, he kissed her and lifted her higher, his hands on her bottom. With a whimper she complied by wrapping her legs around his hips. She clung tightly to his shoulders, her fingers clenching and stroking fitfully. She felt as taut as a wire, stretched beyond her limits by her all-encompassing desire for this man who held her so securely in his arms.

Michael carried her into the small room at one end of the stables, where the saddles and bridles were kept. Instead of the perfume from a bower of flowers, the air held a hint of linseed oil and leather. Light came from a small glazed window, not romantic, flickering candles. There wasn't even a bed, but only a saddle set on a wooden frame. Neither of them cared.

Unable to release her completely, Michael lowered her until she was sitting sideways on the saddle, her thighs on either side of his. The soft cries she was making were driving him over the edge; the clutching bite of her fingers moving restlessly over him left him almost senseless with the need to be inside her.

He couldn't take his mouth from hers. He couldn't

still his hands to any one place on her body. He couldn't stop. He had to have her or lose what little was left of his mind.

He finally broke away from her lips long enough to tug her sweater over her head. She wore nothing underneath. He lowered his head and captured her breasts, filling his hands and his mouth with the taut, trembling, feminine flesh. Her back arched, and she dragged air into her lungs raggedly as a torrent of sensation washed over her.

"Michael," she said achingly.

"Soon," he murmured. "Soon."

Shaking her head, she clamped her thighs tighter around his hips. "Now."

Needing to feel her against his naked skin, he tore at the snaps of his shirt, exposing his chest. Sliding his hand up her spine, he planted his palm against her back and brought her toward him. A grunt of painful pleasure came from deep in his throat, and he fought to control the raging madness.

He needed more. He needed to be closer. He needed her.

His whole body was throbbing and aching for the release he knew he would find only with this woman. With his one hand still behind her, he held her securely as he swept away the scrap of silk under her skirt. Cursing his shaking fingers, he managed to unfasten his jeans and jerk the zipper down. He groaned against her mouth when his aching length was released from confinement, then raised his head enough to see her face.

Her eyes were glazed with passion, her moist

lips swollen and parted as she met his heated gaze.

"Cassidy," he murmured, her name a plea and a question.

"If you don't," she said shakily, "I'll die of wanting you."

Her long lashes lowered as he eased inside her, her body shuddering against him.

"No," he pleaded. "Don't shut me out. Open your eyes."

She met the dark fire in his eyes and didn't look away when he moved his hips to complete the union of their bodies. Her legs wrapped around him, her hands clutched him as she met his unrestrained thrusts.

Michael felt her flaming heat sheathing him and surged deeper and faster to extinguish the fire burning him up. He pressed his lips to her throat as she threw her head back, shudders of completion racking her slender body. As badly as he wanted to prolong his own satisfaction, he couldn't fight his need when he felt her body tighten around him.

He heard her soft cry of reckless abandon and fell with her over the edge.

Eight

They never made it to the lawyer's office that morning. When they returned to the house, Alvilda announced in a tone of voice that dared them to say they wouldn't eat it that lunch was ready. Even though she expected them to go immediately to the dining room, Cassidy excused herself and dashed up to her room to change clothes. Her skirt had the distinct scent of saddle oil embedded in the fabric and her sweater was wrinkled enough to attract curiosity from the housekeeper.

From her scant supply of clothing she chose an ivory knit dress and fastened a brown leather belt around her waist. Since Michael insisted on going to see her father's lawyer, she preferred to wear something less casual than jeans, or her only other option, the black dress she'd worn to her father's funeral. She was going to have to return to London soon for no other reason than to replenish her wardrobe.

Her hands paused in the act of fastening a gold hoop earring. She met her reflection in the bathroom mirror, then looked away when she saw pain darken her eyes at the thought of leaving Knight's Keep. And Michael.

She closed her eyes as her body reacted to the memory of the lovemaking they'd shared in the tack room. How could she live without the magic between them? Their brief affair would end. She'd known that from the first, but that knowledge hadn't prevented her from giving in to the desire raging through her whenever she was with him.

She opened her eyes and gave herself a rueful look. She wanted him even when she wasn't with him. The thought of resuming her life without Michael in it was almost unbearable. She didn't know how she would do it. But once she returned to London and Michael went back to Montana, she would have no choice but to go on the best she could. Alone.

She pressed her hand to her chest. Her heart was being squeezed by an unkind fate, and nothing was going to make the hurt go away except time. She wasn't sure she was going to survive this brief affair with Michael. He hadn't even left England, and already she was suffering.

Her eyes widened and a tortured sound escaped her throat when she realized why the thought of living without him was so devastating.

She had fallen in love with him.

It was the only explanation. She didn't know how it had happened, or even when. She'd always thought love was something that grew gently between a man and a woman as they got to know each other. She'd known Michael for four days. It didn't seem possible she could have such deep feelings for him so soon.

Her body had known before her mind had, she realized. She would never have made love with him if she hadn't loved him.

She bit her lip and sat down on the edge of the tub. She needed time to think about this, a chance to absorb this enormous discovery which would affect the rest of her life.

A knock sounded impatiently on the bathroom door. "Cassidy, could you hurry it up in there? Alvilda is going to start clearing our lunch from the table if you don't get a move on."

She wasn't ready to face him yet.

He knocked again. "Cassidy, are you all right?" The amusement in his voice had been replaced by concern.

"I'm fine," she answered. "Give me a minute." Or at least an hour, she silently pleaded without any hope of having her wish granted.

Michael obviously wasn't satisfied with her answer. He didn't knock again, but just walked in. Seeing her sitting on the edge of the tub, he murmured, "If you plan on taking a bath, it's better if you take your clothes off first."

She ignored his comment, her gaze running over him. He'd also taken the time to change, and now wore a navy blue suit, white shirt, and a light blue tie with narrow white stripes.

"What's the occasion?" she asked.

"This is my visiting-the-lawyer suit."

"I hope you aren't expecting too much from the

solicitor. I've always found members of that particular profession to be fairly close-mouthed."

"I'm running out of options. I'm hoping he might know where King is. While we're there, I want to get some legal advice concerning your horse too." He took another step toward her. "If we had the house to ourselves, I would take your clothes off for you." He paused and studied her carefully. "Are you feeling all right? You look pale."

She stood up. "I was just catching my breath before going downstairs."

"I know the feeling." He touched her face. "Lord knows you've taken my breath since the first time I saw you. Tell me what's causing you to look as though you've lost your best friend."

She managed a ragged smile. He was so close. And she'd just realized she'd lost her heart.

"It's caused by hunger."

Michael kept his gaze on her as she brushed past him and left the bathroom. He didn't believe her feeble excuse. More than hunger had put that haunted look in her eyes and made her skin lose its color. Eventually she was going to tell him what was bothering her. He would ask nicely first. If that didn't work, he would insist.

Alvilda had whipped up a substantial repast that resembled a banquet for ten people instead of a small lunch for three. Spread across the table was baked ham with Somerset cider sauce, new potatoes, three vegetables, a glass of white wine for Cassidy, and a glass of lager for Michael. After exchanging astonished glances, Michael and Cassidy sat down and began to eat under Alvilda's critical eye.

Their idle conversation kept lapsing whenever Cassidy and Michael happened to glance at each other. Neither of them noticed Alvilda's smug smile of satisfaction.

Halfway through the meal, Michael announced, "Cassidy and I won't be here for dinner this evening, Alvilda." He looked around at the array of dishes spread out over the table. "Not that we're going to be very hungry after all this food, but we're going to be dining out."

Cassidy stared at him. "Are we?"

He grinned. "We are."

"Why?"

"Why not?"

"I think it's a wonderful idea," Alvilda said.

Cassidy persisted. "Why are we dining out?"

Michael took his time cutting a slice of ham. After stabbing a succulent piece on his fork, he met her gaze. "I have an urge to see how you look by candlelight."

Cassidy's breath caught in her throat as she met his intent gaze. "I'm sure Alvilda could scare up some candles for our dinner here."

Alvilda scraped back her chair and stood up. "It wouldn't be the same thing at all, Miss Cassidy." Moving around the table, she began to clear away the dishes. "Since you'll be in Wells, I recommend the Bishop's Kitchen in the Swan Hotel. It's very nice, very romantic. The service is impeccable, the food delicious."

"It sounds as though you've been there before," Michael said. "Has your friend Clive taken you there?"

Alvilda suddenly found the tablecloth fascinating, much to the amusement of Cassidy and Michael. She brushed nonexistent crumbs off the table, a faint flush on her cheeks. Finally she looked up and said cheerily, "Do you know how the town of Wells got its name? At one time there were a great number of water wells there. Pilgrims would travel from far and wide to drink the water, which they thought would cure them of all their ailments."

Michael smiled at Cassidy. "We'll have to be sure to try the water while we're there."

Cassidy doubted if miracle water would be able to cure what was ailing her, but she smiled back.

Michael had seen better smiles on his favorite horse after he'd given him an apple. He pushed his chair back. "We have our marching orders, Cassidy."

They didn't exactly march, but by late afternoon Cassidy felt as though she'd run a marathon. First they stopped at Sparrow Farms so Cassidy could see for herself that Nougat was safe and content. She was frustrated when she was stopped from discussing her horse's boarding fees by Mr. Sparrow's statement that Mr. Knight had taken care of all the arrangements. Before she could ask exactly what those arrangements were, she was whisked inside to have tea with Mrs. Sparrow. This time she had been expecting them and had prepared an elaborate spread of tea cakes, scones, fruit tarts, and crustless cucumber sandwiches. Though Michael and Cassidy were still full from lunch, neither was able to refuse taking one of everything after Mrs. Sparrow gave them a wounded look.

After she and Michael were back in the car and on their way, Cassidy tried to bring up the subject of paying Nougat's fees, but Michael cut her off.

"You heard Mr. Sparrow. It's all taken care of."

"Nougat isn't your responsibility, Michael. I like to pay my own way."

A tractor pulling a wagon of hay was a few cars ahead of them, slowing traffic to almost a standstill. Keeping his gaze on the road, Michael said, "You're going to have to get used to me doing things for you. Now is a good time to start." He slanted a glance at her, accompanied by a slow smile. "If it makes you feel more independent, you can pay for our dinner tonight."

She groaned and gave in to the need to loosen the belt at her waist. "How can you even think of dinner? Between Alvilda's lunch and Mrs. Sparrow's tea, I doubt if I'll be able to eat anything for the next two days."

They arrived in Wells a half hour before their appointment, and took advantage of the time to walk off all the food they'd eaten. Wells Cathedral was in the center of town, a short distance from the building where the lawyer had his office, so they wandered around the medieval building. They still had time to spare, so they walked along the cloisters to the Bishop's Palace ruins.

"The last time I was here was on a school outing," Cassidy said when they ended up on Vicar's Close. "It's just as I remembered it. It hasn't changed at all."

Michael stopped walking, turning to look at her. "Is that important to you? To have things in your life remain unchanged?"

She was surprised by the question. "Considering what I do for a living, I wouldn't think you would have to ask that. I never know what I'll be doing from one job to the next."

"But you've always had Chartridge to go back to if you ever wanted to return home."

She tilted her head to one side. "Is that why you're so intent on trying to persuade me to fight my father's will? You think I need Chartridge for security?"

"You make it sound as though I'm doing this for me. I would try to get your home back for you if you needed it."

She shook her head. "My father was my security. My father was Chartridge. Without him there, it's not my home. In a way it hasn't been my home for years." She put her hand on his arm, feeling the tautness of his muscles. "Michael, you don't owe me anything. If you're trying to arrange for me to get Chartridge out of some misguided attempt to make sure I'll have some sort of security after you leave, you needn't bother. I've supported myself for a number of years without any help and without Chartridge. You can leave with a clear conscience."

His hands curled into fists. It was either that or grab her and shake some sense into her. He stared at her, struggling to tamp down his anger.

"If you believe that," he said roughly, "we still have a long way to go."

Even if Cassidy could have thought of something to say, she doubted she would have had the breath to produce the words. He grabbed her arm, his grip uncompromising and barely short of hurting her. As he strode toward the lawyer's office, she had to walk quickly in order to keep up with him.

The visit to King's lawyer, Mr. Hyde-White, went the way Cassidy had thought it would. The lawyer hadn't heard from King. He had read through a copy of Robert Harrold's will, which he'd arranged to see after Michael had called him. It was perfectly legal, he told them. There were no questionable issues that could be used to take the matter of breaking the will to court. The wishes of the deceased were clear, reasonable, and irreversible.

Regarding the issue of her horse, however, Mr. Hyde-White went on, if she could produce proof of ownership, the animal would not be considered part of the Chartridge property and her stepbrother would have no right to sell Nougat.

Cassidy was more than satisfied with the visit to the lawyer, but Michael wasn't. He took her arm again as they left the building, scowling and obviously not in the mood to talk.

After they'd walked for half a block in silence, Cassidy said, "Michael, I appreciate what you're trying to do, but I didn't expect any other answer from the solicitor. Even if there were a way to change my father's will I wouldn't fight Derek in court."

"I've seen your face when you've talked about Chartridge, Cassidy. You love your home. It's being sold out from under you, and you don't want to fight for it? I don't get it."

"No, I don't suppose you do," she said quietly. "Unlike you, I don't go against my father's wishes."

He stopped and pulled her to the side of the

pavement, out of the way of people walking behind them. "Explain that."

"Because King has plans to sell the Camelot chess set, you've flown all the way here from Montana with the intention of doing whatever you can to stop him. I'm not like that. It was my father's wish that Chartridge be left to Derek. I'm not going to go against what my father wanted. It's the last thing I can do for him."

He stared down at her for a long moment, then grasped her hand and lifted it, holding it against his chest. "It really hurt you when he left everything to your stepbrother, didn't it?"

She could have lied. If it had been anyone else but Michael asking that question, she might have. Lord knows, she'd been lying to herself.

"Yes," she admitted. "When the solicitor first read the will, I was devastated and thought my father was punishing me for leaving home when I did. I know I hurt him when I asked to switch schools after he married Derek's mother. It was you who made me realize a few things about my father I'd forgotten."

"Me? How did I do that?"

"Like you, my father had an old-fashioned outlook when it came to women. We're supposed to be protected and cared for whether we feel we need it or not. Even though he accepted my decision to go to boarding school, then later to live and work in London on my own, he would still have thought Derek was better suited to take on the responsibility of Chartridge than I."

"Well, we both know how wrong he was." Michael kept her hand in his as he started walking again.

"Let me get this straight. You really don't mind that once your stepbrother sells Chartridge, you'll never be able to go there again?"

"I wouldn't go that far. I hate the thought of strangers living in the house where I grew up, but there's nothing I can do to change the situation. You wouldn't believe me, but now you've heard the same from Mr. Hyde-White. Derek can do whatever he wants with my father's property."

"Hyde-White also said that if you have proof of ownership for Nougat, Derek can't sell your horse. Do you have such proof?"

"I should. My father had ownership papers drawn up for Nougat and presented them to me on my birthday a few months after Nougat was born. I haven't thought about them for years, but I should still have them."

Obviously encouraged, Michael picked up the pace, and she had to step lively in order to keep up with him. She tugged his hand. "Could you slow down? I'm a musician, not a marathon runner."

"Sorry," he mumbled, immediately shortening his stride. "Where would your proof of ownership of Nougat be?"

They had reached the car. Cassidy waited until they were both seated inside before she asked, "Do you run your ranch like this?"

"Like what?"

"As though there's no tomorrow. Like a steam-roller flattening anything that is in your path?"

"Pretty much, yeah." He wanted things settled, and quickly. "So where would we find Nougat's ownership papers?"

She shook her head. "You don't give up, do you?"

He started the engine. "You might like to keep that in mind. We have time before dinner. Where do we go?"

"My flat in London," she said, resigned to doing as he wanted. Alvilda was right. It was much easier to give in to the Knight men. In this case, though, she was more than willing to cooperate if it meant she could save Nougat.

Michael didn't need directions until they reached the outskirts of London. From there Cassidy guided him through the maze of streets until they reached Bayswater Road, where she lived. Michael was able to find a parking space just around the corner from her apartment building.

Traffic on Bayswater, which bordered Hyde Park, was constant, with an occasional horn honking and the diesel throb of taxicabs adding to the other city sounds. Crowds of people strolled along the sidewalks on either side. Women pushing baby carriages hurried along with children at their heels. Several older women walked slowly, carrying heavily laden shopping bags.

The noise level was startling compared to the quiet countryside they'd left behind. Michael glanced at Cassidy as he walked beside her to her apartment building. She didn't seem either energized or annoyed by the hustle and bustle around them.

If she preferred city life over country life, he mused, he might have one more problem to deal with before they could be together.

She unlocked the outer security door, then led

the way up a flight of stairs that were to the left of the tiled foyer. On the first landing she turned right, walking to the second door, Number 202.

Michael followed her inside and looked around with interest. This was where Cassidy lived, and he was curious what her surroundings would reveal about her.

His first impression was of plants in all sizes and shapes in the small living room. Some hung near the single window, others sat in large pots on the beige carpet or in smaller ones on the walnut end tables. A love seat and an upholstered chair were the only pieces of furniture other than the tables and the plants. Except for a straight-back chair in front of the window with a music stand positioned several feet away from it. On the wide wooden window ledge was a long leather case that Michael guessed contained her flute. Sheets of music were stacked neatly next to the case.

He heard the sound of drawers opening and closing in another room, and realized she'd passed straight through the front room. Following the sounds, he found what was obviously her bedroom. Leaning against the door frame, he smiled. She was bent at the waist with her head and hands inside a tall walnut wardrobe.

As much as he was enjoying the view, he asked, "Can I help?"

"I know it's in here somewhere," she answered, her voice muffled.

Clothing swayed back and forth on the rod overhead as she moved shoeboxes, purses, and various odds and ends out of her way.

"Ah-ha," she said triumphantly. Turning around, she held three shoeboxes. "I found them."

"Shoes? That is exciting."

She kicked off her high heels and arranged a pillow against the headboard of the bed. "I keep my important papers in these boxes."

"Haven't you heard of metal lockboxes or a safe?"

She settled back and removed the lid of one of the boxes. "Burglars would be tempted to steal a lockbox or break into a safe. I can't imagine any thief being tempted by shoeboxes."

Michael joined her on the bed. "I suppose there is some logic to that. Would you like some help?"

She handed him one of the boxes. "What I'm looking for are legal-size sheets of paper folded in half. There's a red ribbon sewn along one side with two gold seals and signatures at the bottom of the first page."

Her idea of important papers differed from his, he thought as he started digging through the box and came upon a set of instructions for a curling iron. He set them aside and picked up the next item. An assurance policy, which was the British equivalent to life insurance. An expired gift certificate. Her health record showed she had type O blood and had all her shots up-to-date. That one he put in a separate pile. Next he came upon several playbills and programs.

Looking closer at one of the programs, he saw that it was autographed. "To Cassie, whose smile could take ten curtain calls, Larry."

"Cassidy?"

"Hmmm?" She didn't look up.

"Is the Larry who autographed this King Lear program the Larry I think it is?"

She looked up, frowning slightly. Then she smiled. "If you're thinking Sir Laurence Olivier, then you're correct."

Michael whistled softly. "Cassie and Larry? Sounds pretty chummy."

She patted his cheek. "Now, don't be getting all macho possessive on me, Michael. Sir Laurence was very kind to me when I dropped my music, my flute, and my self-confidence in front of him on my way to my first rehearsal after I graduated."

Michael took her hand and touched his mouth to the back of her fingers. "He knew a classy lady when he saw one."

For a moment Cassidy became lost in the dark, sensual depths of his eyes. Then she remembered what they were supposed to be doing.

"Michael," she murmured. "The papers."

He nibbled on the tips of her fingers. "Do we have to? I can think of better uses for this bed than as a paper sorter."

She nodded. "We have to if we're going to find the ownership papers. If I still have them, they would be in one of these boxes."

He reluctantly dropped her hand. Delving back into the box, he rummaged through the remainder of the papers. He now had an added incentive to find the darn ownership certificate.

At the bottom of the box his fingers closed around several heavy sheets of paper folded in half. He pulled them out. A red ribbon trailed down one side. Opening it, he saw gold seals on the first page.

"Bingo!"

Cassidy looked up. "You found it?"

"See for yourself."

She took the sheaf of papers from him and gave them a quick glance. With a small cry of victory, she reached over and hugged him, scattering papers across the bed and onto the floor. His arms closed around her, holding her tight. She'd rarely initiated any physical affection, and he planned to make the most of this.

All too soon she drew back. "Is it too late to take this back to Mr. Hyde-White today? I wouldn't put it past Derek to find out where we've hidden Nougat and use the police to get her away from Mr. Sparrow."

"It would take us two hours to drive back to Wells." He looked at his watch. "I doubt if Mr. Hyde-White keeps evening hours."

"You could call and find out if he would make an exception."

He scowled. "I wanted to wine and dine you and impress you with my romantic side."

She smiled. "That isn't necessary. I've found more romance with you than I ever thought existed."

Murmuring her name, he buried his face in her neck. "How can I refuse you anything after that?"

He kissed her long and hard, then released her reluctantly when the bonging of the carriage clock next to the bed reminded him they were pressed for time.

"We'd better straighten up this mess first," he said. Seeing her look of indignation, he grinned.

"Excuse me. As soon as we put away your valuable papers, I'll phone Mr. Hyde-White."

He was about to put papers back into the box, when a small, partially buried booklet caught his eye. It was her passport. While Cassidy was tucking the papers away, he slipped the passport into his back pocket.

Nine

While Cassidy put her shoeboxes back into the wardrobe, Michael went into the living room to use the phone.

The thought of driving back to Wells wasn't as pleasant as sitting across from Cassidy in a candlelight restaurant was. But he would drive all night if it meant eliminating one more obstacle between them. He fingered the shiny leaf of a small vine on the table next to the phone while he waited for the lawyer's office to answer.

A few minutes later he slammed the receiver down and swore under his breath. "Cassidy!"

Responding to the urgency in his voice, she came out of her bedroom. "What is it?"

"We have to get back to Knight's Keep right away."

"Why? What's wrong?"

He took her arm, grabbing up her coat and

tossing it at her before reaching for his. "I'll tell you on the way. Come on."

She ran into the bedroom for her purse, shoving Nougat's ownership papers inside. As she hurried back to join Michael, he was holding the door open, impatient to leave. She had no idea what had happened, but by the rigid set of his jaw, it wasn't good. She didn't waste time asking questions, but left with him.

Michael didn't explain the reason for the change in plans until he was on the M4 and no longer had to concentrate on heavy city traffic.

"When I called Hyde-White's office," he said, his voice as hard as the expression on his eyes, "the secretary had an urgent message from Alvilda to call her."

Tension coiled in her stomach. "What happened now?"

A muscle in his jaw clenched as Michael remembered Alvilda's rush of disjointed words. "The fire brigade had just arrived, she was calmer than she'd been when she'd tried to track us down at the lawyer's office."

Twisting in her seat, Cassidy put her hand on his arm. "The fire brigade? Where was the fire?"

"In the stables."

She bit her lip. "The horses?"

"The gardener was bringing back some tools and was the one who discovered the fire. He managed to get the stall doors opened so the horses could get out. Then he ran to the house to have Alvilda call the fire brigade."

Cassidy didn't ask questions that Michael couldn't possibly answer. He wouldn't have any idea how badly the stables were damaged. She didn't have to ask, though, what had caused the fire. Or, rather, who.

It was her fault. She hadn't actually set the fire, but she was indirectly responsible for the damage to King's property. Because of her emotional ties to a horse, she had inflicted harm on an innocent party. King had been kind to her, and this was how she rewarded his kindness.

She'd involved Michael as well. He'd gone out of his way to help her hide Nougat, help her keep her horse from being killed. Because of her stubbornness, her stepbrother had retaliated against the people who had helped her.

She had to make things right—and she had to stop expecting Michael or King to fight her battles for her. She should never have burdened Michael with her problems with Derek.

They arrived at the estate in record time, and Michael parked the car at a safe distance from the fire engines. Smoke hovered in the sky over the stables, but they couldn't see any flames. The two-story building was intact without any external signs of damage. Water stood in large puddles on the cobblestones, and firemen moved around, cleaning up.

Cassidy was unhooking her seat belt when Michael flung out his arm to prevent her from getting out of the car.

"I want you to go to the house, Cassidy." He placed his fingers over her lips when she started to object. "There's nothing you can do here. The firemen apparently have the fire under control. I want to talk to them to see if they know what caused it."

"We both know what caused the fire, Michael."

He didn't bother contradicting her. "They might have proof the fire was set. If we're lucky, we can find something to give Clive as evidence. You can't protect your stepbrother from this, Cassidy. This time he's gone too far."

"I won't interfere, Michael," she said quietly.

She didn't need to hear what the firemen said anyway. She had all the answers she needed. She deserved the note of censure in Michael's voice. If she'd handled Derek differently, there wouldn't have been a fire. "Let me at least help round up the horses, Michael."

"The way things have been going, you'll just end up getting hurt." His voice was taut, the tone of a man who'd reached the end of his patience. "Do me a favor and stay in the house."

She got out of the car and walked toward the house, concentrating on putting one foot in front of the other. It took a great deal of effort to leave Michael to clean up a mess that had been her fault.

Alvilda met her at the door and ushered her into the front reception room. "Doesn't this beat all? First a burglar, now an arsonist. Whatever will be next?" She silently offered Cassidy a glass of sherry.

"No thank you." She watched Alvilda pour a generous amount of sherry for herself. The situation obviously called for something stronger than tea. "I'm sorry." she said quietly.

Alvilda looked at her after taking a restorative

sip. "What in the world are you sorry for, child? None of this is your doing."

Cassidy sat down at one end of the plush Victorian sofa. "Not directly, but I feel responsible."

"What nonsense," Alvilda said stoutly, then helped herself to another dose of sherry.

"No, it isn't nonsense. You might as well know, Miss Gump. I believe my stepbrother was behind the fire in the stables. I doubt if he actually set it himself, but some of the people he's invited to stay at Chartridge could have been talked into doing the job for him. I believe he was also the one who broke into the stables to attempt to take my horse."

"One advantage of age," Alvilda said kindly, "is that one realizes that things happen for a reason. Many times, in fact most of the time, we have no idea why they happen. You could call it fate if you like, kismet. But sometimes all one can do is wait and hope for the best."

Cassidy smiled faintly. "And sometimes we know the reasons and are forced to do something about them rather than just leave everything to fate."

"That sounds like something King would say." Alvilda chuckled. "Or do. If things aren't quite to his satisfaction, he sets about to do something till thcy are."

Alvilda tossed back the last of her sherry, then turned to set the glass down. When she looked back at the sofa, Cassidy was gone. Thinking nothing of it, she crossed the room to the door. As she put her hand on the latch, she felt it turning and stepped back as the door opened.

Michael glanced around the room, then looked at Alvilda. "Where's Cassidy?"

"She was here just a moment ago." She wrinkled her nose at the smell of smoke clinging to him. He'd removed his suit coat and tie, and his white shirt was smudged with ash on the sleeves and his chest. "Is everything under control at the stables?"

"The fire is completely out and the horses are safe. We'll keep them in the barn until the smoke clears from the stables. The fire had started in the back room, but thanks to the gardener spotting it when he did, it didn't reach the flammable salves and oils."

"That was fortunate. Can I get you anything? Coffee, tea, or perhaps something stronger?"

"Nothing for me, thanks, but the firemen could use something to drink."

"I'll see to it."

She started past him, but stopped when he asked, "Did Cassidy say where she was going?"

Alvilda shook her head. "Not that I recall. Perhaps she's gone to her room."

"Wait here."

Michael took the stairs two at a time. A minute later he was back. "She's not in her room."

Alvilda frowned. "I hope she hasn't done anything foolish."

"What makes you think she might?"

Alvilda wrung her hands. "Maybe I should have taken her more seriously when she said the fire was her fault."

Michael took her hands to stop her restless

movements. "Why would she say that? It wasn't her fault."

"I know that and you know that, but apparently Miss Cassidy doesn't agree with us."

"Tell me what she said."

It looked like every light had been turned on in Chartridge when Cassidy drove up the lane in Michael's rented Jaguar. She would have walked through the woods if she'd had to, but luckily Michael had left the keys in the ignition. Going through the woods would have taken time, and she wanted to get this over with as soon as possible.

She wouldn't put it past Derek to do something even more stupid than what he'd already done. He wasn't hurting her as much as he was hurting King, and she had to stop him.

She parked the car and got out, locking the doors. As she approached the steps leading up to the front door, she heard loud rock music. It wasn't going to be easy to talk to Derek privately.

She didn't need her house key, nor did she bother using the door knocker. The front doors had been left open day and night since her father's funeral.

She winced as she stepped into the foyer and saw a cigar had been stuck in the visor of the suit of armor that stood to one side of the door. The sound of female laughter drew her attention to the curved stairway at the other end of the foyer. A woman wearing one of Cassidy's silk robes was coming down the stairs with a man who was in the process of tucking his shirt into his slacks.

"Dory, I believe you've just been replaced," the man drawled, staring at Cassidy. "You look as though you could use a drink, luv. Name your poison and I'll fetch it for you."

Cassidy stepped aside as he attempted to put his arm around her shoulders. "I'm looking for Derek Pembroke. Would you know where I can find him?"

He made a scolding sound. "Now, what does old Derek have that I can't provide?"

Cassidy looked at the woman who was standing at the base of the stairs. "Would you know where I could find Derek?"

The woman shrugged. "He and a couple of blokes said something about getting some flowers for us girls. Guess they went into town."

Cassidy didn't bother explaining that there were plenty of flowers available in the Chartridge greenhouse. She turned around and walked back out the front door. Going through the house was a more direct route to the greenhouse, but there were too many people wandering around who might delay her.

She made her way around the side of the house. She had no problems seeing where she was going since the lights from the house shone out onto the grass from every window. Through a line of poplars on her left she saw the outdoor lights for the tennis court had been turned on. The sound of drunken laughter from that direction indicated the court was being used.

The toe of her boot hit something and sent it

rolling across the grass. Looking down, she saw an empty bottle of Scotch lying on its side.

She walked faster. She wanted this over with. If she had only given Derek what he wanted earlier, neither Chartridge nor Knight's Keep would have been damaged. If she'd signed over the house, Derek would have cleared out his partying friends and would have left the Knights' property alone.

The door of the greenhouse had been left open, letting cold air in and the warm, humid air out. Stepping inside, Cassidy looked around and spotted Derek standing in front of her father's prize orchids. He was clipping off the exotic blossoms and piling them into a wicker basket.

She hadn't expected to find him alone. "Derek, I'd like to talk to you."

He glanced in her direction, then resumed beheading the orchid plants with relish. "Well, fancy seeing you here, sister dear. Where's your bodyguard?"

"I want this to end, Derek."

"If you mean the party going on inside your father's charming abode, you know how to get them all to leave."

"That's why I'm here."

He paused with the shears held open near a large cattleya bloom. "Spell it out, Cass. I want to make sure we're talking about the same thing."

She hesitated. It was more difficult than she'd thought it would be. "I'm willing to sign over the house to you."

The cattleya blossom fell onto the brick floor. "Are you? And what prompted this turnaround?"

"You know very well what changed my mind,

Derek. I haven't come here to play any of your word games that you enjoy so much. Do you want me to sign over the house to you or not?

"Of course, but what's the rush?" His voice hardened and he ruthlessly clipped off another delicate bloom. "The lady of the manor says jump and I'm supposed to say how high? Those days are over, princess. Daddy handed the property over to me, remember?"

"I'm fully aware of that." She stepped back when he took a step toward her. "I also recall you insisted I sign the house over to you. That's what I'm agreeing to do."

He came closer. "You're forgetting one little thing, dear sister. There's the matter of that old nag you've stolen."

Cassidy tightened her hold on her purse. "Nougat belongs to me, Derek, and I have the papers to prove it. Be satisfied with the house and the rest of my father's property. You aren't going to destroy my horse."

He flung out his arm, knocking over several plants. "Damn you, I want it all."

She backed toward the door, alarmed by the violence. "You have it all. Everything of value that belonged to my father is yours."

"No, I don't. The inventory includes a mare named Nougat. The horse isn't in the stables."

"Why do you want my horse just so you can destroy her?"

"Because you love that horse."

Still backing away, she'd reached the door and stumbled as her heel caught in one of the flag-stones outside the greenhouse. Catching her balance, she took another step back. "Do you really hate me that much, Derek?"

"Oh, yes, little sister. I've waited a long time to see you stripped of everything you love.

"You've always had everything you ever wanted, without lifting a finger, while I always got everyone's leavings. How I hated traipsing along behind dear mummy after she finally landed your father."

"My father always treated you well, Derek."

"I was treated like a charity case while you, the little princess, was the apple of Daddy's eye."

"That's ridiculous."

He slid his forefinger over one of the blades of the shears. "I thought I had all your prize possessions covered, but you've added another one. It's been a challenge to come up with a way to include your new boyfriend in my revenge."

"You mean Michael?"

He made snipping motions in the air. "Yes, your big, tall, handsome cowboy. He is an elusive devil, isn't he?"

"Not really," Michael said as he walked up behind Cassidy. "You just need to know where to look."

Until Michael appeared, Cassidy hadn't realized how frightened she was. When he put his arm around her waist, she had to force herself not to sag against him and let him hold her.

Derek sneered at Michael. "Now, to what do I owe this honor, Mr. Knight? Do you plan on using me as a punching bag again?" The shears made a clicking sound as he opened and shut them. "I'm not empty-handed this time, so take your best shot."

Michael's smile held no amusement. "Not tonight, unless you make a move toward Cassidy with those shears. We're going to have a civilized little chat, Pembroke. Just as soon as Cassidy leaves."

She turned to face him. "I'm not going anywhere, Michael," she said firmly. "I want this settled tonight."

"So do I. And it will be. Go back to Knight's Keep, Cassidy." His taut voice brooked no argument. "I'll make sure your stepbrother understands the way things are."

"Michael, I've already told Derek I'll sign the title of the house over to him, and he knows Nougat is legally mine. There's nothing left to discuss with him."

Anger darkened his eyes. "You told him, but you didn't tell me." He shook his head. "I'd ask you to trust me to handle this, but it's obvious you don't. Take my car and drive back to Knight's Keep."

"Michael," she began, though she was unsure what she could say to make him change his mind.

He responded by drawling her name in the same impatient tone. "Cassidy."

He started to go on, but the sound of glass breaking in the house interrupted him. Cassidy jerked her head around in time to see one of her father's antique lamps shatter on the ground. Someone had thrown it out a window.

Michael had automatically grabbed Cassidy the instant he'd heard the glass break. Keeping hold of her, he moved so that she was looking at him again. "When you get to my father's," he said, "get

Clive's number from Alvilda and call him. Tell him to send some policemen out to Chartridge right away."

The mention of the police was enough for Derek. He tried to sneak away, but had taken only two steps when Michael growled, "Don't try it, Pembroke. I'm not through with you yet."

With a final push, Michael persuaded Cassidy to do as he asked. He kept his gaze on her until she disappeared around the corner of the house. Then he turned back to her stepbrother.

"Now, Pembroke. I'm going to make you an offer you won't refuse."

When Cassidy returned to Knight's Keep, she ran up the front steps and pulled open the door. She called out for Alvilda as she walked quickly through the foyer. She looked in the morning room for her, then dashed back out and raised her voice. "Alvilda!"

"Good Lord, girl," a deep voice answered. "You don't need to shout."

Cassidy stopped abruptly and stared at the man standing in the doorway of the study. "King! What are you doing here?"

"I live here, my dear," he said with amusement. His expression changed when he realized she wasn't making a social call. "What is it, Cassidy? Has something happened to Michael?"

"Not yet, but it might if we don't get the police."

"You'd better explain," he said as he took her arm and guided her toward the dining room. "But wait until we get to the kitchen. Our esteemed chief constable is there chatting up Alvilda and eating me out of house and home. You can tell us all what's going on."

Clive and Alvilda were sitting at the kitchen table. Alvilda caught the urgency of the situation as soon as she saw Cassidy's face and gathered up two more cups and saucers.

King invited Cassidy to take her coat off and sit down, but she was too restless and worried about what was happening at Chartridge. She merely draped her coat over the back of a chair, then faced the three curious people. As quickly and as clearly as she could, she explained what was happening at Chartridge. When she was through, Clive pushed his chair back and walked over to the phone. After calmly issuing orders for two of his officers to head over to Chartridge House, he hung up and sat back down at the table.

Cassidy stared at King, who was casually spooning sugar into his cup of tea. She glanced over at Clive and back to King again. "Aren't you going to go to Chartridge to help Michael?"

"I have every confidence in my son. He doesn't need any help dealing with Pembroke. Clive's men will be sufficient to take care of the rowdies at Chartridge. All we need to do is wait for Michael to return and give us a report."

Thinking of the sharp shears in Derek's hand, she didn't agree. "I don't believe this." She grabbed her coat. "If neither one of you are going to help Michael, I will. You don't know Derek as well as I do. He's capable of doing anything, and Michael could get hurt."

Her coat was taken away from her before she

could put it on. King tossed it back over the chair and cupped her elbow. "Come along with me, my dear. I think the occasion calls for something a little stronger than tea." To Clive he added, "You can find us in my study when you get a report from your men."

"Very good, sir."

Cassidy went along with King, but not willingly. "I can't just sit around here," she said as they crossed the dining room, "not knowing what's happening to Michael."

"Michael can take care of himself." King's hold on her arm was gentle yet firm as he led her into the study. "While we're waiting, you can tell me all about this situation regarding your stepbrother."

He waited until she was seated in the same chair she'd occupied the evening of her father's funeral. "What has Derek done now?"

"As you know, my father left all of Chartridge Manor to Derek, except for the house. Derek was going to destroy my horse unless I signed the deed to the house over to him. Thanks to Michael, Nougat is safe, but I told Derek tonight that I would give him the house if he would stop damaging your property."

King raised a gray eyebrow. "You left a few things out of your description of the situation. Alvilda has filled me in on the break-in at the stables and the fire, but she neglected to mention Derek's involvement. You were right to leave it to Michael to straighten your stepbrother out."

"I didn't have any choice," she said bitterly. "Michael made me leave. I've already caused enough problems for your family, King. It was up to me to deal with Derek."

"By giving him your inheritance? Michael is right to handle it his way."

"No matter what Michael says to Derek, I'm still signing over the house to him. It's impossible the way things are now. It might not be what my father wanted, but I can't help that. He should have left Chartridge to the National Trust instead of creating an impossible situation."

"Robert wanted you to have a home to come back to whenever you needed it."

"Chartridge hasn't been my home for a long time, King. You know that better than anyone."

He nodded. "I know you misunderstood the reason your father married Derek's mother. Robert thought you needed a woman's influence, so he set out to provide you with that. Unfortunately, his choice of women could have been better."

Cassidy looked away. "It doesn't matter what happened in the past. It's the present and future that I'm more concerned about, which is why I'm giving Derek the house."

"Speaking of the present and future." King changed the subject. "I'd like to discuss your relationship with my son."

She glanced warily at him. "Don't you think that's something you should be asking Michael?"

King chuckled. "I could, but I think I stand a better chance of getting an answer from you."

"I met Michael four days ago, King. There hasn't been much time for us even to get to know each other, much less develop a relationship."

King sat down. "It isn't very polite of me to call

you a liar, my dear, but I saw your face when you scolded us for not rushing to Michael's rescue. You care about my son."

Needing to release some of her tension, she stood up and walked over to the glass case. Looking down at the Camelot chess set, she said, "I'd rather not talk about this, King. Whether I care about Michael or not isn't important right now."

"All I seem to be doing is disagreeing with you, Cassidy. But personally I can't think of anything more important than love."

She wrapped her arms around her waist and turned to face him. "I didn't say I love Michael."

"You didn't say you didn't love him either. If your father were alive, he would say the same thing. He loved you very much."

Maybe under other circumstances she would have denied her feelings for Michael, but she was too worried about him to evade the truth.

"I tried not to love him, King," she said softly, "but I do."

"I am perhaps prejudiced, but why would you try not to fall in love with Michael?"

She threw her hands up in exasperation. Like father, like son, she thought. "Think about it, King. I live in England and Michael lives in Montana. That doesn't leave a great of deal of hope for a long-lasting relationship."

"That's geography, my dear."

She walked over to the window and looked out, though she was unable to see anything but her own reflection. "That's a fact, King."

King started to argue, but he was interrupted by the door of the study bursting open.

Michael stood in the doorway. Propping his hands on his hips, he stared across the room at Cassidy.

"You have some explaining to do, sweetheart."

Ten

"Now, Michael," King said as he stood up. "That's not the way to talk to a lady. Come in, sit down, and be civilized."

For a moment Michael simply stared at King, then he crossed the room in a few long strides and hugged his father. Stepping back, he scowled.

"Dammit, King. What the hell are you doing here now? You weren't supposed to be back for two more days."

"This is the second time I've had to defend being in my own house. It's good to see you too, Michael. Am I correct in assuming that matters have been taken care of satisfactorily at Chartridge?"

"I don't know about satisfactorily. Depends on your point of view. The house has been cleared of the rabble that Derek had littering the place. Since the house is still legally Cassidy's, the police told them they were trespassing and sent them on their way."

"Very good. Now, will you sit down and behave like a rational man?"

Michael shook his head. "I can't manage that at the moment, Dad."

He marched over to Cassidy and, without warning, grabbed her at her waist and hauled her up over his shoulder.

The wind went out of her, and her sound of protest was an unladylike grunt. The room spun for a few seconds as he turned around and strode toward the door.

"King," she gasped. "Do something."

"Certainly," King said.

Grinning widely, he walked quickly to the door and opened it.

"Thanks," Michael said. "I'll talk to you later."

"I won't wait up, son."

Cassidy started kicking, and Michael clamped his arm over her thighs. "Hold still."

"Put me down!"

"I will. Eventually." As he approached the stairs he saw Clive and Alvilda standing in the doorway to the dining room. "Thanks for the help, Clive," he said as he started up the stairs.

"Don't mention it," the chief constable replied.

Michael continued climbing the stairs, ignoring Cassidy's fists pounding his back. A solid kick opened her bedroom door, and he kicked it again to close it.

"This is no longer amusing, Michael. The blood is rushing to my head."

"Good. Maybe your brain will start working better."

"Michael! Put me down this instant."

"Your wish is my command," he drawled, and dumped her onto the bed.

She bounced several times, which made her dizzier. The canopy overhead rocked back and forth. Finally getting her balance, she sat up and wiped her hand impatiently across her face, brushing back the hair that had tumbled down.

"Have you gone completely mad?"

He stood beside the bed, his arms folded across his chest. "Oh, I'm mad, honey. In fact, I can't remember ever being this mad before."

"I'm sorry if you've had a difficult time with Derek, but I did tell you that I didn't need your help. I'd already dealt with Derek."

"Yeah, so I heard. It was quite a revelation to learn you're handing your heritage over to that idiot. What I'd like to know is why you didn't discuss something that important with me first."

Staring at him, Cassidy realized that behind Michael's angry facade he was actually hurt. "That's why you're angry with me," she said in a softer voice. "It's not because of Derek at all."

"You've at least got that figured out. And since you're on a roll making decisions here, I'd like you to agree to send your horse to my ranch. She'll be well taken care of, I promise."

"You want to take Nougat to Montana?"

"It's a great idea, isn't it?"

She had to admit she liked the thought of her horse spending her last days on Michael's ranch. "It's a wonderful idea, Michael."

He let out a long breath and dropped his arms to his sides. "Good. That was easier than I thought. However, one of the things we have to work on after we're married is this little matter of communication."

The color drained from her face. She managed to choke out one word. "Married?"

Michael swore under his breath. "This isn't the way I meant to bring up that particular subject. It was supposed to be over a candlelight dinner with soft music in the background, but we never made it to the restaurant."

What he'd said and what he meant had finally sunk in. Cassidy scooted to the other side of the bed and got off. She needed the distance between them.

"You can't be serious," she said.

"Oh, I'm serious, sweetheart." He took a step toward her around the foot of the bed. "I've never been more serious in my life."

"Do you usually plan to marry a woman after knowing her for only a few days?"

"I can honestly say this is the first time." He took another step. "And the last."

Hope battled with shock inside her. If she could only believe he wanted to spend the rest of his life with her. If she could only believe he loved her.

"Michael," she began hesitantly, "we need to talk about this."

He was standing in front of her now. "You bet," he murmured, his gaze on her mouth. "And we will. Later."

"Michael," she whispered as he raked his fingers through her hair. "We need to talk now."

He shook his head slowly. "I need this more."

His invasion of her mouth made her senses reel.

She sighed. He deepened the kiss. She groaned. His hands stroked and caressed.

Desire stirred and swirled in the air around them, enclosing them in sensual sensation. Knowing what awaited them made their hearts beat faster, their blood run hotter.

Michael broke away, his breathing tortured as he pulled her closer and pressed his mouth to her throat. Her taste and scent tangled his emotions, and the feel of her sent his blood searing through his veins.

Sighing raggedly, he raised his head. Other things had to be taken care of before he gave in to his powerful need for her. The dazed longing in her eyes almost made him change his mind. Groaning, he set her back onto the bed and stepped away from her.

"That answers one question," he said.

Cassidy couldn't make any sense out of his comment. She didn't really want to, though. Her body was craving his touch. "What question is that?"

"Whether you want me as much as I want you."

The laugh that escaped from her had a slight hysterical edge to it. "I don't think there's any doubt of that. That has never been our problem."

"I needed to be reminded." He walked around the bed, toward the door. "It will make the next couple of days easier to get through."

She turned her head, eyes wide as she watched him open the door. "Michael! Where are you going?"

"I need to talk to King. Why don't you get some sleep?"

She couldn't leave things the way they were. "Don't leave now, Michael. We have to talk."

"And we will in the morning, honey. If I stay, we won't talk."

Cassidy stared at the closed door after he left. Then she flung her arms over her head in exasperation and fell back onto the bed.

When Cassidy entered the dining room the next morning, she found King seated at the large table eating his breakfast. He was alone.

Looking up from his plate of bacon, eggs, grilled tomato, and fried bread, he smiled at her. "Good morning, my dear. Did you sleep well?"

"If you call closing my eyes for thirty minutes before dawn sleep, then yes, I slept well."

"One of the things my wife took great pride in was the comfort of our guests. For some strange reason, neither you nor my son appear to have been able to rest last night. Michael kept me up until a ridiculous hour of the morning. He's up and about already, out checking the stables."

Cassidy pulled out the chair across from King and sat down. At least, she thought, King didn't think the reason for their sleepless night was that she and Michael had been together. It was important to her that King didn't think she had slept with his son last night.

"I feel I owe you an apology, King. My stepbrother has caused a great deal of damage to your property, and I have to take some of the responsibility."

"We can take responsibility only for our own

behavior, Cassidy. Whatever actions Derek has taken is not your fault."

"I wish I could agree with you. I haven't handled this situation very well. If I had given Derek title to the house at the beginning, you wouldn't have a hole in your foyer ceiling and damage to your stables."

"I think you're being too hard on yourself."

"Maybe. But I can't help thinking I could have prevented Derek from damaging both your property and Chartridge Manor. Miss Gump and Michael have been wonderful, but I certainly disrupted their lives during the last week."

"It was good for them. Let's talk about more pleasant matters." Calmly cutting his grilled tomato, King said, "I believe congratulations are in order."

Cassidy gave him a blank look. "Whatever for?"

"Michael announced last night that you two are going to be married." He looked up and saw her astonishment. "Your father would be very pleased," he added smiling. "Shortly before his death, he and I discussed how wonderful it would be if we could tie our two families together by marriage. Robert was very concerned that you would be alone once he was gone. He had done what he could by arranging for Derck to oversee Chartridge and provide you with a place to return to when you needed it."

"You've said that before, about my father leaving Chartridge to Derek for my sake."

"He was of the old school, Cassidy. He thought a woman needed a man to take care of her. He would have approved of marriage between you and my son."

The sound of the front door slamming caused King to smile again. "He never did learn to close a door quietly." Raising his voice, he called, "We're in the dining room, Michael."

A few seconds later Michael strolled into the dining room. His coat was open, his hair blown by the wind. His blue chambray shirt was the same color as his faded jeans.

Cassidy felt her mouth go dry at just the sight of him.

He walked over to her side of the table and bent down to kiss her briefly. Glancing at the empty space in front of her, he asked, "Haven't you had breakfast?"

"Not yet." She made a startled sound when she felt his hand on her thigh under the table, covering it with a cough.

Alvilda chose that moment to enter the dining room, pushing a tea cart brimming with tea, scones, and a pot of coffee for Michael. "Good morning. Did you see that lovely sunshine? It's going to be a wonderful day." Pouring tea and coffee, she asked, "Now, what would you like for breakfast?"

"Nothing for me," Cassidy said.

Michael thanked Alvilda for the coffee and said, "I don't have time for breakfast this morning. I have to leave in a few minutes if I'm going to catch the flight I booked."

Cassidy's hand jerked, knocking her teacup off its saucer. Jumping up, she dabbed at the spilled tea with her cloth napkin, but Alvilda took over.

"Don't worry about this. I'll get you another cup."

Cassidy shook her head. "Don't bother, Miss Gump. I don't care for any." Seeing the amusement in Michael's eyes, she wished she hadn't spilled the tea. She would have liked to have thrown it in his face. "Do you think it's funny that I'm a klutz, or are you simply happy to be leaving?"

Pushing back his chair, he glanced at his father. "Excuse us, Dad. It looks like I have a little explaining to do. I'm going to use the study, okay?"

"Of course." King pushed back the cuff of his shirt to look at his watch. "You'd better be quick, Michael. It's a long drive to Heathrow."

"I'll make it." Clasping Cassidy's hand, he tugged her to her feet. "Come on, sweetheart."

She jerked her hand away and preceded him out of the room. She didn't know who she was angrier at, Michael or herself. She had almost believed him, had wanted to believe him when he said he wanted to marry her. Maybe it was fortunate she'd found out now that he hadn't been serious, before she was too badly hurt. The pain she felt now was lethal enough

She entered the study, walking straight over to the glass case that held the chess set. Michael closed the door behind them, then followed her, putting his arms on her shoulders as she looked down at the game.

"King has no intention of selling it," Michael said. "He told me last night."

She shrugged his arms off and took several

steps away from him. "So you can return to Montana without worrying about your father."

"Don't you want to know why he sent the fax in the first place?"

"Does it matter? You accomplished what you came to do."

"And then some," Michael murmured, his gaze following her as she walked over to the window and looked out. Beams of sunlight shone through the glass onto her hair, making a halo of the blond tresses. "King used the threat of selling the Camelot set to get my butt over here so I could meet you."

She whirled to face him. "Your father was playing matchmaker?"

"That's what it boils down to. I told him it worked."

Her gaze dropped. "For a while. You're leaving, remember?"

"Come with me, Cassidy."

"What?"

"I don't know how long it'll be before I can get back. I don't want to be without you for even one day. Come with me."

As hard as she tried to prevent it, tears filled her eyes. "Michael, I don't understand what's going on," she said shakily. "One minute you tell me you want to marry me, then you say you're leaving. Now you ask me to go with you. One minute I want to shake you, the next I want to . . ."

When she didn't finish the sentence, he crossed the room and cupped her face in his hands. "You want to what?"

"It doesn't matter," she muttered, lowering her gaze so he couldn't see the emotion in her eyes.

"Honey, it's the only thing that does matter. I know I'm rushing you. I wish we had months to work out every little detail, but circumstances aren't cooperating. I don't trust anyone else to take Nougat to the ranch, so that means I'll be gone a couple of days. I need to wrap up a few things there before I can leave my foreman in charge again. Four, maybe five days should do it. I'd like you to come with me."

She tried to pull away, but he wouldn't let her. "Michael, too much has happened in too short a time. I don't know what to think about anything anymore."

He wiped away a drop of moisture that had escaped from the corner of her eye. "There's only one thing you need to think about right now."

"Only one?" she asked with a shaky laugh.

"Only one. Do you want to live with me the rest of your life, Cassidy?"

No would be easier to say than yes. If she told him she didn't want to live with him, he would go back to Montana and she would never see him again. If she said yes, she would be risking all that she had achieved for herself on the hope that he loved her enough to overcome the many barriers between them. And one of the major ones was convincing him that she was an independent woman capable of making her own decisions.

Taking the biggest step in her life, she met his gaze and said, "You were wrong, Michael. There's something else I have to think about. I love you."

Shock filled his eyes, but was quickly replaced

by desire. He pulled her into his arms. "Cassidy," he groaned against her mouth.

He kissed her with all the passion of a man who had bet his last dollar and just discovered he'd won the jackpot.

A rapping on the door stopped Michael from showing Cassidy in intimate detail all that she meant to him. He would be back for her in record time, even if he had to charter the Concorde.

"Since you won't come with me," he said, "stay here with King. I need to know you'll be safe while I'm gone."

"Michael!" King yelled through the door. "You need to leave now if you're going to make your flight."

"Damn," Michael muttered.

Cassidy pulled away from him. "You'd better go." He swore again when he saw the uncertainty back in her eyes. His choices were limited to only one, and that was to leave. He didn't like it, but he had the consolation that once he came back for her, he wouldn't be separated from her again.

Two days later, Michael was sitting behind his desk at the ranch, yelling into the phone. Just as he'd done the night before.

"Dad, this is ridiculous. I've got to talk to Cassidy. Last night you said she was at Chartridge arranging for her personal possessions to be moved. I asked you to tell her to call me, but she didn't. Now you're saying she went to London for the day. What's going on?"

His father's exasperation came clearly over the

international phone lines. "When you asked me to take care of her, you didn't say I was supposed to chain her to the house, Michael. She's a free agent, you know."

"Not for long."

"She doesn't seem to realize that. You might not have left things as clear-cut as you think."

The knot in Michael's stomach tightened. "Look, Dad, I'm not in the mood for your brand of prodding. You explained why you had me rush to England. Cassidy and I are going to get married, so what more do you want?"

"I'm perfectly happy with the results, Michael. It's Cassidy who doesn't seem too pleased with the present situation."

"I'm not ecstatic about this separation either. I'm trying to arrange things so I can take a month off for our honeymoon. Once we're married, we'll be able to sort everything out."

"I have no doubts you will make things right, my boy. But I'm not the one who's unsure."

"I'll be back on Saturday." He gave his father his flight number, airline, and the time he'd be arriving. "I'll try to call again at the same time tomorrow night. Ask Cassidy to stick around. I just might survive if I can at least hear her voice."

"I'll do what I can." King changed the subject, asking about Michael's siblings. A few minutes later, they said good-bye.

Even though the sun had gone down, Michael didn't turn on the lights in his office. The phone call hadn't eased the clutch of fear in his gut. As he'd flown back to the ranch, he'd had second thoughts about leaving Cassidy so abruptly. He'd been in a hurry to get things settled so he could go back to her. It was too late now, but he had the feeling he should have stayed until Cassidy was more comfortable with their future.

For someone who thought he had all the answers, he was suddenly asking himself an awful lot of questions.

The line to clear customs at Heathrow Airport crawled along, unbelievably slow. Michael impatiently shifted his carry-on bag from one hand to the other.

He hadn't allowed himself to hope that Cassidy would be waiting at the airport until now. During the week they'd been apart, he hadn't spoken to her once and he'd increasingly felt as though he were walking on a very thin line. One wrong word to her and he'd fall into oblivion.

When he finally managed to get through Customs, he scanned the crowd of people waiting behind the barrier. He saw a number of blond women, but none of them were the one he wanted. Lord, how he wanted. The week had seemed like a year.

He was about to move on when he spotted a placard with his name written on it. He walked over to the man dressed in a chauffeur's uniform who was holding it.

"I'm Michael Knight."

Taking the carry-on bag out of his hand, the chauffeur said formally, "This way, sir."

Since the man had his bag, Michael had no choice but to follow him. If this was King's idea, he thought, his father had better have arranged for a chauffeur who used to drive a race car. Michael didn't want to waste another second getting to Cassidy.

Outside the terminal, the chauffeur opened the rear door of a white Rolls-Royce. Michael slid inside. He waited until his bag had been placed in the trunk and the chauffeur was settled behind the wheel before asking who had sent the car.

"I have no idea, sir."

Michael didn't bother questioning the man again. Especially when he didn't head the Rolls toward the M4 which would take them to Somerset. He tapped his fingers impatiently on his thigh as he waited to see what his destination was.

When the Rolls stopped in front of a familiar apartment house on Bayswater Road, every nerve in Michael's body was jangling.

He didn't wait for the door to be opened for him. He was already striding up the steps to the front door when the chauffeur called him back.

"Your bag, sir."

Michael hurried back and grabbed the bag out of the chauffeur's hand. When he reached for his wallet, the driver's nose lifted even higher in the air, although Michael didn't see how that could be possible.

"The gratuity has been provided, sir."

Michael didn't wait around to argue with the man. He took the steps two at a time, then nearly tore the security door off its hinges when it wouldn't open. After a frustrating moment, he heard a buzzer and a click, and pulled the door open.

A few seconds later he was standing in front of

Cassidy's door. He didn't bother knocking. Something told him the door wouldn't be locked.

He planted his hand on the center of the door, but before he could push, the door opened. Off balance, he stumbled into the apartment. Before he could speak, Cassidy pressed her hand over his mouth.

"Not a word, Michael. Not a single word."

He made a muffled sound against her hand, and she scowled. "Not a word."

He raised a hand in a gesture of peace and nodded.

She took his arm and led him over to the room's one upholstered chair. "I want you to sit down and listen. I realize this might be difficult for you, but do give it your best attempt."

Michael didn't know whether to be furious or amused. If it were anyone else, he would have been angry. And if she moved any farther away from him than arm's length, he would be. She was wearing a khaki-colored skirt and matching cotton V-neck shirt, with an ivory vest over it. Both the skirt and shirt buttoned down the front, and he briefly considered how easily he would be able to get her out of those clothes.

She stood in front of his chair, her arms folded across her chest as she waited for his answer.

Lifting one hand, he gestured that the floor was hers.

"Ever since we've met," she began, "you've done all the talking, and now it's my turn. I've had six days to think about this and—"

He held up seven fingers.

She gave him a weak smile. "I've had seven days

to think about whether or not we should be married. It's a very important decision, probably the most important one I've ever had to make." She paced in front of him. "I had to take into consideration that we've known each other a very short time. I also had to weigh the fact that your home is quite a distance from England. Of course, what made my decision really difficult was that I have fallen in love with you."

She clamped her hands on her hips when he started to push himself out of the chair. "Michael, you promised."

He fell back against the cushion and threw up his hands.

"Thank you," she said formally. Pacing again, she continued. "The night I confronted Derek at Chartridge you were furious with me because I didn't tell you I had decided to let my stepbrother have the house. Yet I am supposed to go along with all the plans you've made without consulting me. Do think that is fair?"

He opened his mouth to answer, then shut it, settling for shaking his head.

"I don't either, but we can work on that. In fact, the conclusion I finally came to is that all of the problems I thought we had are things we can work out with time. Except for one essential item."

He raised a brow when she didn't say what that essential item was. Making a waving motion with one hand, he urged her to go on.

Cassidy had given a great deal of thought to how she was going to handle this meeting with Michael. She'd presented her case unemotionally, as she had planned. She'd said what she had wanted to say. Now it was time to ask him the most important question. His answer would determine her happiness.

She stepped between his legs. Bracing her hands on the arms of the chair, she bent down close to him.

"Everything I've thought about boils down to one salient point, one question. Why do you want to marry me?"

He held her gaze with his and remained silent.

When he didn't speak, Cassidy almost lost her nerve. Then it occurred to her that he was still obeying her command that he not speak.

"Now you can talk," she said.

He didn't answer right away. His gaze lowered to her mouth when she nervously licked her dry lips.

"Please, Michael. This hasn't been easy for me. Answer my question. Why do you want to marry me?"

"I love you," he said simply. "I can't imagine living without you."

She had to tighten her grip on the chair arms to keep from sinking to the floor, her relief was so great. She ended up there anyway when Michael moved unexpectedly, taking her in his arms and easing her down onto the carpet.

He did what he'd been wanting to do for seven torturous days. He kissed her, hard and hungry, letting her feel the love and desperation that was deep inside him. Her legs parted so he could nestle his hips against hers, and he nearly lost his control at that natural gesture of invitation.

Propping his upper body on his elbows, he

brushed his hands over the sides of her face and threaded his fingers into her silky hair.

"I thought you knew," he said.

"How could I have known? You said we were going to get married. You never mentioned you loved me."

"I've never made love with a woman like I made love with you. Didn't that give you any hint as to how I felt?"

She slid her hands over his lean hips. "I could ask you the same thing. You weren't sure I loved you until I said so."

"I'm not going to apologize for rushing you, sweetheart." He brushed his mouth over hers, "If I'd had my way, we would have taken off for the church the day after I met you. We have our whole lives to work out all the things you've been worried about."

"Like where we'll live?"

"We can spend six months in Montana and six months here. I'll purchase Chartridge for you if that's what you want. I'll do whatever I have to in order for us to be together."

Her eyes glittered with desire and love. "Didn't you say we have the rest of our lives to work out everything?"

"I can guarantee it."

She smiled, a private, intimate smile. "Then why don't you shut up and show me what I have to look forward to as a rancher's wife?"

Need seized and seared him. He stood and in one easy movement lifted her into his arms. "I can see I'm going to have my hands full being married to you." He kissed her as he carried her into her bedroom. "I can hardly wait to start."

Hours later, Cassidy raised her head from Michael's shoulder. "There's one stipulation I forgot to mention that has to be met before I'll marry you."

Judging from his contented murmur, he didn't sound too concerned. "What is it?"

She rose up on an elbow and looked into his eyes. "What's your first name?"

He chuckled and pulled her back down to him. "You'll find out the day we get married. I'll have to put it on the marriage license."

She smiled against his lips. "I guess we'd better start thinking of names of knights for our children, since this appears to be a tradition."

He rolled her onto her back. Grinning down at her, he said softly, "Later."

THE EDITOR'S CORNER

There are certain stories we all know and love, whether they're fairy tales, classic novels, or unforgettable plays. We treasure them for the way they touch our heart and soul, make us laugh or cry—or both—and next month LOVESWEPT presents you with a bounty of **TREASURED TALES,** six wonderful romances inspired by beloved stories. With special messages from the authors and gorgeous covers featuring black-and-white photographs that reflect the timelessness of these stories, **TREASURED TALES** are worth a king's ransom!

Starting the lineup is Helen Mittermeyer with **'TWAS THE NIGHT,** LOVESWEPT #588, a stirring version of **BEAUTY AND THE BEAST**. It was on Christmas Eve that Rafe Brockman and Cassie Nordstrom first met, but then they parted as enemies. Now, years later, fate brings them together again on Christmas Eve, and they learn that the gift of love is the true Christmas miracle. A heartwarming story from one of the genre's most popular authors.

In **THE PRINCESS AND THE PEA,** LOVESWEPT #589, Fayrene Preston gives her heroine something more intriguing—and gorgeous—to deal with than a troublesome legume. Though Cameron Tate is the perfect hunk to star in a jeans commercial, all Melisande Lanier wants from him is his bed. But Cameron will sell only if workaholic Mel slows down long enough to fall in love with him. Fayrene's winning charm makes this enchanting story shine.

Like Sydney Carton in Charles Dickens's *A Tale of Two Cities,* Nick Atwell is a rebel with a taste for trouble, but his **RENEGADE WAYS,** LOVESWEPT #590 by Terry

Lawrence, can't dissuade Connie Hennessy from believing the handsome diplomat might be just the hero she needs. And she quickly lets Nick know she's willing to barter heated kisses for Nick's help in a perilous mission. Terry really lets the sparks fly between these two characters.

With **NIGHT DREAMS,** LOVESWEPT #591, Sandra Chastain gives us a hero as unforgettable as the Phantom from *The Phantom of the Opera*. No one knows the truth behind the legend of Jonathan Dream, the playboy who'd vanished after building an empire. But when Shannon Summers is taken to his castle to help his disabled daughter, she learns of his scars and his secrets—and burns with the wildfire of his desire. Sandra tells this story with stunning force.

Snow White was contented living with the seven dwarfs, but in **THE FAIREST OF THEM ALL** by Leanne Banks, LOVESWEPT #592, Carly Pendleton would like nothing better than for her seven loving, but overbearing brothers to let her have her own life. Longtime friend Russ Bradford agrees, especially since he has plans to claim her for his own and to taste the sweetness of her ruby-red lips. Leanne delivers a wonderfully entertaining read.

Peggy Webb will light up your day with **DARK FIRE,** LOVESWEPT #593. Although Sid Granger isn't as short on looks as Cyrano de Bergerac, he doesn't dare court the beautiful Rose Anne Jones because he thinks he can never match her perfection. Instead he agrees to woo her for a friend, but the thought of her in another man's arms sends the fighter pilot soaring to her side. Peggy has once again created an irresistible, sensuous romance.

On sale this month are four fabulous FANFARE titles. From *New York Times* bestselling author Amanda Quick comes **RECKLESS,** a tale of a tarnished knight, a daring maiden, and a sweet, searing, storybook love. When

Phoebe Layton needs help to carry out a quest, she can imagine no one more suited to the job than Gabriel Banner. But the Earl of Wylde has a quest of his own in mind: to possess Phoebe, heart and soul.

The Delaneys are here with **THE DELANEY CHRIST-MAS CAROL!** For this long-awaited addition to this enduring family's saga, Kay Hooper, Iris Johansen, and Fayrene Preston teamed up once again, and now we're thrilled to give you three tales of three generations of Delaneys in love and of the changing face of Christmas—past, present, and future. Enjoy our special holiday offer to you.

If you missed Tami Hoag's novel **SARAH'S SIN** the first time around, you can pick up a copy now and discover a warm, moving story of two cultures in conflict and two hearts in love. Matt Thorne is every fantasy Sarah Troyer has ever had. And though there's a high price to pay for giving herself to one outside the Amish ways, Sarah dares to allow herself a brief, secret adventure in the arms of a forbidden man.

Maureen Reynolds has been described by *Romantic Times* as "a very HOT writer," and the tempestuous historical romance **SMOKE EYES** will show you why. Katherine Flynn has worked hard to overcome the double prejudice she faced as a woman and an Arapaho half-breed, but she can't win against the power of desire when Zach Fletcher abruptly returns to her life.

Also on sale this month in the Doubleday hardcover edition is **CONFIDENCES** by Penny Hayden. In the tradition of Danielle Steel, **CONFIDENCES** is a deeply moving novel about four "thirty-something" mothers and a long-held secret that could save the life of a seventeen-year-old boy.

Well, folks, it's around that time of year when people usually take stock of what they've accomplished and look forward to what's ahead. And one of the things we've been taking stock of is **THE EDITOR'S CORNER**. It's been a continuing feature in LOVESWEPT books since LOVESWEPT #1 was published. That makes almost ten years' worth of previews, and we wonder if it's still something you look forward to every month, or if there's something else you'd like to see perhaps. Let us know; we'd love to hear your opinions and/or suggestions.

Happy reading!

With warmest wishes,

Nita Taublib
Associate Publisher
LOVESWEPT and FANFARE

OFFICIAL RULES TO WINNERS CLASSIC SWEEPSTAKES

No Purchase necessary. To enter the sweepstakes follow instructions found elsewhere in this offer. You can also enter the sweepstakes by hand printing your name, address, city, state and zip code on a 3" x 5" piece of paper and mailing it to: Winners Classic Sweepstakes, P.O. Box 785, Gibbstown, NJ 08027. Mail each entry separately. Sweepstakes begins 12/1/91. Entries must be received by 6/1/93. Some presentations of this sweepstakes may feature a deadline for the Early Bird prize. If the offer you receive does, then to be eligible for the Early Bird prize your entry must be received according to the Early Bird date specified. Not responsible for lost, late, damaged, misdirected, illegible or postage due mail. Mechanically reproduced entries are not eligible. All entries become property of the sponsor and will not be returned.

Prize Selection/Validations: Winners will be selected in random drawings on or about 7/30/93, by VENTURA ASSOCIATES, INC., an independent judging organization whose decisions are final. Odds of winning are determined by total number of entries received. Circulation of this sweepstakes is estimated not to exceed 200 million. Entrants need not be present to win. All prizes are guaranteed to be awarded and delivered to winners. Winners will be notified by mail and may be required to complete an affidavit of eligibility and release of liability which must be returned within 14 days of date of notification or alternate winners will be selected. Any guest of a trip winner will also be required to execute a release of liability. Any prize notification letter or any prize returned to a participating sponsor, Bantam Doubleday Dell Publishing Group, Inc., its participating divisions or subsidiaries, or VENTURA ASSOCIATES, INC. as undeliverable will be awarded to an alternate winner. Prizes are not transferable. No multiple prize winners except as may be necessary due to unavailability, in which case a prize of equal or greater value will be awarded. Prizes will be awarded approximately 90 days after the drawing. All taxes, automobile license and registration fees, if applicable, are the sole responsibility of the winners. Entry constitutes permission (except where prohibited) to use winners' names and likenesses for publicity purposes without further or other compensation.

Participation: This sweepstakes is open to residents of the United States and Canada, except for the province of Quebec. This sweepstakes is sponsored by Bantam Doubleday Dell Publishing Group, Inc. (BDD), 666 Fifth Avenue, New York, NY 10103. Versions of this sweepstakes with different graphics will be offered in conjunction with various solicitations or promotions by different subsidiaries and divisions of BDD. Employees and their families of BDD, its division, subsidiaries, advertising agencies, and VENTURA ASSOCIATES, INC., are not eligible.

Canadian residents, in order to win, must first correctly answer a time limited arithmetical skill testing question. Void in Quebec and wherever prohibited or restricted by law. Subject to all federal, state, local and provincial laws and regulations.

Prizes: The following values for prizes are determined by the manufacturers' suggested retail prices or by what these items are currently known to be selling for at the time this offer was published. Approximate retail values include handling and delivery of prizes. Estimated maximum retail value of prizes: 1 Grand Prize ($27,500 if merchandise or $25,000 Cash); 1 First Prize ($3,000); 5 Second Prizes ($400 each); 35 Third Prizes ($100 each); 1,000 Fourth Prizes ($9.00 each) ; 1 Early Bird Prize ($5,000); Total approximate maximum retail value is $50,000. Winners will have the option of selecting any prize offered at level won. Automobile winner must have a valid driver's license at the time the car is awarded. Trips are subject to space and departure availability. Certain black-out dates may apply. Travel must be completed within one year from the time the prize is awarded. Minors must be accompanied by an adult. Prizes won by minors will be awarded in the name of parent or legal guardian.

For a list of Major Prize Winners (available after 7/30/93): send a self-addressed, stamped envelope entirely separate from your entry to: Winners Classic Sweepstakes Winners, P.O. Box 825, Gibbstown, NJ 08027. Requests must be received by 6/1/93. DO NOT SEND ANY OTHER CORRESPONDENCE TO THIS P.O. BOX.

The Delaney Dynasty lives on in

The Delaney Christmas Carol

by Kay Hooper, Iris Johansen, & Fayrene Preston

Three of romantic fiction's best-loved authors present the changing face of Christmas spirit—past, present, and future—as they tell the story of three generations of Delaneys in love.

CHRISTMAS PAST by Iris Johansen

From the moment he first laid eyes on her, Kevin Delaney felt a curious attraction for the ragclad Gypsy beauty rummaging through the attic of his ranch at Killara. He didn't believe for a moment her talk of magic mirrors and second-sight, but something about Zara St. Cloud stirred his blood. Now, as Christmas draws near, a touch leads to a kiss and a gift of burning passion.

CHRISTMAS PRESENT by Fayrene Preston

Bria Delaney had been looking for Christmas ornaments in her mother's attic, when she saw him in the mirror for the first time—a stunningly handsome man with sky-blue eyes and red-gold hair. She had almost convinced herself he was only a dream when Kells Braxton arrived at Killara and led them both to a holiday wonderland of sensuous pleasure.

CHRISTMAS FUTURE by Kay Hooper

As the last of the Delaney men, Brett returned to Killara this Christmastime only to find it in the capable hands of his father's young and beautiful widow. Yet the closer he got to Cassie, the more Brett realized that the embers of their old love still burned and that all it would take was a look, a kiss, a caress, to turn their dormant passion into an inferno.

The best in Women's Fiction from Bantam FANFARE.
On sale in November 1992   AN 428 9/92

FANFARE

On Sale in November

RECKLESS
☐ 29315-X $5.50/6.50 in Canada
by Amanda Quick

New York Times bestselling author of
RENDEZVOUS and RAVISHED

THE DELANEY CHRISTMAS CAROL
☐ 29654-X $4.99/5.99 in Canada
by Kay Hooper, Iris Johansen, and Fayrene Preston

UNSUITABLE COMPANY
☐ 29712-0 $5.99/6.99 in Canada
by Judith Green

SARAH'S SIN
☐ 56050-6 $4.50//5.50 in Canada
by Tami Hoag
author of STILL WATERS and LUCKY'S LADY

SMOKE EYES
☐ 29501-2 $4.99/5.99 in Canada
by Maureen Reynolds
"A very HOT writer." --*Romantic Times*

☐ Please send me the books I have checked above. I am enclosing $ _____ (add $2.50 to cover postage and handling). Send check or money order, no cash or C. O. D.'s please.

Name _____

Address _____

City/ State/ Zip _____

Send order to: Bantam Books, Dept. FN84, 2451 S. Wolf Rd., Des Plaines, IL 60018
Allow four to six weeks for delivery.
Prices and availability subject to change without notice.

Ask for these books at your local bookstore or use this page to order.   FN84 12/92

FANFARE

On Sale in December

THE TIGER PRINCE
☐ 29968-9 $5.50/6.50 in Canada
by Iris Johansen
Bantam's "Mistress of Romantic Fantasy"
author of THE GOLDEN BARBARIAN

LADY DEFIANT
☐ 29574-9 $4.99/5.99 in Canada
by Suzanne Robinson
Bestselling author of LADY GALLANT
and LADY HELLFIRE

"Lavish in atmosphere, rich in adventure, filled with suspense
and passion, LADY DEFIANT is a fitting sequel to
LADY GALLANT. Suzanne Robinson brilliantly captures the
era with all the intrigue, costume, drama, and romance that
readers adore." --*Romantic Times*

PRIVATE SCANDALS
☐ 56053-0 $4.99//5.99 in Canada
by Christy Cohen
A stunning debut novel of friendship,
betrayal, and passionate romance

A LOVE FOR ALL TIME
☐ 29996-4 $4.50/5.50 in Canada
by Dorothy Garlock
One of Ms. Garlock's most beloved romances of all time

Ask for these books at your local bookstore or use this page to order.

☐ Please send me the books I have checked above. I am enclosing $ _____ (add $2.50
to cover postage and handling). Send check or money order, no cash or C. O. D.'s please.

Name _____

Address _____

City/ State/ Zip _____

Send order to: Bantam Books, Dept. FN85, 2451 S. Wolf Rd., Des Plaines, IL 60018
Allow four to six weeks for delivery.
Prices and availability subject to change without notice.

FN85 12/92

HIGH PRAISE FOR JENNIFER ASHLEY!

THE PIRATE NEXT DOOR

"A witty and splendidly magical romance."
—*Booklist* (Starred Review)

"*The Pirate Next Door* is a fast-paced, enjoyable story, one guaranteed to throw a bright spot into a dreary fall evening."
—*The Romance Reader*

"A delightful treat."

—*All About Romance*

"*The Pirate Next Door* is a wonderful tale full of humor, passion, intrigue, excitement, and non-stop adventure."
—*Romance Reviews Today*

"I was teased, tantalized, and enthralled while reading *The Pirate Next Door*! Full of twists and turns, adventure, love and lust, and betrayals, this is a great new addition to the pirate books of romance!"

—RomanceJunkies.com

PERILS OF THE HEART

"Deliciously fun, delightfully entertaining. Featuring impeccably crafted characters and laced with both humor and danger, this historical romance is simply superb."
—*Booklist*

"This is one of those lightning-fast roller-coaster rides loaded with escapades and plot . . . a wonderful escape from a stressful day."

—*Romantic Times*

"*Perils of the Heart* is just plain fun. It has action and adventure, lust, and a sweetly naïve heroine with nerves of steel."

—*All About Romance*

"An incredible first novel that has everything a reader could ask for and more with a story so well told, it's one not to be missed."

—*Romance Reviews Today*

"Pamela Morsi is witty, wise and wonderful.
I'm a huge fan."
—*New York Times* bestselling author
Susan Elizabeth Phillips

PAMELA MORSI

Forty-something Ellen Jameson is currently
downsizing her life, a term she prefers over ones like:
widowed, *broke* and *homeless*. After her husband's
untimely death, she was forced to sell his business
and their family home to pay off the debt. Now, with
her party-hardy, 21-year-old daughter, Amber, in tow,
along with Amber's three-year-old daughter, Jet, Ellen
has moved home with her mother, Wilma, a serial
bride for whom *stability* is a dirty word.

But life is what you make it, and in colorful
San Antonio, Texas, four generations of women
discover that the most important thing about
having a past is letting it go.

LETTING GO

Available the first week of March 2003
wherever paperbacks are sold!

Visit us at www.mirabooks.com   MPM656

She looked like an angel, acted like a vixen
and sang like an alley cat.

NAUGHTY MARIETTA

Marietta Stone had a glorious future ahead. But it did not include
being kidnapped by Cole Heflin, a ruthless, conniving scoundrel
who'd been paid to bring her back to the one place she'd vowed
never to set foot again—home.

Cole had never met a woman he didn't like, nor one he wasn't happy
to love. Until Marietta. But even with her benefactor's hired gunmen
on their trail and a dangerous frontier ahead, the trip home was not
nearly as dangerous as the temptation naughty Marietta inspired….

NAN RYAN

"Beautifully crafted characters, a powerful story and sizzling
sensuality have always made Nan Ryan's romances special."
—*Romantic Times*

MIRA®

*On sale April 2003
wherever paperbacks are sold!*

Visit us at www.mirabooks.com   MNR676

New York Times **Bestselling Author**

STELLA CAMERON

Adam Chillworth, the mysterious portrait artist of
7C Mayfair Square, is passionately in love with Princess Desiree,
but he has constantly refused her ardent adoration. He's convinced
he's too old and worldly for her—and he is only a commoner.

Still, Desiree has a plan. She'll show him that she has matured.
She'll treat him as an old friend—even if every time she's with
him, all she feels is passion. But when ruthless enemies from
Adam's past place them both in peril, Desiree discovers that
Adam Chillworth is a dangerous man to hate—and to love.

ABOUT ADAM

*Available the first week of March 2003
wherever paperbacks are sold!*

MIRA®

Visit us at www.mirabooks.com

MSC666

but as she watched they opened. One brow rose in query.

Suddenly shy, she dropped her gaze to where her fingers played in the folds of his cravat. "Will you take me to see the Fragonards?"

As a deep chuckle rumbled through his chest, she blushed vividly. But when she glanced again into his face, his expression was perfectly serious.

"Maybe you should see them. Just so you know what kind of man you're marrying."

His lips twisted into a smile that held a gentle promise. The glow in his eyes thrilled her to the core. Feeling suddenly light-headed, her heart thundering, Georgiana managed to nod her agreement.

A few minutes later they left the drawing-room with some semblance of normality and started up the stairs, Georgiana going ahead. On the landing they met Duckett, on his way down. As he drew abreast of his butler, Dominic paused to murmur, *sotto voce,* "Just remember, Duckett, this is all your fault."

Duckett's rigidly correct demeanour did not alter. He inclined his head. "Very good, m'lord."

Duckett continued down the stairs, pausing at their foot to listen to the soft murmur of lovers' voices, cut off by the closing of a door overhead.

Then he smiled. "Very good, m'lord."

her mind away from its preoccupation with the gentleman beside her and turned it to consideration of something—anything—else.

Lord Ellsmere's actions, for instance. Why had he gone to Lord Alton, rather than directly to Bella? That Bella should have summoned her brother was no surprise, but why had Lord Ellsmere done so? No answer occurred to her. Giving up on that issue, she wondered how to acceptably ask what he had done when he had re-entered the inn. She felt she had a right to know; it might prove important in any future disputation with Charles. Surreptitiously, she glanced at him.

In the light thrown by the lamps of a passing carriage, she saw a bloody scratch across the knuckles of his right hand.

"Oh! You've hurt yourself!" Without a thought for propriety or the consequences, Georgiana captured his hand in hers, holding it closer to examine the wound in the dim light. "You've been...been milling with Charles!" Settling the large hand firmly in her lap, she whipped out her small handkerchief and wrapped it tightly over the cut, tying a small knot in the lace edging to keep it in place. "There was no need, I assure you."

A deep sigh greeted her protestations. "Oh, there was every need. Charles needed to be taught a lesson. No gentleman goes about scheming to ruin a lady's reputation."

"What did you do to him?"

His head back against the squabs, Dominic tried to read her expression. "Don't worry, he still lives." When she continued to wait patiently, he grimaced and added, "He was unwise enough to make a number of suggestions I found distinctly ungentlemanly. I took great delight in making him eat his words."

"But you might have been hurt! You *were* hurt." Georgiana looked again at the hand which still lay in her skirts, gently cradled between hers. Suddenly recalling the impropriety of holding a gentleman's hand in her lap, she reluctantly released it, thankful the dim light hid her blushes.

His lips twisting in a smile he knew she could not see, Dominic equally reluctantly withdrew his hand from where it lay, stilling the all but automatic impulse to reverse the situation and capture her hand in his. He had initially been stunned into immobility by her impulsive actions. When his wits returned, he had seen no reason to shorten a moment which had touched him strangely. Now, sensing her unease, he sought for some comment to distract her.

"Anyway, I doubt you'll be troubled by Charles again."

Georgiana heard and nodded, but, suddenly feeling ridiculously weak, sought refuge in silence. Too many emotions swirled in her breast, conflicting with all the accepted precepts, and his nearness only compounded her confusion. She fixed her gaze on the scene beyond the window, the shadows of trees merging into the darkness. Yet her mind remained centred on the man beside her.

Perceptive enough to sense her turmoil, Dominic smiled into the darkness and, smothering a small sigh of frustration, put aside his plans for furthering his suit. She was nervous and on edge. Doubtless, her recent brush with the despicable Charles had contributed its mite to her state. In fact, now he came to think on it, it was wonderful that she hadn't treated him to the vapours. Most young women would undoubtedly be weeping all over him by this juncture, not concerning themselves with his minor hurts. In the dark, his fingers found the lace edging of her handkerchief wrapped tightly about his hand.

The moment was not right, either, for bringing up the subject of the masked ball. He was far too experienced even to contemplate making love to her now, while she was so touchy. There was, after all, tomorrow. And the day after tomorrow. And all the days after that. For, if nothing else had been settled this evening, he had definitely decided that Georgiana Hartley was not going to be allowed to slip out of his life. Whether she realised it or not, she was there to stay.

He paused in his mental ramblings to glance down at the slight figure beside him. She sat absorbed in her thoughts, her hands tightly clasped in her lap. Another half-hour would see them in Green Street. With another smile for the darkness, Dominic settled his head comfortably against the well stuffed squabs and closed his eyes, the better to indulge his fantasies.

Georgiana sat silently, taking herself to task for her forward behaviour. A lecture on the unwisdom of allowing her fanciful dreams to lead her to read more into Lord Alton's actions than was intended followed. He was very fond of Bella. She should remember that he had come to find her in response to Bella's request—brotherly devotion was the emotion which drove him to protect her, nothing else. Her stern admonitions made her flinch inwardly but did little to ease the tightness around her heart.

Gradually, without conscious direction, her tired mind drifted to consideration of its main preoccupation. Of course he had no interest in her. If he had known who she was at the masked ball, he would have mentioned the fact by now. She knew little of the ways of gentleman rakes, but felt sure a coach trip, together alone, must rate as one of those opportunities too good to let slip. Yet the man beside her remained silent. She stole a glance at him from beneath her lashes. His eyes were closed. Emboldened, she allowed her gaze to skim the contours of his face, the wide forehead and squared chin, his firm, well shaped lips... Finding her mind frolicking in fantasies of how those lips would feel against hers, Georgiana forcibly withdrew her gaze and returned it to contemplation of the darkness beyond the window.

Ravello. The image of the villa there, now hers, materialised in her mind's eye. She seized on it. And was suddenly struck by the obvious solution to her troubles. Charles was a bully and totally unscrupulous. He would continue to threaten her peace of mind while she remained in England. And Bella's brother, too, disturbed her rest and reduced her ability to cope with the daily round of fashionable life. Yet shc was not particularly enamoured of the social whirl; it would cause her no great pain to eschew the life completely. It was a pleasant diversion, nothing more.

With sudden conviction, she made up her mind. She would see out the Season with Bella, as she had promised Arthur she would. Then she would return to Ravello, a great deal older and a great deal wiser. She stifled a small sigh and forced herself to promise—when winter set in, she would be in Ravello.

The increasing light coming from street-lamps as they entered the capital made it worth while for Dominic to desert his imaginings in favour of the real thing. He had been watching Georgiana for some minutes, wondering what it was that kept her so serious, when a point which had thus far eluded him surfaced as a question. ''Georgiana, do you have any idea why Charles wants to marry you?''

As he said the words, he realised they were hardly flattering. Still, he had a high enough opinion of Georgiana Hartley to be sure she was not the sort of flighty young woman who believed all men who wished to marry her were smitten by her beauty. The memory of her numerous suitors, all of whom were most definitely smitten, himself included, brought a wry smile to his lips.

In the flickering, shifting light, Georgiana saw the smile, and her heart turned to lead and dropped to her slippers. To ask a question like that and then smile condescendingly! Well, if anything was needed to convince her Lord Alton had no romantic interest in her it was that. Doggedly, she forced her mind to concentrate on his query. Frowning with the effort, she shook her head and answered truthfully, ''I have no idea.''

''It was the same while you were at the Place?''

Georgiana nodded. ''Exactly the same.'' She paused, then decided she might as well tell Lord Alton the whole of it. He knew so much already. Choosing her words carefully, she explained Charles's claim of a long-standing betrothal.

"And you're certain such an arrangement never existed?"

"Quite sure." Georgiana paused, then added in explanation, "My father and I were...very close. He would never have done such a thing and not told me. Not for any reason."

Lord Alton seemed to accept her assurance. He sat silently beside her as the coach rumbled along the cobbles towards Green Street.

Dominic had no doubt that Georgiana's beliefs were true. He only wished he had known of Charles's claim before he had returned to the inn parlour. The tenseness he had felt but not recognised on his drive to the Hare and Hounds had converted to anger once he had got Georgiana safely away—anger that had demanded some outlet. So he had returned to the parlour, to be quite unnecessarily provoked by Charles's animadversions on his cousin. In the end he had administered a thoroughly deserved thrashing. He knew Charles was close to financial ruin—was, in fact, technically bankrupt. Georgiana's small fortune would not come close to meeting his mounting debts. After suggesting Charles would be wise never to approach his lovely cousin again, he had repeated his offer to buy the Place. The sum he named was far more than Charles would ever get from any other, with the Place situated as it was. Charles had only attempted a sneer through swollen and cracked lips.

Dominic contemplated a late-night return to the Hare and Hounds, to pursue further the reason for

Charles's apparent fixation with marrying his cousin. Even less than Georgiana did he believe Charles would act for the good of the family. There was something in all this that he was missing, some vital clue which would make all clear. But Charles would almost certainly have left before he could return to the inn.

He turned the anomalies of Charles's behaviour, both with respect to Georgiana and to the sale of the Place, over and over in his mind. Suddenly, the two connected. Dominic straightened in his seat.

"Georgiana, have you been to see your father's English solicitors yet?"

Dragged from the depths of a series of most melancholy thoughts, Georgiana shook her head. "No. I suppose I should, but there doesn't really seem much point."

"But…" Dominic paused, then decided he was going to interfere even though he theoretically had no right. Right be damned. He was going to marry the chit, wasn't he? "Correct me if I'm wrong, but I seem to recall you left Italy before notification of your father's death was acknowledged by your English solicitors. Is that right?"

"You mean," said Georgiana, brow wrinkling in an effort to get the question straight, "before they wrote back after they got the letter from the Italian solicitors?" At Dominic's nod, she agreed. "Yes, that's right."

"And you haven't seen your father's will?"

"No…no. That was left with the English solicitors. But I always knew I would inherit all Papa's money. And the villa at Ravello." She paused, puzzled by his line of questioning, not sure of what possibilities he saw. ''But surely if there had been anything more, or anything unexpected, someone would have told me by now?''

''Who are your solicitors here?''

''Whitworth and Whitworth, in Lincoln's Inn.''

''Good. I'll take you to see them tomorrow.''

Georgiana turned to look at him in amazement. She had not previously had much exposure to the autocratic side of Lord Alton's temperament. She surveyed the satisfied expression on his face with misgiving. ''But...why?''

He smiled at her, and she almost forgot her question.

''Because, my dear Georgiana,'' he said as he captured her hand and raised it to his lips, ''Charles, despite all evidence to the contrary, is not a complete gudgeon. His attempts to coerce you into marriage must have some motive behind them. And, as your kinship with him is the only connection between you, I suggest we start looking for the answer with your father's solicitors.''

Despite the clear impression that Lord Alton had a stronger motive for insisting she visit her solicitors, Georgiana got no further chance to question him. He had barely ceased speaking when the carriage pulled up outside Green Street. In the ensuing hullabaloo there was no opportunity to do more than thank him prettily for his rescue and meekly accept his instruction to be ready the next morning at eleven.

GEORGIANA RETURNED Arthur's reassuring smile as the Alton town carriage drew up at the entrance to

Lincoln's Inn. Both she and her host had been taken up by an irresistible force at eleven that morning, their objective being the office of her father's solicitors. Despite her belief that nothing new would be learned from Whitworths, Georgiana was enjoying her first view of an area of London she had not previously had cause to visit.

Lord Alton, sitting beside her, had leant forward to speak to the porter. As he leant back, the carriage lurched forward again, over the cobbles and through the large gate of the Inn. The cobbled yard was surrounded by buildings entirely given over to solicitors and clerks. By each doorway leading on to a stairwell hung the bronze plaques of the practitioners within. The carriage drew up before one such door. Lord Alton jumped down and gave her his hand.

Their destination lay on the first floor. A desiccated clerk of indeterminate years, dressed in sombre grey and sporting a tie wig of decades gone by, bade them seat themselves in the small outer office, "While I enquire if Mr Whitworth will see you." He left Georgiana with the definite impression that to be permitted to see the Mr Whitworths was tantamount to being granted an audience with the Regent.

Minutes later he was back, oozing spurious concern. A Mr Whitworth—the elder, as they later learned—followed close on his heels. A portly man of late middle age, he glanced down at the card he held in his hand, given to the clerk by Lord Alton.

Mr Whitworth looked at the two elegant and eminently respectable gentlemen filling his antechamber and became slightly flustered. "My lord…?"

Dominic took pity on him. "I am Lord Alton," he explained smoothly, "and this is Miss Georgiana Hartley, one of your clients. She is presently in the care of my sister, Lady Winsmere. Lord Winsmere," he added, indicating Arthur for the solicitor's edification, "and I have escorted her here in the hope you can clarify a number of points concerning Miss Hartley's inheritance."

It was doubtful if Mr Whitworth heard the latter half of this speech. His eyes had become transfixed on Georgiana, sitting patiently on a chair between her two protectors. Despite the fact she was now used to being stared at, and knew she looked her best in a soft dove-coloured merino gown with a delicate lace tippet, Georgiana found his gaze unnerving. As Lord Alton finished speaking, and the man continued to stare, she raised her brows haughtily.

Mr Whitworth started. "Miss Georgiana Hartley—Mr James Hartley's daughter?" he asked breathlessly.

Georgiana looked puzzled. "Yes," she confirmed, wondering who else had her name.

"My dear young lady!" exclaimed the solicitor, grasping her hand and bowing elaborately over it. "My dear Miss Georgiana! Well, it's a relief to see you at last! We've been searching for you for months!" Once he had started, it seemed the man hardly paused for breath. "Almost, we had begun to fear foul play. When we couldn't contact you and all our letters were returned unopened and no one seemed to know where you had disappeared to…" Suddenly he paused and seemed to recollect himself. He waved plump hands in sudden agitation. "But what am I thinking of? Please come into my office, Miss Hartley, my lords, and we will sort this matter out at once."

He ushered them into a large office which bore little resemblance to the spartan outer chamber. Here all was air and light, with a rich red Turkey carpet covering mellow polished boards. Through the windows, the branches of the trees in the small lawn in the middle of the yard could be seen, the last yellow leaves tenaciously defying the brisk autumn breeze.

As they entered, a thin, soberly clad gentleman rose from behind one of two large desks. Mr Whitworth, holding the door, proclaimed, "Alfred, Miss Hartley is here!"

The second Whitworth—for, from the similarity of facial features, there was little doubt of who he was—looked startled. He pulled his gold-rimmed pince-nez off his nose, polished the glass, then returned it to its perch the better to view Georgiana. After a moment of rapt contemplation, he sighed. "Thank God!"

Both Whitworths bustled about, arranging chairs for their guests. They set these in front of the large desks which, side by side, faced the room. Once their visitors were seated, they subsided, each behind his own desk.

"Now!" said Whitworth the elder, chins flapping as he settled, hands folded before him. "As you can see, we're delighted to see you, Miss Hartley. We have been trying to contact you since we learned of your father's death, with respect to the matter of your inheritance." He beamed at Georgiana.

"If we might speak frankly...?" enquired Whitworth the younger, his flat tone a contrast to his brother's jovial accents.

Turning to face him, it took a moment before Georgiana understood his query. "Oh, please," she said quickly when light finally dawned, "Lord Alton and Lord Winsmere are my friends. I will be relying on their advice."

"Good, good," said Whitworth the elder, causing Georgiana to swivel again. "Not wise for a young lady so well dowered as you are to be alone in the world."

"Quite," his younger brother concurred drily.

"Now, where to begin?"

"Perhaps at your father's bequests?"

"There weren't many—nothing that interfered with the bulk of the estate."

"A few minor legacies to old servants—the usual sort of thing."

"But the major estate remains intact." Whitworth the elder paused to beam again at Georgiana.

Stifling the impulse to put a hand to her whirling head, Georgiana took the opportunity to quell her impending dizziness. It was like watching a tennis game, the conversational ball passing from brother to brother and back again, before their audience of three. Then his last words registered. "Major estate?"

"Why, yes."

"As the major beneficiary of your father's will, you inherit the majority of his estate."

"Which is to say," Whitworth the elder took up the tale smoothly, "the estate known as the Place in the county of Buckinghamshire…"

"His invested capital," intoned Whitworth the younger. "The house in town..."

"And all his paintings not previously sold."

A pause ensued. Georgiana stared at the elder Mr Whitworth, he who had last spoken. Lord Winsmere, having given up the unequal task of allowing his eyes to follow the conversation, stared out of the window, his lips pursed. Lord Alton, even less enthralled by the vision of the Whitworths, had shifted his gaze long since to the young woman beside him. He showed no surprise at the solicitor's news.

"The Place? But... There must be some mistake!" Georgiana could not believe her ears. "My cousin Charles owns the Place."

"Oh, dear me, no!" said the younger Whitworth. "Mr Charles Hartley is not a client of ours."

"And has no claim whatever on the Place. The estate was not entailed."

"It generally passed through the eldest male..."

"But your grandfather divided his estate equally between his two sons..."

"Your father and his brother, your uncle Ernest."

"Both were given an estate—in your father's case, the Place."

"Unfortunately, Ernest Hartley was a gambler."

"Quite ran through his patrimony, as the saying goes."

"He eventually lost everything and turned to your father for aid."

"Your father was enjoying a great success in London at that time. He had married your mother and was much in demand. Dear me, his fees! Well, quite astronomical, they seemed.'' Mr Whitworth the elder paused for breath.

This time Georgiana could not restrain her need to put a hand to her brow. The world was whirling.

"If we could condense this history, gentlemen?'' Viscount Alton's precise tones jerked both Whitworths out of their rut.

"Er—yes. Well,'' said Mr Whitworth, with a careful eye on his lordship, "the long and the short of it is, your father and mother wished to spend some time in Italy. So your father installed your uncle as steward of the Place, put his ready capital in the funds, leased the house in London, and left the country. I believe you were a child at the time.''

Georgiana nodded absent-mindedly. The Place was hers. It had never been Charles's property, and he had known it.

"When we heard of your father's death,'' broke in the younger Whitworth, warily eyeing the Viscount, "we wrote immediately to you at the villa in Ravello. The letter was returned by your Italian man of business, stating you had returned to England before learning of your uncle's demise and had planned to stay at the Place.''

Whitworth the elder opened his mouth to respond to his cue, but caught the Viscount's eye and fell silent, leaving it to his sibling to continue, "We wrote to you there, but the letters were returned without explanation. In the end we sent one of our most trusted clerks to see you. He reported that the house was shut up and deserted.''

The elder Whitworth could restrain himself no

longer. "No one seemed to know where you'd gone or even if you'd arrived from the Continent."

Following the tale with difficulty, Georgiana saw what must have occurred. Questions hammered at her brain, but most were not for the solicitors' ears. She fastened on the one aspect that held greatest importance to her. "You mentioned pictures?"

"Oh, yes. Your father left quite a tidy stack of canvases—some unclaimed portraits, and others—in England. He always claimed they were a sound investment." The dead tones of the younger solicitor left no doubt of his opinion on the matter.

"But where are they stored?" asked Georgiana.

"Stored?" The elder Whitworth stared at her wordlessly, then turned to his brother for help. But the younger Whitworth had clearly decided this was one cue he would do well to miss. "Er…" said Mr Whitworth, chasing inspiration, "I rather suspect he must have left them at the Place."

"Are you certain they haven't been sold?" Lord Winsmere bought into the conversation. "From what you say, Ernest Hartley sounds the type to hock his grandmother's spectacles. Excuse me, m'dear," he added in an aside to Georgiana.

But the elder Whitworth waved his hands in a negative gesture. "A reformed character, I assure you. After his—er—brush with the Navy, he was so thankful to be pulled free that he was quite devoted to his brother and his interests."

"Devoted?" echoed Lord Alton incredulously. "Have you seen the Place?"

"Unfortunately, Mr Hartley was unsuited to the task

of managing the estate, although he tried his best."
The younger Whitworth drew his lordship's fire. "We
would seriously doubt he would have sold any of his
brother's paintings. He lived quite retired at the Place
until his death, you know."

"So," said Georgiana, struggling to take it all in,
"the most likely place for my father's pictures—the
ones he left in England—is the Place. But they aren't
there. I looked."

Both Whitworths shifted uncomfortably but could
throw no further light on the matter.

Eventually Mr Whitworth the elder broke the silence. "Are there any instructions you wish to give
us, my dear, concerning your property?"

Georgiana blinked, then slowly shook her head.
"I'm afraid I'll need a little time to think things
through. It's all been rather a surprise."

"Yes, of course. No rush at all," said the elder Mr
Whitworth, resuming his genial state. "Mr Charles
Hartley will of course be given due notice to quit."

Then, as there seemed nothing further to say, Georgiana rose, bringing the men to their feet.

"One moment, my dear," came Lord Winsmere's
voice. "It's as well to know all the facts." He smiled
at Georgiana and then turned to ask, "You mentioned
capital placed in the funds. What is the current balance?"

The elder Mr Whitworth beamed. The figure he
named sent Lord Alton's black brows flying.

An enigmatic smile played on Lord Winsmere's lips
as he turned to a stunned Georgiana. "Well, my dear,

I'm afraid you'll have more than your earnest suitors to repel once that piece of news gets around.''

ARTHUR'S REACTION was echoed by Bella when, over the luncheon table, she was regaled with the entirety of Georgiana's fortune. Arthur told the story; Dominic had declined an invitation to join them, pleading the press of other engagements.

''There's no point in thinking you can hide it, Georgie,'' Bella said once she had recovered enough to speak. ''You're an *heiress*. Even if the Place is all to pieces.''

Georgiana was still trying to recover her equilibrium. ''But surely, if we don't tell anyone, no one will know.''

Bella felt like screaming. What other young lady of quality, with her way to make in the world, when informed she was a considerable heiress, would act so? Inwardly, Bella railed again at the unknown who had stolen her friend's heart. Dominic had not yet found him; that much was clear. After his successful rescue of Georgiana the evening before, he had stayed to partake of a cold supper. She could well imagine what he had done to Charles, even without the tell-tale handkerchief she had seen him quickly remove from his hand and stuff into his pocket before he thought anyone had noticed. She was more than ready to believe his assertion that Charles would not trouble Georgiana again, and would in all probability not remain over long in England. But, after arranging for Arthur to accompany Georgiana and himself to her solicitors' this morning, her brother had merely bestowed a fond pat on her cheek and left…left her to struggle with the herculean task of convincing Georgiana to forget her hopeless love and choose between her lovesick beaux.

Sudden inspiration blossomed in Bella's mind. "Georgie, my love, we will really have to think very carefully about how you should go on." Bella paused, carefully choosing her words. "Once it becomes known you're an heiress, you'll be swamped. Perhaps it would be better to make your choice now."

Georgiana's gaze rose from her plate to settle on her friend's face. Bella's attempted manipulation was unwelcome, but, seeing the wistful expression in the blue eyes watching her, and knowing that she only meant to help, Georgiana could not suppress a small smile. But, "Really, Bella!" was all she said.

Abashed, Bella retreated, but rapidly came about. "Yes, but seriously, Georgie, what do you plan to do?"

"I'm afraid, my dear," put in Arthur, "that for once Bella is quite right." Bella grimaced at his phrasing. "Once it becomes common knowledge that you have such a fortune, you'll be besieged."

With a sigh, Georgiana pushed her plate away. They had sent the servants from the room to give free rein to their discussion. She rose to fetch the teapot from the side-table. Slipping once more into her chair, she busied herself with pouring cups for both Arthur and Bella before helping herself. Only then did she answer Bella. "I don't know. But please promise me you'll say nothing to anyone about my inheritance?"

Arthur bowed his acquiescence. ''Whatever you wish, my dear.'' His stern eye rested on his wife.

Bella pouted, but, under her husband's prompting, she gave in. ''Oh, very well. But it won't help, you know. Such news *always* gets around.''

CHAPTER EIGHT

THE ACCURACY of Bella's prediction was brought home to Georgiana before the week was out. Shrewd assessing glances, condescending and calculating stares—the oppressive, smothering interest of the *ton* made itself felt in a dozen different ways. She could only conclude that the clerks in Mr Whitworth's office, or, perhaps, the Mr Whitworths themselves, were less discreet than she, in her naïveté, had supposed.

Bella, of course, behaved as if all the attention was only her due. Her friend continued to hope she would succumb to the blandishments of one or other of her insistent suitors. In fact, thought Georgiana crossly, the entire charade was enough to put anyone off marriage for life. How could she ever hope to convince herself any gentleman was in earnest, that he truly loved her for herself, rather than for the financial comfort she would bring him, when everyone behaved as if her new-found fortune was of the first importance?

With a disgusted little snort, she turned over on the coverlet of her bed, kicking her legs to free her skirts from under her. She had retreated to her room to rest before dressing for dinner and the Massinghams' rout. For the first time since Georgiana had come to Green Street, Bella had also retired for a late afternoon nap.

While she studied the details of the pink-silk-draped canopy, Georgiana considered her friend. Bella certainly seemed more tired these days, though the bloom on her skin showed none of the subtle signs of fatigue. Still, Georgiana couldn't understand how she kept up. Or why. For her own part, the glamour of the balls and parties was rapidly fading, their thrills too meaninglessly repetitive to hold her interest. Now she had no difficulty in understanding Bella's plea of boredom with the fashionable round.

Her eyes drifted to the wardrobe, wherein resided all her beautiful gowns. Bella was always so thrilled when she wore her latest acquisitions. They were worth every last penny just for that. Georgiana grinned. She could hardly deny Bella such a small pleasure when all her friend's energies were directed towards securing her, Georgiana's, future. Nothing seemly likely to turn Bella from her purpose. Her beloved Georgie must marry into the *ton*.

As an errant ray of sunshine drifted over the gilded cords drawing back the curtains of her bed, Georgiana wondered again at the oddity of having a virtual foster-sister. She was fast learning that receiving care and concern laid a reciprocal responsibility on the recipient. But, despite Bella's yearnings, this was one aspect of her life on which she was determined to hold firm. She would marry for love, or not at all.

Just the thought of love, the very concept, brought a darkly handsome face swimming into her consciousness. Vibrant blue eyes laughed at her through a mask, then turned smoky and dark. Resolutely she banished the unnerving image. Dreams were for children.

In truth, if it had not been for Lord Alton's support, she might well have turned tail and fled back to Italy the first day after their discovery at Lincoln's Inn. The puzzle of Charles and his machinations was now clear. Fiend that he was, devoid of all proper feeling, he had decided to marry her before she found out she owned the Place. That way, Dominic had explained, she would likely never have known the extent of her fortune; as her husband, Charles would have assumed full rights over her property.

Dominic. She must stop thinking of him like that, in such a personal way. If she was to preserve her secret, she must learn to treat him with becoming distance. Unfortunately, this grew daily more difficult.

When he had appeared before her at the Walfords' ball the evening after their momentous visit to the Whitworths', she had offered him welcome far in excess of what might reasonably be excused on the grounds that he was her patroness's brother. She hoped he had put it down to a gush of girlish gratitude, no matter how the very thought irked her. But the warmth in his blue eyes had left her with an uncomfortable feeling of no longer being in control, as if some hand more powerful than hers was directing her affairs.

Dominic—*Lord Alton!*—continued to rescue her from the worst of her importunate court. In fact he was now so often by her side that the rest of her admirers tended to fade into the background, at least in her eyes. Georgiana frowned at the wandering sunbeam which had moved to light the bedpost. Now she came to consider the matter, it was almost as if Lord Alton himself was paying court to her.

Another unladylike snort ruffled the serenity of the afternoon. Ridiculous idea! He was merely being kind, giving her what protection he could from the fortune-hunters, knowing she did not like her prominence one little bit. He was her patroness's brother, that was all.

Nothing more.

THE HUM of a hundred conversations eddied about Georgiana, enclosing her within the cocoon of the Massinghams' rout party. The bright lights of the chandeliers winked from thousands of facets, none more brilliant than the sparkling eyes of the débutantes as they dipped and swayed through the first cotillion. Laughter tinkled and ran like a silver ribbon through the crowd. It was a glittering occasion; all present were pleased to be seen to be pleased. The ballroom was bedecked with tubs of hothouse blooms, vying with the ladies' dresses in splashes of glorious colour, perfuming the warm air with subtle scents. A small orchestra added its mite to the din, striving valiantly to be heard above the busy chatter.

Newly entered on the scene, Georgiana had taken no more than three steps before being surrounded by her intrepid admirers, all clamouring for the honour of setting their name in her dance card. With a charm none the less successful for being automatic, she set about her regular task of ordering her evening.

"My dear Miss Hartley, if you would allow me the supper waltz I should be greatly honoured."

Georgiana glanced up and found the serious face of Mr Swinson, one of her earnest suitors, who had become even more earnest over the last few days, hov-

ering beside her. All her instincts cautioned her to refuse his request. The supper waltz, with the implied
intention of going into supper on the gentleman's arm
at the conclusion of the measure, was the most highly
prized of the dances at such a gathering. Whenever
possible, Georgiana strove to grant that dance to one
or other of her refused suitors, so as not to raise any
false hopes among others of her court. But what excuse could she give, so early in the evening? A lie?
Resolute, she opened her mouth to deny Mr Swinson,
hoping he would accept her refusal without excuse,
but was forestalled by a deep voice, speaking from
behind her left ear.

"I believe the supper waltz is mine, Swinson."

Swaying slightly with the dizziness his nearness always induced, Georgiana struggled to keep her expression within the limits of the acceptable, and knew
she failed dismally. Her eyes were alight, her nerves
tingling. She turned and gave her hand to Lord Alton.
She didn't even notice Mr Swinson huffily withdraw,
eyeing the elegant person of the Viscount with marked
disfavour.

Lord Alton bowed low over her hand. "Fairest
Georgiana."

His words were a seductive murmur, rippling across
her senses. Then, knowing it was unwise, but utterly
incapable of resisting the compulsion, Georgiana met
his eyes, and the warmth she saw there spread through
her, leaving dizzy happiness in its wake.

"My lord."

She retained just enough wit to return his greeting,
dropping her eyes from his in a flurry of shyness.

With a gentle smile, Viscount Alton tucked the hand he was still holding into the crook of his arm, thereby making life exceedingly difficult for the numerous other gentlemen waiting to pay court to this most desirable of young ladies. Lord Ellsmere, by his friend's side, grinned. Taking pity on Georgiana, he engaged her in light-hearted conversation.

Georgiana's hand burned where it lay on Lord Alton's silk sleeve. Why was he behaving so? Under cover of paying polite attention to Lord Ellsmere as he related the latest *on dit,* she glanced up to find the Viscount's blue eyes regarding her, an expression she dared not place lighting their depths. Another glance around showed her frustrated court dwindling, leaving only those gentlemen she regarded more as friends than suitors. Unlike those whose interest was primarily pecuniary, none of these gentlemen seemed to find Lord Alton's possessive attitude any impediment to conversing with her.

Possessive? Georgiana's thoughts froze. Then, inwardly, she shrugged. If the shoe fitted… And really there was no other way to describe the way he was behaving. This was the third night in a row he had appeared by her side almost immediately she had entered a room. By his mere presence he eased the crush about her, bringing relief which would doubtless be acute if she could feel anything through the sheer exhilaration of having him so near.

With an effort Georgiana forced herself to attend to the conversation, grateful for the distraction of Mr Havelock, who now joined them. By imperceptible degrees, the circle about them grew as more acquaintances stopped to talk. Gradually the sense of being, in some strange way, identifiably his receded, leaving only a subtle feeling of security.

When Lord Aylesham approached to claim the next dance, Lord Alton relinquished her with no more than a warm smile and a whispered reminder of their later appointment.

Released from the mesmerising effect of the Viscount at close quarters, Georgiana determinedly devoted a large part of her mind to a detailed analysis of his actions and motives. None of her partners noticed anything amiss; she was now too thoroughly practised in the arts of dancing, conversing and general entertaining to need to assign more than a small portion of her attention to these endeavours.

Of all the questions revolving in her head, the most insistent was, *Why?* Why was he doing all the things he was? Why was he behaving as he was? Again and again, only one answer came. It was impossible to attribute his actions to any other cause. *He was making her the object of his attentions.* Delicious shivers ran up her spine when she finally allowed her mind to enunciate that fact. Mr Sherry, whose arms she graced at the time, looked at her askance. Georgiana smiled dazzlingly upon him, completely stunning the poor man.

The next instant her sky clouded again. How could she believe such a magnificent man, with all the advantages of birth, position and fortune, would seriously look in her direction? That he was contemplating anything other than the acceptable was unthinkable. But perhaps he wasn't contemplating anything at all.

Maybe she was just an amusing aside, his sister's protégée who needed looking after. Was she simply a naïve foreigner, reading far more into the situation than was intended? Georgiana forgot to suppress her sigh, and was forced to spend the rest of the dance soothing a ruffled Mr Sherry.

While Georgiana struggled with question and answer, alternating between cloud nine and prosaic despondency, the object of her thoughts strolled about the rooms, stopping here and there to chat as the mood seized him. Dominic was in a state of pleasurable anticipation. To his mind, his course was clear. While it was not one he had followed previously, he did not doubt his ability to carry the thing off. The major problem was time—or, rather, the patience required to see the campaign through.

The necessity for taking things slowly was self-evident. This time the object of his desires was not an experienced woman, capable of playing the game with a facility on a par with his. This time he wanted a green girl, an innocent, an angel whose conquest meant more to him than all the others combined. She needed gentle wooing. So the habits of the last ten years were set aside in favour of the strict dictates of propriety. With a wry grin at no one in particular, Dominic wondered how long he could harness the coiled tension that was growing, day by day, beneath the surface of his suave urbanity.

"Dominic! What ho, lad! Up from the princely delights of Brighton?"

Dominic swung to face the speaker, a smile lighting his face. "My lord." He nodded to Lord Moreton, one of his late father's contemporaries. "As you say, sir, the amenities of Brighton palled."

"Palled before the attractions of the young ladies, eh?"

Unperturbed by the close scrutiny of a pair of sharp grey eyes overhung by bushy brows, Dominic smiled in his usual benign way and agreed. "Oh, Prinny's no competition, I assure you."

Lord Moreton guffawed. Slapping Dominic on the back, he resumed his peregrination through the crowd, allowing Dominic to do likewise.

It was, Dominic supposed, inevitable that people would start to speculate. The very fact that he was here, attending all the balls and parties of the Little Season, rather than pursuing a very different course, in very different company, positively invited the attention of the gabble-mongers. No one was as yet sufficiently bold to put their speculation into circulation, but doubtless that, too, would come. For his part, he didn't give a damn what the gossips said. He'd weathered far worse. But he would need to be vigilant to ensure no disturbing whispers reached his Georgiana's ears. In truth, he was not sure how she might respond. But, with first-hand knowledge of the spitefulness of some among society's civilised hordes, he was not prepared to take any chances.

For the first time, at the ripe old age of thirty-two, he was seriously wooing a young lady. The pace grated. The slowly compounding returns, when set against the constantly high expense in time and restraint, were hard to bear, particularly for one to whom instant gratification of the smallest whim, however

fleeting, had become the norm. And unusual absti-
nence only aggravated his state.

Still, there was at least one shining beacon on the
horizon, holding the promise of safe haven in the end.
He was too experienced not to be able to read the
signs. Her response to him was gratifying, even at
thirty-two. Who would have imagined he would be so
susceptible to such flattery? Dominic allowed a slow
grin to twist his lips. The pull he sensed between
them—that magnetic attraction that drew man to
woman and bound them together with silken strands
of desire—was so strong that he felt sufficently confident to leave her, essentially unwatched, for half the
evening. The other half, of course, would be his. At
least this way the gossip-mongers would have to wait
a little longer for their *on dit*.

"What on earth are you grinning at?"

Startled, Dominic turned to find Bella at his side.
His slow smile surfaced. "Pleasant thoughts, my
dear." His eyes scanned her face, noting the pallor she
had attempted to hide with rouge. "How goes it with
you?"

A small frown worried at Bella's arched brows.
"Oh, so-so." she paused, then went on in a rush, "If
I wasn't so concerned about Georgie, I declare I would
have stayed at home with Arthur. These affairs are
becoming a dreadful bore."

The quavering note in her voice alerted Dominic to
her state. He drew her hand comfortingly through his
arm, stroking it soothingly, a small gesture he had used
since she was a child. It had the desired effect. While
his sister regained her composure, it occurred to him

that time, his present arbiter, was about to place a limit on his courtship. The Season had only two more weeks to run. Then the *ton* would retire to their estates for Christmas and the worst of the winter. He was unsure if Bella had yet recognised her condition. Typically she was not one to coddle herself and could be relied on to fail to consider such possibilities until they became too obvious to ignore. But Arthur was not so sanguine. He would undoubtedly wish to remove from London as soon as the Season ended. Which raised the question of Georgiana's future plans.

On impulse, Dominic turned to his sister. "Incidentally, what are you planning for Christmas?"

Diverted, Bella gave him a clear blue stare. "Christmas?" Then, recovering from her surprise, "I haven't given it much thought." She shrugged. "I suppose we'll go down to Winsmere, as usual."

"Why not come to Candlewick? You haven't spent Christmas there since you married. I want to open the house up—just us, but the place needs warming."

Bella was taken aback by the invitation, but the more she considered it, the more value she could see in the suggestion. While she was very comfortable at Winsmere Lodge, it couldn't compare with the graciousness of Candlewick. Nothing could. "I'm sure Arthur wouldn't mind. I'll speak to him tomorrow."

Dominic nodded. "What about Georgiana?"

Bella's brow clouded again. "I've already asked, but she seems set on returning to Italy. I've tried to talk her out of it, but she's so stubborn!"

His suspicions confirmed, Dominic, repressing a

grin at his sister's disgruntled tone, said, "Leave it to me. I'll see what my persuasions can do."

Big beseeching blue eyes met his. "Oh, Dominic. If you could only persuade her to stay, I just know she'll make a good match once she gets over this horrible mystery gentleman of hers." Remembering her brother's promise, Bella added, "You haven't found out who he is yet, have you?"

It was Dominic's turn to frown. Amid the delights of wooing Georgiana, he'd forgotten the existence of her "secret love". Now, considering the matter carefully, knowing what he did of that young lady, he was hard put to it to credit the notion. If she had ever in truth had a "secret love", then the man was all but forgotten already. The unwelcome idea that Georgiana's partiality could vacillate like a darting sunbeam, now here, now there, awoke in his mind. Resolutely he quashed it. Quite simply, he had no intention of allowing her the leeway neccesary to vacillate. Seeing the worry etched in Bella's face, he yielded to the impulse to reassure her. "Don't worry your head about your protégée. From all I've seen, she's well on the way to achieving a highly creditable alliance."

The glow in Bella's face brought a smile to Dominic's lips.

"Who? Where…? I haven't noticed any particular gentleman… Oh, Dominic! Don't tease! Who is he?"

But Dominic only shook his head, smiling at her chagrin. "Patience, sister, dear. Don't crowd out the action. Just keep your eyes open and you'll doubtless see it all. But," he said, returning to a sterner tone, "believe me, there's no need for you to worry."

Bella grimaced up at him.

Dominic's brows rose, with that faintly supercilious air that warned Bella he was in earnest. Her rejoinder was destined to remain unuttered as Viscount Molesworth approached to claim her for the cotillion just forming.

Free again, Dominic continued his amble, determined to eschew Georgiana's company until the supper dance provided him with adequate excuse. At the door to the card-room, he was hailed by his brother-in-law.

"Thought you were at home," Dominic said, strolling up and nodding to Lord Green, standing beside Arthur.

"Finished my last box earlier than I'd thought. You've seen Bella?"

Dominic nodded. "She's dancing with Molesworth."

"In that case, come and join us."

"Just a quiet hand," put in Lord Green with a smile, "but at least more life than you're likely to find out here."

The smile on Dominic's face broadened. "Not tonight. I have other fish to fry."

"Ah." Arthur's pensive eye met his brother-in-law's bright blue gaze. "And what a shock that must be to the system."

Dominic's lips twitched, but he responded calmly. "As you say."

"Still," said Arthur, his eyes now on the figure of his wife twirling down the set with Viscount Molesworth, "it's worth it in the end."

With a nod and a smile, Dominic moved on. The cotillion had ended, and the dancers were taking their places, with a great deal of noisy laughter, for a set of country dances. His eyes were drawn to where Georgiana was standing, partnered by Julian Ellsmere. Dominic stood unobtrusively between a sofa occupied by two turbaned dowagers and a potted palm and watched the dancers, anticipation growing keener by the minute.

Suddenly the irritation of being stared at caused him to lift his eyes and look over the dancers' heads. Directly opposite, Elaine Changley stood watching him.

She smiled as their eyes made contact. Then, completely ignoring the ladies beside her, she glided across the ballroom in his direction.

It was a bold move. Under his breath, Dominic uttered an oath, completely forgetting the proximity of the elderly dowagers. As he watched her progress between the sets, he allowed himself to examine, as if from a distance, her attractions. Other than as a passing diversion, she had failed to activate his interest. He had never encouraged her to believe otherwise. It amazed him that she could confuse the emotion he felt for the lady he would marry with the fleeting passion he had indulged with her.

Elaine Changley was desperate. Just how desperate, she had not known until she had seen the handsome form of Dominic Ridgeley across the room and realised the smile on his face was caused by the sight of his sister's protégée. Her present play was a gamble. By the time she reached his side, she realised how dangerous a gamble it was.

Dominic greeted her with a formal bow and a cold, "Elaine."

Inwardly, Lady Changley winced, but she kept a bright if brittle smile fixed on her lips and attempted to inject some warmth into her habitually cold gaze. "Dominic, darling," she purred, "how pleasant to find you here. Have you come to alleviate the singular boredom of this party?"

Dominic allowed his gaze, which had returned to the dancers immediately after greeting her, to come slowly about to rest on her face—a handsome face, pale and perfectly featured, but devoid of all softness, all womanly feeling.

The music stopped.

Suddenly nervous, Elaine Changley plied her fan, fluttering it delicately just below her eyes.

Curtly Dominic bowed. "If you'll excuse me, my lady, I am engaged for the next dance."

With that, he left her, aware of the avid interest of the dowagers, and of Elaine Changley's eyes, following him.

Paler than ever, Elaine Changley had no move left on the board. She had perforce to remain where she was, her temper in shreds, and bear the sly feminine whispers of the ladies from across the room and the less subdued cackle of the witches on the sofa beside her. Her apparently impetuous approach to Lord Alton had been designed to draw all eyes. His leaving her after no more than a minute made his uninterest as clear as if the town crier had announced it. And he had gone straight to Miss Hartley's side! Seething and impotent, Lady Changley stood rigid as a post, forced to accept the most comprehensive defeat of her varied career with what very little grace she could muster.

A sudden tingling rippling along her nerves told Georgiana, chatting easily with Lord Ellsmere, that her next partner was close. She turned slightly to find her hand taken in a firm grip and placed, equally firmly, on Viscount Alton's arm. Chancing an upward glance, she found his lordship's blue eyes smiling down at her, that curiously warming expression readily discernible.

"Julian, I believe Arthur is looking for a fourth in the card-room."

Lord Ellsmere laughed at the overt dismissal and, with a smiling bow over Georgiana's free hand, he left them.

There was a slight break betwen the country dances and the waltz, while the musicians retuned their instruments. Lord Alton seemed quite content to spend the time staring at her. Unnerved, and knowing she would very likely dissolve entirely if she permitted him such licence, Georgiana strove to find a suitably distracting conversational gambit.

"All the *ton* seem to be attending tonight. The rooms are quite full, don't you think?" Breathless and quivering, it was the best she could manage.

"Are they?" Lord Alton replied, brows rising, but his gaze remaining fixed on her face. "I hadn't noticed."

The expression in his blue eyes and the seductive tenor of his voice infused his words with a meaning far in excess of the obvious. Georgiana blushed.

Dominic smiled. "But you remind me of something I had to ask you."

"Oh?" Georgiana struggled to reduce their inter-action to the commonplace. If she could only keep talking, and avoid those soft silences that he used so well to steal her mind and her wits and her very soul, she might just survive. "What was that?"

"Why, only that I wondered what your plans for the winter months were." The music restarted, and Dominic drew her gently into his arms and into the swirling drifts of couples on the floor.

Her feet circling dutifully, Georgiana made a des-perate effort to focus her mind on his words. "Ah…" She moistened suddenly dry lips with the tip of her tongue, then tried again. "I… That is to say…" She caught his amused look. A sudden little spurt of anger allowed her to regain her composure. Putting up her chin, she stated calmly, "I expect to be returning to Italy."

A woebegone sigh met her declaration. At her look of surprise Dominic said, "Mrs Landy and Duckett will be so disappointed. I'm sure they would love to see the eminently fashionable young lady you have become, if only to congratulate themselves on their far-sightedness."

Georgiana looked her puzzlement.

Effortlessly guiding her about the turns required to negotiate the end of the room, Dominic waited until they were once more precessing up the length of the ballroom before smiling down into her large eyes. "I have invited Bella and Arthur to spend Christmas at Candlewick. It is my earnest hope you will join us."

Wise in the ways of his Georgiana, Dominic watched her thoughts in her eyes. He waited until the desire to accept his invitation had been overcome by her instinctive fears, and a reluctant refusal was about to leave her lips, before allowing a pained expression to infuse his features. "Before you come to any hasty conclusion, I beg you will consider what a refusal would mean to me, my love."

His evident distress, the unacceptable endearment, combined with her own conflicting emotions, which he had skilfully invoked, left Georgiana's head in a whirl. "What...? Why, what on earth can you mean, my lord?" Her eyes widened. "What did you call me?"

He ignored her last question, and continued in despondent vein, "You must see that it really won't do."

Dizzy, Georgiana made a grab for sanity. She drew a deep breath. "My lord—"

"Dominic."

Georgiana blushed, and was further confounded by his lordship's rising brows and the words, "If I'm to go about calling you 'my love', it's only reasonable for you to use my Christian name."

Georgiana was so flustered that she could think of nothing to say.

"Now where were we?" mused his lordship. "Ah, yes! You were about to accept my invitation to spend Christmas at Candlewick."

Her resolve to flee to the safety of Ravello as soon as she possibly could was melting under the warmth in his sky-blue eyes. "But—"

"No buts," countered Dominic. "Just think of poor Arthur and myself, condemned to a mournful Christmas with Bella all mopey because you've gone off and left her in the dismals again.'' Glancing down into her sweet face, and seeing that desire was winning his battle, Dominic withheld the news of Bella's condition. He would keep that as an ace up his sleeve, in case of future need. ''You couldn't possibly be so cruel.''

The music ceased, and for one silent moment they stood, eyes locked. Then, suddenly frightened she would see the strength of his desire in his eyes and be alarmed, Dominic smiled and broke the contact. He raised one long finger to caress a golden curl that hung by her ear. The finger, with a will of its own, moved on to trace the curve of her jaw.

At his touch, Georgiana shivered, pure pleasure tingling along already overstretched nerves.

Dominic's eyes widened slightly. His gaze returned to her eyes, large and luminous under softly arching brows. Instinctively he sought to reassure her. ''Besides,'' he said, his voice no more than a whisper, ''there's no reason for you to run away.''

Georgiana's tired brain accepted the statement, with all its layered meanings. She understood he knew she had no pressing need to return to Italy, but also, in her heart, heard his vow that she would have no cause to flee him.

''Say you'll come. I promise you Christmas at Candlewick will be everything you could wish.'' Dominic had not the slightest hesitation in making that vow. He had every intention of seeing it fulfilled.

Entranced, with his darkened eyes demanding only one answer, Georgiana found herself nodding.

A brilliant smile was her reward. Warmed through

and through, she allowed him to settle her hand on his arm once more.

The other dancers were leaving the floor, heading for the supper-room. Dominic's appetite had no interest in food, and, from her pensive expression, his Georgiana was not in the mood for lobster patties either. With an imperious gesture he commandeered a footman and sent him on a search for two glasses of champagne.

With the foresight of a man accustomed to success in the field, he had already made arrangments to allow him to appropriate much of the rest of Georgiana's evening without raising any scandalised eyebrows. When the footman returned with their drinks, Dominic handed one to Georgiana and, taking the other himself, steered her away from the crowded supper-room towards the entrance to the ballroom.

With the fizz of champagne tickling her throat, Georgiana held her peace until it became clear he did indeed intend leading her out of the ballroom. Then she raised her face, her eyes meeting his in mute query.

Dominic smiled slowly, allowing just enough time for her to sense his thoughts and blush delightfully, before saying, "I thought you might like to see the Massingham art collection. It's quite impressive, and includes, I'm told, a number of your father's works."

It was, of course, the perfect ploy. Georgiana was all eagerness to view her father's protraits of the last generation of Massinghams. And no one would remark on their absence on such an errand, particularly not when Dominic had had the forethought to request permission from Lord Massingham to show his sister's protégée around the collection, dispersed about the gallery and the large library downstairs.

Delighted with their excursion, Georgiana relaxed entirely in the enjoyment of fine paintings, many of which she, with her tutored eye, could accurately place and appraise. To her surprise, Dominic proved to have a sound knowledge of the painters whose works were displayed. She eventually forced him to admit to an extended Grand Tour, which had included many of the galleries and great houses of Europe.

He did not press her to speak when they stood before one of her father's portraits, but stood back and perceptively left her to her musings.

After long moments of studying again the brush strokes she knew so well, Georgiana sighed and moved on, coming up again level with Dominic, smiling tremulously at his now serious face with its gently questioning look. She allowed him to take her hand. He raised it and, to her surprise, brushed it gently with his lips before returning it to its accustomed place on his sleeve. Strangely comforted, recognising her need only by its relief, Georgiana felt herself curiously but totally at ease by the side of this man who more normally reduced her to quivering mindlessness.

With no need for words, they descended the staircase and crossed the chequered-tiled entrance hall to the library. The door stood open, glasses and a decanter on a tray bearing witness to the Massinghams' care for their guests, all of whom had apparently succumbed to the lure of the lobster patties. The room was empty. Ushering Georgiana in, Dominic quietly closed the door behind them.

The walls boasted two Tintorettos, a Watteau and one Hartley—a small protrait of one of the sons of the house. It hung between two sets of long windows. Dominic appropriated a three-armed candelabrum from a sidetable and placed it on the sofa table beneath the portrait.

Head on one side, Georgiana studied the small picture. Dominic watched her. The flickering candlelight gleamed on her golden tresses, striking highlights deep in the silken mass, like flames in molten ore. His fingers itched to tangle in those glorious curls, to see her golden eyes widen in surprise, then darken with delight. He could not see the expression in those bewitching eyes, but her lips, warmly tinted and full, were pursed in thought, pouting prettily, all but begging to be kissed. Desperately he sought for some distracting thought. If he continued in this vein, he would never be able to resist the temptation posed by the deserted room.

"It's one of his better works," said Georgiana. She smiled up at her companion, so still and silent beside her. His face was a polite mask, telling her nothing of his thoughts, but his eyes, so intensely blue that they seemed, in the weak light, to be almost black, sent skittering shivers along her sensitised nerves. She found herself wishing she had not donned the latest of Fancon's creations—a sheath of bronze satin which revealed rather more of her charms than she was presently comfortable with. She reminded herself to keep talking. "Papa always said that children were especially hard to do. Their features are so soft—almost unformed—that he claimed it was excessively easy to make them look vacuous.''

Dominic, with no interest in anything save the flesh-and-blood woman beside him, asked, ''Are there any portraits of you?''

Alerted by the rasping huskiness of his voice, Georgiana moved slightly, ostensibly to gaze out of the uncurtained window, thereby increasing the distance between them. ''Of course,'' she replied, surprised at her even tone. ''There are three at the villa in Ravello, and there was supposed to be one, done when I was very young, left in England.''

If Georgiana had seen the smile which curved Dominic's lips as she stepped into the window embrasure, she might have recognised the unwisdom of the move. As it was, it was only when, after a moment's silence had further stretched her nerves to tingling awareness, he closed the distance between them, coming to stand behind her, that she realised she was effectively trapped, unable to retreat, her exit blocked by his large body. And he was so close that she dared not turn around.

Dominic's smile was devilish as he moved so that no more than an inch separated them. His hands came up to stroke her upper arms gently, where her ivory skin gleamed bare above her elbow-length gloves. He leant forward so that his lips were close by her ear, and whispered, ''In that case, we'll have to make a special effort to locate these mysterious paintings.'' He grinned at the shiver that ran through her. ''Perhaps, now that you own the Place, you should institute a search.''

"Mmm-mmm," murmured Georgiana, her mind far from her father's missing paintings. He was so close! Through the thin satin gown, she could feel the radiant heat of him. His breath wafted the soft curls by her ear, sending all sorts of feelings skittering through her body. The caressing hands, drifting so gently over her skin, had ignited a funny warm glow deep inside her, quite unlike any sensation she had previously experienced. She decided she liked it.

Caught up in her novel discoveries, Georgiana was unaware of her instinctive movement, of leaning back against the hard chest at her back, letting her coiffed head rest against one broad shoulder, exposing the long column of her throat and a creamy expanse of shoulders and breasts to the blue gaze of the man behind her.

Dominic stopped breathing. This wasn't how he had planned it. Suddenly the rules of the game seemed to be shifting, leaving him confused, struggling to control a rampant desire which had somehow slipped its leash. His eyes flicked to hers, and found them half closed, heavy-lidded with the first stirrings of passion. Her lips, luscious and ripe, were slightly parted, her breathing swift and shallow. Full understanding of the effect he was having on her hit him with the force of a sledge-hammer.

A muffled groan escaped him, then, unable to resist, he bent his head and touched his lips to where the pulse beat strongly beneath the soft skin of her throat.

Georgiana stiffened at the intimacy, then, as his lips

moved over her skin, warm and gentle, yet teasing, so teasing, promising more of the delicious delight, she relaxed fully against him, accepting and wanting to know more as the fires within her grew.

The click of the door-latch brought Dominic's head up.

"This place is nice and quiet. So much noise up there, can't hear yourself think!" The old Duke of Beuccleugh stumped into the room, accompanied by two equally ancient cronies. They headed across the room towards the deep armchairs by the hearth, but pulled up to stare at the couple engaged in rapt contemplation of the picture on the wall between the long windows.

"Very nice brush strokes, don't you agree?" said Viscount Alton, gesturing towards the painting.

Georgiana choked.

Dominic turned, as if just realising they were no longer alone.

The Duke peered at him, then recognition dawned. "Oh, it's you, Alton."

"Your grace." Dominic bowed.

"Admiring the view?" enquired the Duke, hard grey eyes glinting.

With an expression of bland innocence, Dominic explained, "Miss Hartley's father painted the portrait."

"Ah." His Grace's grey gaze switched to Georgiana, curtsying deeply. "Painter chappie, heh? Vaguely recall him, if m'memory don't serve me false." He nodded benignly at Georgiana, then recalled his purpose in the room. "Dancing's started again upstairs."

Dominic took the hint. "In that case, we should perhaps return." He turned to Georgiana and offered his arm. "Miss Hartley?"

Very correctly, Georgiana placed her hand on his sleeve and allowed him to escort her back to the ballroom. She was deeply shaken. Never would she have believed she would enjoy such a scandalous interlude. Yet she had not only enjoyed it; even now, with her eyes wide open, and no longer under his hypnotic spell, she was conscious of how deeply she resented the interruption that had brought a premature end to proceedings. Her concupiscence shocked her.

Unknown to Georgiana, her response had also shocked Dominic although, in his case, the feeling was purely pleasurable. On the stairs he recalled his as yet unfulfilled intention of making clear to the beautiful creature on his arm that he had, most definitely, known who she was at the masked ball the week before. Determined to be rid of this potential source of misunderstanding, he waited until they had reached the upper landing before stopping to glance down at a still flushed Georgiana. Unable to resist a knowing smile, drawing sparks from her huge hazel eyes, he chose what he thought was a simple but effective means of conveying his information. "I most heartily approve of that dress, my love," he said, his voice a sensuous murmur. "It will doubtless vie for prominence in my memory with that topaz silk creation you wore at the masked ball."

Georgiana blushed furiously, completely missing the implication in her thoroughly unnerved state. With an enormous effort, she gathered sufficient control to incline her head graciously and say, "I think perhaps we should return to the ballroom, my lord."

A deep chuckle answered her. "I'm sure you're right, my love. You've had quite enough adventure— for tonight."

There was a wealth of promise in his suggestive tone, none of which was lost on Georgiana. She willed her jittery nerves to compliance and, with the most serene expression she could muster firmly fixed on her face, allowed him to lead her back into the cacophany of the ballroom.

NOT UNTIL she was wrapped in the darkness of the Winsmere carriage on the long drive home from the Massinghams' did Georgiana allow her mind to dwell on the events of the evening. Even in the shielding gloom, she felt herself blush as she recalled those long moments in the library. How could she have been so…so positively *wanton?* Easily, came the damning reply. And now he knew. The thought made her shiver. Drawing her cloak more closely about her, she snuggled into its warmth, feeling the silk lining brush across her bare shoulders. These outrageously fashionable gowns of Fancon's hardly helped. Somehow, scantily clad in satin and silks, she was much more aware of a peculiar need to be held, to be stroked and caressed as she had been that evening. Repressing a little snort of derision, she told herself she could hardly claim it was the dresses which made her feel as she did. They simply made it easier to feel so…abandoned.

Jettisoning that unproductive line of thought, she

blushed again as she remembered Dominic's rapid actions when the Duke and his friends had threatened discovery. She had sensed his suppressed laughter and had had to struggle to subdue her own, bubbling up in reply. It was odd, now she came to consider the matter, that she felt no sense of shame, only frustration.

Abruptly refocusing her thoughts once more, she tried to remember what he had said later, before they had gained the ballroom. Her mind promptly supplied the caress in his eyes as they had roamed appreciatively over her face and shoulders before he had complimented her on her gown. What had he said? Something about it being as pretty as her topaz silk.

The carriage jolted over a rut and she slipped sideways on the seat. She resettled herself in her corner, sightlessly watching the house fronts slip past the window.

Then her mind caught hold of the elusive memory, and his words replayed in her head. "It will doubtless vie for prominence in my memory with that topaz silk creation you wore at the masked ball."

Georgiana gasped.

"Georgie? Are you all right?"

Struggling to draw breath, Georgiana managed a reassuring phrase, then, feeling winded, curled up in her corner and gave her full attention to her staggering discovery.

He had known!

Which, as she had long ago worked out, meant... Her mind went completely blank, unable to accept the implication. Yet it was the only explanation possible.

Her heart beating in double time, a host of quivery, fluttery feelings crowding her chest, Georgiana forced her mind to grapple with the unthinkable. He had known, therefore he was... Oh, heavens!

THE NEXT THREE DAYS passed in a haze of happiness. Georgiana hardly dared to believe her deductions, yet, whenever she met Lord Alton, every word, every action, confirmed them. He was paying court to her. Her—little Georgiana Hartley!

Bella seemed quite unaware and, yielding to the promptings of some sixth sense, Georgiana did not explain the source of her sudden elation to her friend. Bella had, certainly, noticed her glow. Uncharacteristically, she had yet to enquire its cause. But Georgiana was too much in alt to worry about such inconsistencies.

She had artfully managed to drop the information that Dominic had invited her to Candlewick for Christmas and she had accepted. Bella had feigned complete surprise, but Georgiana suspected she had known of her brother's intent. The subtle smugness in her smile suggested as much.

It was Lady Chadwick's gala tonight. She would see Dominic there, she was sure. They had yet to meet outside a ballroom, but it had only taken a moment or two to work out his strategy. Young and naïve as she was, even she knew any overt gesture on his part, any attention which could not be credited to a natural assistance to his sister's protégée, would make them the focus of the most intense speculation. She had no wish to figure in the latest *on dit,* and was grateful for his care of her reputation.

So she had to make do with the caress in his eyes every time they met, the gentle promise of his smile, the touch of his fingers on hers. It was nowhere near enough. She contented herself with the thoughts that, when the time was right, he would surely advance their courtship to the stage where the heady delights he had introduced her to in the library of Massingham House would once again be on their agenda.

Bella had retired to rest before the Chadwick gala. Georgiana had come to her room with a similar intention. But her thoughts denied her sleep. Restless, she jumped off the bed and paced the room in small, swirling steps, then broke into a waltz, spinning about as anticipation took hold. Whirling almost out of control, she did not see the door open, and cannoned into Cruickshank as she entered.

"Oh!" Georgiana put a hand to her whirling head. "Oh, Cruckers! What a start you gave me."

"I gave you?" said her dour maid, righting herself and shutting the door firmly. "Now, Miss Georgie, whatever's got into you? Whirling about like a heathen, indeed!"

Georgiana giggled, but made no other reply. She was in love, but she had no intention of letting anyone into the secret. Anyone other than Dominic.

Cruickshank sniffed. "Well, if you're so wide awake, I'll get your bath-water brought up. We may as well spend the time beautifying you."

Georgiana, thinking of the admiration she would see in a pair of bright blue eyes, gladly agreed.

THERE WAS NO supper waltz at the Chadwicks' gala. Dominic had, instead, claimed both the first and the last waltzes of the evening. Twirling down the long ballroom, under the glare of the chandeliers, Georgiana suddenly realised why it was he always chose a waltz. He was holding her far closer than was the norm. And, when she blushed, all he did was laugh softly and whisper, ''As I cannot steal you away, my love, to a place where we might in safety pursue our mutual interest, you can hardly deny this lesser joy.'' The look that went with the words only made her blush more.

At the end of the dance, the last waltz of the evening, she was breathless and very nearly witless. Laughingly declining a most sensually worded invitation to take the air on the terrace—a highly dangerous undertaking, she had not a doubt—she whisked herself off to the withdrawing-room. A glass of cool water and a few moments of peace and quiet were all the restorative she needed. It would never do to let Bella see her return from a dance with her brother in such a state. There was, she felt sure, a limit to her friend's blindness.

When she entered, the withdrawing-room, a large bedchamber on the first floor, was empty of other guests. While she sipped the cool water an attentive maid brought her, Georgiana strolled to the long windows. The cool night air beckoned; Georgiana stepped out on to the small balcony. Behind her, the door of the withdrawing-room opened and shut, but she paid the newcomers no heed.

Not until the words, ''Alton's such a cynical devil.

D'you think he means marriage this time?'' riveted her attention.

Slowly Georgiana turned to face the room. Standing still and silent in the shadows of the billowing draperies, she was concealed from the occupants, two matrons of considerable years and similar girth. They had dropped into two chairs and were busily fanning themselves while they considered the night's entertainment.

"Oh, I should think so," opined one, the fatter, pushing a wilting ostrich plume from over one eye. "After all, why else would he be dancing attendance as he is?"

"But she's hardly his sort," countered the other, resplendent in blue bombazine. "Just look at Elaine Changley. What I want to know is why an out-and-outer like Alton should suddenly succumb to a sweet young thing whose charms can't possibly compare to those he's become accustomed to."

"But haven't you heard?" The fat matron leaned closer to her companion and lowered her voice in conspiratorial fashion. "It's her land he's after." She sat back in her chair and nodded sagely. "Seems she's inherited a section of land Alton's been chasing for years."

"Oh. Well, that sounds more like it. Couldn't imagine what had come over him." The blue bombazine rustled and shuffled, then stood and stretched. "Come on, Fanny. If we don't get back soon, that boy of yours will catch something you'll wish he hadn't."

Frozen, her senses suspended, Georgiana remained on the balcony while the two ladies fussed over the frills on the gowns before departing for the ballroom.

The Place. Georgiana wished she had never heard of it. And, of course, the words rang all too true. According to Bella, it was an obsession of her brother's. Georgiana's heart turned to ice, a solid chilled lump in her breast. Slowly, hardly aware of what she was doing, she came back into the room, pausing to place the glass she was carrying on a side-table.

Then she looked up and caught sight of herself in the mirror above the dressing-table. Huge haunted eyes stared back at her, stunned and distressed. She couldn't go back to the ballroom looking like that.

Drawing a deep breath, Georgiana shook herself, then straightened her shoulders and blinked several times. Pride was not much comfort, but it was all she had left. Determined to think no more about what she had heard until she had the privacy to indulge her tears, she left the room.

Once back in the crowded ballroom, misery hovered, threatening to engulf Georgiana if she relaxed her superhuman effort to ignore the matrons' words. She had to survive the rest of the gala. But Bella, seeing the stricken look in her friend's eyes, was immediately concerned.

"No, Georgie! We'll leave right now. There's no reason at all we need stay for the rest of this boring party."

With a determined frown, Bella silenced Georgiana's protests, and, within minutes, they were ensconced in the carriage and on their way to Green Street.

Bella yawned. "One thing about leaving just that little bit early—you can always get your carriage straight away.'' She stretched and settled herself. ''Now, what's the matter?''

But Georgiana had had time to get herself in hand. She had anticipated the question and strove to deflect Bella's interest. ''Nothing specific. It's just that I seem to have developed a migraine. I find it hard to go on once it comes on.''

''Oh, you poor thing!'' exclaimed Bella. ''You just lie back quietly. As soon as we're home, I'll get Cruickshank to brew a tisane for you. I won't speak to you any further. Now try to rest.''

Grateful for Bella's silence, Georgiana sank into her corner of the seat and gave herself up to her chaotic thoughts. After several minutes of totally pointless recollection, she forced herself to view the facts calmly. First of these was the relationship she knew existed between Lord Alton and Lady Changley. There was no doubt it was real—not just from the gossip, but from the evidence of her own eyes, on the terrace that fateful night. The memory of the passionate kiss Lord Alton had bestowed on Lady Changley was imprinted indelibly on her mind. He had never kissed her—let alone with such ardour. She recalled her early conviction that his attitude to her was merely that of helpful friendship, giving what assistance he could to his sister in her efforts to find a husband for her protégée. And his behaviour at the masked ball? Well, she had always thought he had not known who the lady in the topaz silk was. When had he told her he knew? Only a few days ago, long after he had learned of her inheritance. He could easily have found out what she had worn to the ball—from Bella if no one else. And then, too, Bella's ready acceptance of her sudden happiness could be easily explained if her friend knew her brother was paying court to her.

Georgiana stifled a sob. A few hours ago her world had looked rosy indeed. Now all her hopes lay in ashes about her. She had thought he was different, blessed with all the virtues, strong and steady and protective. Now it seemed he was no different from the rest. His love for her was superficial, assumed, of no great depth, called forth only by her possession of the Place. His main interest in life was status and wealth, with all the trappings. Why, he was not much better than Charles. And Bella thought nothing of Dominic's marrying her to gain title to the land. In all probability, he planned to keep Lady Changley as his mistress, even after they were married.

Georgiana tried to whip up her anger, her disdain. She must despise him, now she knew of his plans. But, as the miles rolled by, a cold certainty crept into her heart. She loved him far too much to despise him. Surely love wasn't meant to hurt so much?

Disillusioned on every front, she huddled into her corner and wept.

CHAPTER NINE

A SLEEPLESS NIGHT filled with hours of crying was no remedy for Georgiana's ailment. Bella took one look at her in the morning and insisted she spend the day in bed. Georgiana was in no mood to argue. But she winced at Bella's last words, floating in her wake as, having insisted on tucking her in, she tiptoed out of her bedroom. "For don't forget, we've the Mortons' ball tonight, and that's one event we can't miss."

Georgiana closed her eyes and let misery flow in. But she knew Bella's reasons for attending the ball, the Mortons being old family friends, and knew she could not avoid going. She had revised her opinion of Bella's part in her brother's schemes. No one who was as kind as Bella could possibly be party to such cold-blooded manipulation. And there was Arthur, too. Try as she might, it was impossible to cast Bella's husband in the light of a hard-hearted character who would idly watch while a young girl was cajoled into a loveless marriage. No. Neither Bella nor Arthur knew of Dominic's schemes. Not that that made life all that much easier, for she could hardly ask them for advice on such a matter. Still, she was glad she had at least two friends she could count true.

The evening came all too soon. Under the combined

ministrations of Cruickshank and the redoubtable
Hills, supervised by Bella herself, the ravages of her
imaginary migraine were repaired until only her lack-
lustre eyes and her pallid complexion remained as witness to her inner turmoil.

Those items were sufficient, however, to immediately draw Dominic's attention to her distress. As was
his habit, he gravitated to her side immediately she
appeared in the ballroom.

"Georgiana?" Dominic bowed slightly over her
hand, his eyes searching her face.

Flustered and weak, Georgiana retrieved her hand
immediately, not daring to meet his intent gaze. Her
heart was thudding uncomfortably, bruised and aching.

Dominic frowned. "My dear..."

At his tone, desperation flooded Georgiana. She
raised her head, but still could not meet his eyes. "I'm
afraid, my lord, that my dance card is full."

The silence on her left was complete. She had just
entered the ballroom—he must know she was lying.

Dominic felt his face drain of expression. His jaw
hardened. The impulse to call her bluff was strong.
Then he noticed again her pallor, and the brittle tension in her slim frame, and swallowed his anger.

Stiffly, he bowed. With a cold, "My dear," he
forced himself to walk away.

Dominic spent the first two dances watching Georgiana from the side of the room, unsure of his feelings,
unsure, for what seemed like the first time in his life,
of what to do. What the hell was going on? Then,
finding himself the object of more than a few curious
glances, he took himself off to the card-room.

He was rapidly inveigled into playing a few hands, but his mind was not on the game, and no one demurred when he left the table and returned to drift idly about the ballroom, keeping an unobtrusive eye on Georgiana. He had been careful enough for their association to have passed for mere acquaintance. If he displayed too overt an interest now, it would be tantamount to a declaration. But the impulse to cross the floor and haul her out on to the terrace and demand an explanation for her extraordinary conduct grew.

If she had betrayed the slightest hint of partiality for any other gentleman, he would have done it, and the consequences be damned. Luckily, she seemed unusually subdued, dancing only with those he knew she deemed her friends, refusing all others.

Slowly, his mind calmed and he started to sort through the possibilities in a more methodical fashion. At the Chadwicks' gala, all had been well, until after their last dance. She had gone off to the withdrawing-room, and he, careful of appearances, had gone to make one in the card-room. When he had returned to the ballroom, he had found the Winsmere party had decamped. That had not surprised him at the time, knowing Bella's condition. But perhaps there had been some other reason for their early departure.

Useless to speculate, when he had no idea what might have occurred. But between that last waltz and this evening, something had happened to destroy the carefully nurtured bond between himself and Georgiana.

Feeling very like hitting someone, but having no idea whom, Dominic scowled and strode out on to the balcony. The cool air brought some relief to his fevered brain. This was ridiculous. He was thirty-two, for heaven's sake! The effect Georgiana's withdrawal was having on him was both novel and highly unnerving. He didn't like it. And he'd be damned if he'd endure it for a minute longer than necessary.

Drawing a deep breath, he frowned direfully at the young couple who, giggling softly, came up out of the secluded garden. Surprised to find him there, arms folded and looking so grim, they fled back to the ballroom. Dominic sighed. If he did not have to be so circumspect, he could have taken Georgiana into the garden and made delicious love to her—

Abruptly he cut off the thought. Right now, it seemed as if she wasn't even speaking to him.

He would have to find out what was upsetting her. From the few comments he had exchanged with his sister, Bella clearly had no idea what had happened— she still had no idea of his interest in Georgiana. He needed to see Georgiana alone. For several moments, he pondered various schemes for attaining this end, finally settling on the one which, although it would not allow the fiction of the avuncular nature of his interest to stand, had the best chance of success.

With his decision made, he left the terrace to lay the necessary groundwork to put his plan into action.

GEORGIANA had no idea how she survived the Mortons' ball. It remained, long afterwards, a dull ache in her memory. She was glad, she kept telling herself, that Lord Alton had accepted her dismissal so readily. It would have been too much to bear if he had insisted she speak with him. Perhaps he had realised she had come to understand his motives and would not be the easy conquest he had expected. Hopefully, he would stay away from her now. Depressed and weary, she slept the sleep of exhaustion, and awoke the next morning, refreshed at least in body, if not in spirit.

Despondent, she trailed into the breakfast-room.

"Georgie! Are you feeling better this morning?"

Bella's solicitude brought Georgiana to her senses. She had no right to wallow in misery and act like a raincloud over her friend. Summoning a wan smile, Georgiana nodded. "Yes. I'm fine."

Bella's face suggested she did not look fine, but, instead of harping on the subject, Bella started chattering about the events that would fill the next week and bring the Little Season to an end. Georgiana listened with half an ear.

As Bella's catalogue ran its course, Georgiana realised she could not just up and flee to Italy tomorrow, much as she might wish to. She had made a bargain with Arthur, who had stood her friend when she had been in need. She could not shrug off her indebtedness. So she would have to see out the rest of the Season with what interest she could muster, trying not to dampen Bella's enjoyment with her own unhappiness.

She apparently returned sufficiently accurate, if monosyllabic, responses to Bella's opinions, for they rose from the breakfast-table in perfect amity.

"Oh, Georgie! I nearly forgot. Dominic noticed you looked a bit peaked last night, so he's coming to take you for a drive this afternoon."

Bella had preceded Georgiana through the door, so did not see the effect her announcement had on her friend.

"It's really a great honour, you know. I can't even remember the last lady Dominic took up for a drive in the park. He doesn't normally do so—says it's too boring. You must wear your new carriage dress; it'll be just the thing."

Reaching the parlour, Bella turned expectantly.

Georgiana had had enough time to school her features to a weak smile. "I really don't know if—"

"Oh, nonsense!" said Bella, dismissing whatever megrim Georgiana had taken into her head. "Some fresh air is just what you need to blow the cobwebs away."

Sinking on to the window seat and taking up her embroidery frame, Georgiana could not think of any reasonable excuse to decline Lord Alton's invitation. At least, not without explaining a great deal more of the situation to Bella. And that she was definitely not up to doing. Quite clearly, Bella was still in the dark regarding the state of affairs between her brother and her protégée.

Throughout the day, Georgiana formulated and discarded a string of plans to avoid the afternoon drive. In the end, her schemes became so wildly far-fetched that her sense of humour came to her rescue. What on earth did she imagine he'd do to her in the sanctity of the park? Besides, she knew him too well to believe he'd do anything scandalous—at least, not with her. She spent a moment in dim regret over that point, then determinedly stiffened her spine. She would go with

him and hope to impress on him that she did not wish
to see him again. Perhaps, with one major effort, she
could avoid having to live with the dread of dancing
with him at every evening entertainment, of being held
in his arms, with his blue gaze warming her.

With a despairing sigh, she went upstairs to change.

Cruickshank was waiting with the carriage dress
laid out. Having seen the sudden change in her mistress, and having more than a suspicion of the cause,
Cruickshank fretted and snorted over every pleat in
the elegant brown velvet dress with its snug-fitting
jacket. Georgiana, knowing she could hide little from
her maid's sharp eyes, was thankful to escape her
chamber without a lecture. As she descended the curving staircase, the villager hat she had chosen dangling
by its ribbons from one hand, Georgiana imagined
such a scene, and what Cruickshank might actually
say. The possibilities brought a smile to her face, the
first for the day.

A sudden tingling brought her head up. Her eyes
met blue—bright blue. Lord Alton was standing in the
hall below, Bella by his side, watching her. For an
instant she froze. Then, drawing what courage she
could from knowing she looked as well as might be,
Georgiana descended to the hall and placed her hand
in his, curtsying demurely.

He raised her and carried her hand to his lips, and
there was no doubt of the warmth in his gaze. Georgiana blushed vividly; her heart fluttered wildly. She
had forgotten how devastatingly charming he could be.

She turned to Bella, who remained rooted to the
spot, an arrested look on an otherwise blank face. But

before Georgiana could make any comment, Dominic
said, "We'll be back in about an hour, Bella." And,
with a nod for his sister, he firmly escorted Georgiana
outside.

Handed into a curricle of the very latest design,
Georgiana quickly tied her hat over her curls. The
breeze was brisk, stirring the manes of the two black
horses stamping and sidling between the shafts. A
small tiger held their heads. Dominic climbed up beside her and, with a flick of the reins, they were off,
the tiger scrambling for his perch behind.

As he threaded his team through the traffic, Dominic
realised that his supposedly straightforward plan to
have an hour's quiet conversation with his love had
already run off the tracks. For a start, there were no
horses which could be described as docile in his stables. Until the present, this had not proved a problem.
The pair he had unthinkingly requested be harnessed
to the curricle were Welsh thoroughbreds, perfectly
capable of stomping on anyone or anything they took
exception to. And they had not been out for days and
would willingly run a hundred miles if he would just
drop his hands and give them their heads. Stifling a
sigh, he gave them his undivided attention.

Once the park gates were reached, he set the horses
to a trot, letting them stretch their legs at least that
much. They tossed their heads impatiently, but eventually responded to the firm hand on the reins and
accepted their lot. Only then did he turn to view his
second hurdle. What on earth had possessed her to
wear that hat? He knew perfectly well that the outfit
she wore—the very latest in carriage wear—should

have been completed by a tight-fitting cloche, perhaps with a small feather or cockade on the brim. The temptation to tell her as much burned his tongue, but he left the words unsaid. At the moment, he did not think a demonstration of his familiarity with feminine apparel was likely to further his cause.

"Someone is waving to you."

Dominic looked about and returned the salutation, ignoring the invitation to draw up his carriage by Lady Molesworth's barouche.

Georgiana's fingers were clutching her reticule so tightly that she could feel the thin metal brim twisting. She wished he would say something, or that she could think of a safe topic to discuss. Finally, sheer desperation drove her to say, "I believe the weather is turning more cold..." only to hear her voice clash with his.

They both fell silent.

Dominic glanced down at the top of her hat and grimaced. Without being able to see her face, he felt he was groping in the dark. He dropped his voice to a softer tone. "Georgiana, my dear, what's wrong?"

His experience with his sister, on top of his extensive expertise in related spheres, enabled him to get the tone just right, so that Georgiana felt that if he said another word in such a gentle way she would burst into tears in the middle of the park and shame them both. She waved her small hands in distress. "My lord... Please..." She had no idea what to say. Her mind wouldn't function, and her senses, traitorous things, were too much occupied with manifestations of his presence other than his conversation. "There's nothing wrong,'' she eventually managed in a very small voice.

Swallowing his frustration, Dominic wondered just what he had expected to achieve with a question like that in the middle of the park. He should have guessed that whatever it was that had upset her would prove too distressing to discuss reasonably in such surroundings. The situation wanted improving, and he would get rid of that hat, too.

Without the least effort, he instituted a conversation on recent events, none of which could be construed as in any way disturbing. Gradually, he won a response from Georgiana.

Grateful for his understanding, and believing the worst was behind her, Georgiana set about recovering her composure, and her wits, eventually contributing her half of the conversation. As they bowled along, the horses' hoofs scattering the autumn leaves, the breeze whisked past her cheeks, bringing crisp colour to hide her pallor. Bella had been right: fresh air was just what she needed. By the time they had completed their first circuit, she was chattering animatedly when, to her surprise, the curricle headed for the gates. They had been out for less than half an hour. ''Where are we going?''

''Back to Green Street,'' came the uncompromising reply. ''I want to talk to you.''

The ride back to Winsmere House was, not surprisingly, accomplished in silence. Georgiana stole one glance up at Dominic's face, but, as usual, his features told her nothing.

The curricle swayed to a halt. Before she could at-

tempt to climb down, he was there, lifting her effortlessly to the pavement. Breathless, she stood for one
moment within the circle of his arms and dared to look
up into his face. "There's really no need—"

"There's every need." Dominic's face remained
shuttered. His hand at her elbow drew her up the steps.

Georgiana, trembling inwardly with an odd mixture
of exhilaration and sheer terror, drew a deep breath
and swung to face him. "My lord—"

"Ah, Johnson."

Georgiana turned to find the door open and Bella's
butler bowing deferentially. The next instant she was
in the hall.

"We'll use the drawing-room, I think."

Borne inexorably over the threshold, Georgiana
gave up all hope of avoiding the coming interview and
crossed the room, her fingers fumbling with the ribbons of her hat.

Dominic shut the door and watched with relief as
she cast the offending headgear aside. He moved to a
side-table and stripped off his driving gloves, dropping
them on the polished surface.

"Now—"

The door opened.

"There you are!" Bella came tripping over the
threshold, big eyes bright.

Georgiana looked on her with undisguised relief.

Dominic looked on her with undisguised irritation.
"Go away, Bella."

Brought up short, Bella turned to stare at him. "Go
away? But whatever—?"

"Bella!" The dire warning in his voice was enough

to send Bella about and start her for the door. Then she remembered she was in her own house and no longer needed to heed her brother's orders. She stopped, but before she could turn again a large hand in the small of her back propelled her out of the room.

The drawing-room door shut with a sharp click. Stunned, totally bewildered, Bella turned to stare at its uninformative panels.

Inside, Dominic turned to find Georgiana regarding him with distinct trepidation. Wondering how long his patience was going to last, he crossed the room and took her hands in his, covering her cold fingers with his warm ones. "Don't look at me like that. I'm not going to eat you."

Georgiana smiled weakly.

"But you are going to tell me what's wrong."

Glancing wildly up at him, eyes wide, Georgiana drew breath to reiterate that there was nothing wrong, when she caught his sceptical look and fell silent.

"Precisely." Dominic nodded sternly. "I'm not addle-pated enough to swallow any tale you might concoct, so the truth, if you please."

Standing there, her hands warm in his, the temptation to cast herself on his broad chest and sob out all her woes was dreadfully strong. In desperation, Georgiana sought for some way out, some tale he would accept for her not seeing him again. But another upward glance under her lashes convinced her the task was hopeless.

"It's... It's just that our...our association has become sufficiently marked that people might start talking and..." Her voice trailed away altogether.

She looked up to find an oddly amused expression on Dominic's face.

He smiled. "Actually, our association has, until today, been sufficiently well hidden. However, I dare say they will start talking now."

Distracted, Georgiana frowned. "You mean after our drive in the park?"

Still amused, Dominic nodded. "That. And tonight." At Georgiana's puzzled look, he explained, "It's the Rigdons' ball. And as from now, I'm going to be so very attentive to you that even the blindest of the gossips will know my intentions."

"Your intentions?" Georgiana's voice had risen strangely.

Dominic regarded her with some slight annoyance. "My intentions," he repeated. After a moment he sighed and went on, "I know I haven't proposed, but surely, Georgiana, you are not so scatter-brained you don't know I'm in love with you and intend asking you to marry me?"

Georgiana stared at him. Of course she knew he intended to marry her. But that he loved her? No, she knew that wasn't right. Gently, she tried to ease her hands from his, but he would not allow it.

Dominic frowned. "Georgiana, love, what is the matter?"

Becoming more nervous by the minute, Georgiana shook her head, not daring to look up at him. "I can't marry you, my lord." There, she had said it.

"Whyever not?"

The calm question took her breath away. Inwardly Georgiana groaned. She closed her eyes and wished herself anywhere but where she was. Yet when she opened them again, a pair of large, well formed hands were still clasped firmly around hers. She risked a glance upwards. He was calmly waiting for an answer. Nothing in his face or stance suggested he would let her go without one.

Dominic stood silently and hoped she would hurry up. The effort of keeping his hands on hers, rather than sweeping her into his arms and kissing away whatever ridiculous notions she had taken into her head, was draining his resolution. In the end, he repeated his question. "Why can't you marry me?"

Georgiana drew a deep breath, closed her eyes, and said quite clearly, "Because you're in love with Lady Changley and were planning to marry her."

Sheer surprise kept Dominic immobile and slackened his hold on her fingers.

Instantly Georgiana whisked away and, on a broken sob, rushed from the room.

Even after the door closed behind her, Dominic made no move to follow her. How on earth had she come to that marvellous conclusion? How on earth had she learned of Elaine Changley? Feeling remarkably sane for a man who had just had his first ever proposal thrown in his face, before he had uttered it, Dominic strolled to the sofa and sat down, the better to examine his love's strange ideas.

Within a minute a subtle smile was curving his lips. Another minute saw him chuckling. So that was what all this fuss was about. His ex-mistress. It really was absurd. Undoubtedly Elaine would be thrilled if she ever knew she was the cause of such difficulties. And

Julian Ellsmere would laugh himself into stitches if he ever heard. He spent a moment wondering which busybody had told Georgiana of Elaine Changley, then dismissed the subject from his mind. There were any number of loose tongues about town.

Standing, Dominic stretched, then relaxed. He would just have to arrange to explain to his love the subtle difference between what a gentleman felt for the woman he made his mistress and the emotions he felt for the woman he would make his wife. It was, as it happened, a point he was supremely well qualified to expound. His smile broadened. He had told her he would see her at the Rigdons' that night. As he recalled, Rigdon House had a most intriguing conservatory, tucked away in a corner of the mansion, unknown to most guests. The perfect place. As for the opportunity, there would be no difficulty arranging that.

Strolling to the door, relieved of his strange burden of not knowing what had gone wrong, Dominic felt on top of the world. Then, out of the blue, two phrases, heard at widely differing times, coalesced in his mind. He froze. Georgiana's secret love was a man she had met during her earliest days in London who she believed was in love with and about to marry another woman. He had searched her acquaintance to no avail—there was no such man. Now she had just admitted that she thought *he* was in love with and had been about to marry Lady Changley. *Ha!*

Dominic's smile as he left Winsmere House could have warmed the world.

IT WAS WITH a strange mixture of trepidation and relief that Georgiana entered the Rigdon House ballroom. She had initially felt devastated and drained after her interview with Lord Alton, but a peaceful hour in her bedchamber had convinced her that it was all for the best. At least he now knew she would not accept an offer from him and why. She told herself her problems were over. Yet, deep down inside, she was far from sure he would accept her dismissal. And buried even deeper was the uncertainty of whether she really wanted him to.

She had not left her chamber until, arrayed for the evening, she had descended for dinner. Arthur's presence would, she had hoped, inhibit Bella's ability to question her closely about her brother's strange behaviour. As it transpired, Bella had evinced not the slightest degree of curiosity, even in the privacy of the carriage on the way to the ball. Dimly Georgiana wondered if Bella's brother often did such outrageous things.

After being presented to Lord Rigdon, whom she had not previously met, she and Bella drifted into the crowds of guests, chattering avidly while they waited for the dancing to begin.

Joining a circle of young ladies, many of whom she now knew, Georgiana went through the usual process of filling in her dance card, allocating the vital supper waltz to Lord Ellsmere. To her surprise, he also requested another waltz, earlier in the evening. She was puzzled, for he had rarely danced twice with her since she had refused his suit. Still, she numbered him among her most trusted cavaliers and gladly bestowed on him the first waltz of the night.

It was while she was circling the ballroom in Lord Ellsmere's arms that she first became aware of a change in her status. A number of dowagers sat on chairs lining the walls. From the direction of their sharp glances and the whisperings behind their fans, she realised with a jolt that she was the subject under discussion. A few minutes later, as the waltz ended and, on Lord Ellsmere's arm, she joined a small group of young people, she surprised a look of what could only be envy on the face of Lady Sabina Matchwick, one of the Season's *incomparables*.

Slowly, it dawned that, as Dominic had prophesised, people were beginning to talk. Finding Bella by her side, and momentarily alone, Georgiana could not help but ask, "Bella, tell me. Is it really so very unusual for your brother to drive a lady in the park?"

Bella's candid blue gaze found her face. "Yes. I told you. Dominic's never taken any lady driving before."

"Oh."

At her stricken face, Bella burst into a trill of laughter. Impulsively, she hugged Georgiana. "Oh, Georgie! I'm so happy!"

The approach of their partners for the next dance put an end to any confidences. Georgiana dipped through the cotillion and barely knew what she did. As dance followed dance, she realised the nods and smiles denoted not scandalised horror, but a sort of envious approval. Heavens! Just by taking her for a drive, Lord Alton had all but publicly declared himself. How on earth was she to rectify the mistaken impression? Then Georgiana reminded herself that in a few short days her Little Season would be over. And she would go back to Ravello and forget all about Lord Alton and his very blue eyes.

It was almost time for the supper waltz. Lord Ellsmere came to claim her. By some subtle manoeuvre, he separated her from her court and proceeded to stroll down the long room with her on his arm.

"My dear Georgiana, I do hope you won't forever hold it against me, but I've a confession to make."

Startled out of her abstraction, Georgiana stared at him. "Confession?" she echoed weakly. Oh, dear. Surely he was not going to start pressing her to marry him, too?

As if sensing her thoughts, he smiled at her. "No, no. Nothing to overset you. At least," he amended, frowning as if suddenly giving the matter due thought, "I hope it won't upset you."

Georgiana could stand no more. "My lord, I pray you'll unburden yourself of this horrendous secret."

He smiled again. "It's really quite simple. I engaged you for this waltz in proxy, as it were."

Her heart was beating an unnerving tattoo. "Who...?" Georgiana didn't bother finishing her question. She knew who. And as if to confirm her suspicions, she felt a familiar tingling sensation start along her nerves, spreading from the bare skin of her shoulders and neck in a southerly direction. No, Lord Alton had not accepted his dismissal.

"Ah, here he is."

With a smile and an elegant bow to her, Lord Ellsmere surrendered her to the suavely elegant gentleman who had come to stand beside her.

Georgiana felt her hand being raised and the warm pressure of his lips on her fingers.

"Georgiana?"

His husky tone rippled across her senses. Despite all her intentions, she could not prevent herself from looking up. And she was lost. His eyes caught hers and held her gaze effortlessly. Somewhere in her unconscious the subtle perfection of his attire registered, along with an appreciation of face, form and figure, all apparently designed with her own prejudices in view. But her conscious mind was only aware of the total mastery he exerted over her senses, the hypnotic tug which drew her, unresisting, into her arms. Before she knew it, they were waltzing.

With an effort, Georgiana managed to free enough wit to realise he was smiling at her in amused appreciation, quite certain of his conquest. Then, as her senses probed the ballroom about them, the enormity of his strategy hit her. They might have been waltzing amid a host of other couples, but every eye in the ballroom was on them. She blushed vividly.

This evidence of her sudden awareness drew a deep chuckle. "Don't worry. You look radiantly lovely. Just think what a handsome couple we make."

Georgiana tried to summon enough anger to glare at him, but her overwhelmed emotions were not up to it.

Dominic looked down at her, her golden eyes and creamy skin, the glorious riot of her golden curls filling his vision. More than satisfied with her capitulation thus far, he made a mental note to play on her senses more often—a subtle torture, at present, but so very rewarding.

The music drew to a close, Georgiana waited to be released, but, instead of bowing and escorting her back to Bella's side, Dominic simply tucked her hand into his arm and walked out of the ballroom. Entirely unable to resist, and with a sinking feeling that it would be singularly pointless to try, Georgiana found herself wandering the corridors on Lord Alton's arm.

Suspecting that the amble had more purpose than was apparent, Georgiana turned an enquiring gaze upwards, to be met with a smile of quite dazzling effect.

''I thought, my love, that, given your apparent misconception regarding my feelings towards you, we should find a quiet spot where I might endeavour to disabuse your mind of its strange notion.''

Georgiana tried, really tried, to come up with some suitable response, but not a coherent phrase came into her head. At the end of the long corridor, Dominic turned right, opening a glass-panelled door and ushering her through.

Vines and species of *ficus* grew out of large tubs artfully arranged to give the impression of a tropical forest. Cyclamens provided bursts of exotic colour amid the greenery. A small fountain played a lonely tune in the middle of a circular tiled courtyard. Of other humans, there was no sign.

With no real idea of what he meant to say, Georgiana was caught between a desire to hear his words and a conviction that it would be unwise to do so. But she was given no choice in the matter as, smoothly compelling, Dominic led her to a rustic ironwork seat. At his nod, she sat, and he sat beside her, retaining possession of her hand and showing no inclination to release it.

Sensing her skittering nerves, Dominic smiled reassuringly and raised her fingers to his lips, placing a leisurely kiss on each rosy fingertip, his eyes all the while holding hers. He watched as her golden eyes widened and her breathing suspended, then started again, more shallowly and less evenly. Entirely satisfied, he grinned wickedly. "Now where were we, when you so abruptly left the room this afternoon? Ah, yes! You believe I'm in love with Lady Changley and was intending to marry her." He directed a look of patent enquiry at Georgiana, clearly seeking confirmation.

Trapped, in every way, Georgiana coloured.

Smiling again, Dominic continued, his voice light but perfectly serious. "I'm not, I'll have you know, in favour of the idea of a gentleman discussing his paramours with anyone, least of all with his intended bride. Young ladies are not supposed to be cognisant of the sorts of affairs women such as Lady Changley indulge in. However, as you have already heard of her, I'll admit we enjoyed a short liaison, which ended some weeks before I met you."

Dominic paused to allow the full implication of his words to sink in. Georgiana's attention was complete; she was hanging on every word, and he doubted not that she would remember what he said, even should she fail to immediately register its import.

Pensively he began to stroke her fingers with his

thumb. "Like all rich and single peers, I am high on the list of prey for such as Lady Changley. She, unwisely, believed I was besotted enough to offer marriage. At no stage did I do so. You'll have to take my word for that, although you will notice no public charges for breach of promise have been levelled at me. That's because she knows no one would believe I would be so lost to all propriety as to offer to make her my Viscountess."

To Georgiana his words were every bit as intoxicating as the sensations produced by the insistent pressure of his thumb over the sensitive backs of her fingers. Then his eyes lost their far-away look and his gaze became intent, capturing her own as if to focus her entire being on him. Georgiana felt herself drowning in blue.

Without releasing her from his spell, deliberately, Dominic raised her hand to his lips, but this time turned it to press a warm kiss to her palm. He smiled at the marked shiver the caress produced, but his eyes were nevertheless perfectly serious as he said, "The feelings I have for you, my love, are far removed from the lust a man feels for his mistress, a fleeting emotion which dissipates, usually in months if not weeks. No man marries his mistress. No man falls in love with his mistress."

Georgiana could not have moved if the ceiling fell. She was mesmerised—by his voice, by his eyes, by him. Drawing a shuddering breath, she waited for what was to come, knowing she could not prevent him from saying the words, knowing that, once said, they would bind her, no matter how hard she struggled, tying her to him, not by his love, but by hers.

Dominic continued to devour her with his eyes, following her reactions. He waited until full awareness returned to her, then said, "What I feel for you is far removed from mere lust. I can hardly deny I know what that is and can readily define it. What I feel for you is not that. I fell in love with you the first moment I saw you, asleep in my armchair by the drawing-room hearth at Candlewick. You belong there." He paused, knowing that his next move was chancy, but, confident he had gauged her responses, and her temperament, accurately, he smoothly continued, "Regardless of what you may say, regardless of how many times you deny it, I know you love me in exactly the same way I love you."

His words, delivered in a low, deliberate, slightly husky tone, sent shivers up and down Georgiana's spine. He was right, of course, at least in defining her love. Oh, what temptation he posed! Still trapped in his gaze, she knew immediately his attention shifted. His eyes were now fixed on a golden ringlet hanging beside her face. One long finger came up to caress the soft curl, then moved on with tantalising slowness to outline the curve of one brow, then the length of her pert nose, and then traced, oh, so lightly, the full bow of her lips. The roaming finger slipped under her chin and tilted her face upwards. Georgiana's eyelids drooped. His lips touched hers in the gentlest of kisses.

When he drew back, she could barely cope with the sense of loss, could barely restrain herself from throwing her arms about his neck and behaving like a wanton. Again, she blushed rosily, not at his actions but at her thoughts.

Entirely satisfied with progress thus far, Dominic sat back and waited patiently until her breathing slowed, watching her through half-closed lids. When she had recovered sufficiently to glance at him once more, he took up his dissertation. "As you've realised, the rest of the *ton* are now *au fait* with my intentions. Our affairs are thus public knowledge, and should, given your age, proceed with all due circumspection."

He smiled, his eyes lighting with a certain devilment that awoke an answering spark in Georgiana. She found herself smiling back in genuine empathy.

"Thus, you will now be wooed in form. I will drive you in the park every afternoon, weather permitting. I will escort you to whichever evening functions it is your desire to attend. The *ton* will be edified by the sight of me at your pretty feet. Therefore, having attained that position, it will be no great difficulty to propose to you at the end of the Season."

Whereat you'll accept me. And thank God there's only a week of the Season to go! Dominic left his last thoughts unsaid, contenting himself with another warm smile. Dropping a last kiss on Georgiana's fingers, he rose.

"Come, my child. We should return you to the ball before the dowagers start having the vapours."

THE INTERLUDE in the conservatory disturbed Georgiana more than she had believed possible. She had never before been exposed to, let alone been called upon to withstand, anyone as compelling as Bella's brother. The magnetic force he wielded was of a magnitude that rendered mere reason impotent. Settled in her corner of the *chaise* on their way home from Rigdon House, she was conscious that the attractions of Ravello and freedom were dimming in the light of the flame Lord Alton was skilfully igniting.

That he meant to do it, she had not a doubt. Deliberate, calculated, he made no effort to hide his tactics. He wanted the Place. In the darkness of the carriage, Georgiana shivered.

Their discussion had at least relieved her mind of one nagging, guilty worry. He did not and had never loved Lady Changley. Of that, she was certain. She could not decide whether it was the hint of humour that had coloured his voice when he had spoken of his mistress or the coldly unemotional way he had considered her machinations that had convinced her. But convinced she was. Lady Changley might or might not have believed he was in love with her. Whichever way it was, she was only another victim of his lordship's potent charm.

Unfortunately, all that did was prove he had the ability to make women fall deeply in love with him. It hardly proved that he loved her.

The more she considered the matter, the more she doubted the possibility. Why would such a handsome man, so eligible in every way, with all of the last ten years' débutantes to choose from—*incomparables* included—have decided to opt for her? Little Georgiana Hartley, whose head barely topped his shoulder, who knew next to nothing of the fashionable life of England, let alone the political side with which he was so intricately involved. Why had he picked her?

The Place. It was the only answer.

Miserable all over again, Georgiana lay sleepless for a long time after Cruickshank had snuffed her candles. In the dark, she wrestled with demons who all too often had bright blue eyes. He professed love, and she longed to believe him. Yet, when it came down to it, his actions belied his words. Admittedly she had been brought up in Italy, but she couldn't believe national boundaries changed human nature so very much. True love always brought desire in its wake, as was only right and proper. Yet the chaste kiss he had bestowed on her had held no hint of burning passion. And she knew that wasn't how he kissed a woman he desired.

Again and again, her thoughts brought her back to the same depressing conclusion. He was an expert in seduction; she was a novice. Her hand in marriage would secure the Place, so he had calmly set about capturing it. In the world of the *ton,* it would be considered a very fair exchange—her land for the position and wealth he could provide.

As the hours of the night gave way to a grey dawn, Georgiana considered for the first time whether she might be wise to listen to the promptings of her heart, to accept the proposal he had told her was coming, even knowing that her love wasn't shared. She knew he would always treat her well—with respect and affection, if not with the love she craved. She would fill the position of his wife, be able to care for him, bear his children.

A vision of Candlewick swam before her, and she

spent some time imagining what might be. But she could not place him in the picture beside her. Instead, he appeared as a nebulous figure, arriving in the dead of night, leaving with the dawn.

With a sob, Georgiana buried her face in her pillow. No. It was impossible. If she couldn't have his love, the rest was meaningless. She would leave for Ravello as soon as the Season ended.

CHAPTER TEN

"HUMPH!"

The loud snort brought Georgiana awake with a start. Cruickshank stood by the bed.

"You'd better wake up and take a look at these."

With a grim look, Cruickshank drew back the bed curtains. The window drapes had already been opened, letting weak morning sunshine bathe the room. For an instant Georgiana stared uncomprehendingly at her maid, then her attention was drawn to the door. It opened to admit a young girl, one of the parlour maids, all but concealed behind a huge stand of cream roses.

The girl peeked at Georgiana around the delicate blooms, then, with a giggle, crossed to deposit the vase on a table by the window.

To Georgiana's astonishment, her place in the doorway was immediately taken by another maid, similarly burdened. When a third maid entered, with yet more cream roses, Georgiana put her hands to her hot cheeks. Cream roses in October!

Hundreds of cream roses.

By the time the procession of maids had transferred all the blooms delivered to the house by the florist's that morning to her bedroom, Georgiana was speechless. She sat and stared. The sheer outrageous extravagance of the gesture numbed her. About her, the delicate perfume of the flowers took hold, flavouring the air with their subtle enchantment.

She needed no card to tell her who had sent them.

At the Rigdons' ball, he had vowed to woo her formally. His public courtship had started that night, when he had returned her to Bella's side but remained possessively beside her, discouraging all her partners but those he approved of simply by being there. The next day he had swooped down on her morning and taken her driving to Richmond, later producing a picnic hamper for lunch and taking her to the Star and Garter for tea. It was impossible to stand firm against the invitation of his smile. He would accept no denials. Powerless to prevent his whirlwind courtship, she had, unwillingly, reluctantly, been swept along, mesmerised by the blue of his eyes. The following evening she had seen the effects of his strategy. As far as the *ton* was concerned, only the ceremony was required to establish her as the Viscountess Alton.

In the four days that had followed, each filled with unsought joy and a hidden despair, he had succeeded in convincing everyone that theirs would be a marriage made in heaven, until it seemed to Georgiana that only she guessed the truth.

Her moods fluctuated wildly, from ecstatic pleasure when he was with her, to blackest despair when he was not. She was counting the days to the end of the Season, to when Bella and Arthur departed for Candlewick and she could flee to Ravello and safety. She had even tried to sound Arthur out on the possibility of leaving before then. But he had looked at her blankly, seeming not to understand her oblique reference. Incapable of being more explicit, she had been forced to let the matter drop.

Cream roses surrounded her. Her consciousness was filled with him to the exclusion of all else. Georgiana sighed.

Only Cruickshank remained in the room, fussing over laying out her clothes, sharp eyes stealing covert glances, trying to assess her reaction.

Shaking free of despondency, Georgiana slipped out of bed. Cruickshank held up a blue morning dress for her approval. Through narrowed eyes, Georgiana studied its clean lines. Then, abruptly, she shook her head. "No, Cruckers. The new green velvet, please."

Cruickshank's eyebrows rose comically, but she made no comment beyond the predictable snort.

Stripping off her nightgown, Georgiana washed her face and donned her soft muslin undergarments while Cruickshank brought out the latest of her purchases from Fancon. If her association with Lord Alton had taught her anything, it was to value the added confidence appearing before him in new and fashionably elegant gowns gave her. Besides, in a few days' time, she would no longer have the pleasure of appearing before him at all. Despite the heaviness of her heart, weighed down by unrequited love, she was determined to live these last few days as fully as she could, to store away the bittersweet memories to warm the long winter days, and nights, in Ravello.

THE EAST WIND was chilly. Grey clouds scudded low across the tops of the trees, skeletal fingers emerging

to trap them as the summer cloaks were stripped, leaf
by leaf, away. Everywhere summer was in decline,
giving way to the gusts of autumn, chill harbingers of
year's end.

Perched on the box seat of Viscount Alton's curricle, Georgiana was immune from the cold. Refusing
to face her bleak future, she revelled in the warmth of
the moment. Her wind-whipped cheeks glowed and
her eyes, when she managed to wrench them free of
his lordship's steady gaze, sparkled with life and love.
She had left her inhibitions in Green Street and was
happy.

Beside her, Dominic was host to a range of emotions, some of which were both novel and, to one of
his experience, distinctly disturbing. That he loved
Georgiana Hartley, in the complete fullness of the
term, he no longer doubted. But that she could invoke
in him the full gamut of desire, to the point where his
mind became prey to salacious imaginings, was not
something he had expected. She was a young, innocent, inexperienced, green girl. A golden angel. Yet,
no matter how many accurate adjectives he heaped
about her name, nothing detracted from the sensual
spell she cast over him. She was learning quickly. But
she had no idea, he felt sure, of the risks she courted.
His well honed skills, all but automatic, were in danger
of carrying them away.

There were few people in the park. The cold
weather had kept most of the fashionable indoors.
They completed one circuit, then went about again,
content to prolong their time in such unaccustomed

seclusion. Few words were exchanged. Their eyes spoke, and that was enough.

When the gates hove a second time into view, Dominic acknowledged the passing hours and headed his team for the street. His gaze flicked to Georgiana's face, catching her wide-eyed hazel stare, and he knew she had enjoyed their time together as much as he had. In that instant, he made his decision.

He had postponed asking her to marry him, wanting his courtship of her to be a recognised fact before any announcement. Quick betrothals between men such as he and sweet delights such as she had a way of being remembered and whispered about. He wanted no breath of a question to touch her.

But there were only two more days of the Season to go. And there was no doubt of their state. And no reason at all to procrastinate.

As the park gates fell behind, Georgiana was conscious of the day closing in, of a dimming of her joy. For the past hour she had been happy. It was so easy to forget, to imagine instead how things might have been. But always reality eventually intruded, reminding her of the real reason for his interest in her.

By the time Green Street was reached and he lifted her down she was thoroughly depressed once more. He escorted her indoors, and she inwardly shrank at the coming meeting with Bella. Her hostess, to whom she owed so much, was *aux anges* at the prospect of having her for a sister-in-law.

She was shaken out of her dismal thoughts by the words, "The drawing-room, I think, Johnson. You needn't inform your mistress that we've returned."

Before her weary mind had time to do more than register that quite improper order, Dominic had deftly ushered her into the drawing-room and shut the door.

Suddenly conscious of the desirability of putting as much space as possible between them, Georgiana quickly crossed the room. Her heartbeat, which had slowed somewhat since they had left the park, picked up its tempo.

From his stance just inside the door, Dominic viewed her impetuous movement, which had about it the air of flight, and frowned. Then, when he saw the agitated flutter of her small hands, clasping and unclasping before her, a slow smile erased the stern look. She was nervous, no more. A strange rapport existed between them. So she sensed his intention and, true to her age and innocence, was disturbed. His features softened. He crossed to stand beside her.

"Georgiana, my love..."

A small gesture silenced him. Georgiana could stand the strain no more. "Dominic, please," she whispered, infusing every particle of persuasion she could into her tones.

After the briefest of pauses, she continued, "My lord, I am most sensible of the honour you do me, but I cannot marry you."

Dominic suppressed the instinctive retort that he hadn't yet had a chance to ask her and, to his surprise, found himself fascinated, rather than furious. "Why?"

Despite her highly strung state, Georgiana spared a moment to curse silently the incredible evenness in temper that could yield such a mild response. If truth be known, she would infinitely have preferred a more melodramatic reaction. That, she would have known how to deal with. Instead, his deceptively simple question was anything but easy to answer.

In fact, as the minutes stretched, she realised she couldn't answer it at all. In growing panic, she shook her head, dropping her gaze to her nervously clenching fingers.

Dominic sighed. "Georgiana, my love, I should perhaps inform you that I am not one of the school which holds it right and proper that a young lady should refuse her chosen suitor at least three or four times before accepting him, so as not to appear too eager." He waited to see what effect that had, and was not entirely surprised to see her ringlets dance a decided negative.

Allowing silence, so often his ally, to stretch still further, Dominic, close behind her, watched her growing agitation, and chose his moment to murmur, "Sweetheart, I've not got infinite patience."

The gentle tone of his voice cloaked the steel of the words. Georgiana did not miss the implication of either. Her nerves singed by his nearness, she abruptly took a step away, then turned to face him. She had to make him understand the futility of his enterprise.

"My lord, I...must make it plain to you. I will not marry you."

Dominic wasn't really listening. She had not answered his question, which, in itself, was answer enough. He was not in the mood to listen to missish denials, not when her eyes were so soft and her lips, gently parted, just begged to be kissed.

Seeking to impress on him the inevitability of her refusal, Georgiana allowed her eyes to meet his. And, as had happened so often before, in the warm blue of his gaze, she felt their wills collide and hers melt away. Mesmerised, she could barely breathe as he moved closer, one long finger rising to trace the curve of her cheek, stopping at the corner of her mouth. Unable to move, she watched as his eyes fixed on her lips. Unconsciously, her tongue slipped between them to run its moist pink tip along their suddenly dry contours. He smiled. Then, tantalisingly slowly, his head drew nearer, his lips hungry for hers.

As her eyelids drooped, panic seized Georgiana. In desperation, she put her small hands up before her and met the wall of his chest. She turned her head away. She felt him hesitate. In that instant she seized the tattered remnants of her sanity and, on a choked sob, fled the room.

In utter disbelief, Dominic watched her go. As the door shut behind her he uttered one comprehensive oath and, thrusting his hands deep in his breeches pockets, swung about to glare at the window.

After a moment he glanced around, half expecting the door to open and for her to return. When nothing happened, he muttered irritably and ostensibly gave his attention to a minute inspection of Bella's lace draperies. What the devil did Miss Georgiana Hartley think she was playing at? What the devil did she think *he* was playing at?

When the ticking of the mantelpiece clock made it plain any hope of Georgiana's return was forlorn, Dominic let his head fall back. Scowling at the ceiling, he vented his disapproval in one sharp and pungent phrase, then strode purposefully to the door, his face like granite.

Johnson, unperturbed and imperturbable, met him in the hall.

"Dominic!"

In the act of shrugging on his greatcoat, Dominic swung to meet his brother-in-law's sharp gaze.

Arthur stood in the library doorway. Now he took a step back in clear invitation. "I've some information you might find of interest. If you can spare the time…?"

Even from across the hall Dominic could sense the amusement in the older man's voice. He knew Arthur understood his intentions towards Georgiana. And approved of them. With another shrug, he divested himself once more of his coat and, leaving the heavy garment in Johnson's hands, strolled with as much nonchalance as he could muster past his brother-in-law and into the library.

A delighted chuckle was his reward.

Elegantly disposing his limbs in one of the heavily padded leather chairs, Dominic raised eyes limpid with enquiry to Arthur's face.

Sinking into the chair behind his heavy desk, Arthur met the cool blue glaze with one of unalloyed amusement. "You know, for a man of such vast experience, you're being singularly obtuse in your present campaign."

Dominic's black brows rose haughtily. "Oh?"

"From Georgiana's loss of composure and your own black looks, I assume you've offered for her and been rejected."

From narrowed eyes, Dominic surveyed his brother-in-law. They had always got on well. In truth, there was no one he trusted more. So he dropped his reserve and answered with a languid air, "If you must know, I haven't as yet proposed. I have, however, been refused. Twice."

With an effort that was obvious, Arthur swallowed his laughter. Finally, when he was sure he could command his voice, he said, "Well, that's hardly surprising."

The blue eyes watching him narrowed again. After a pregnant pause Dominic murmured, "Arthur, if you weren't who you are, I rather think I'd take exception to that comment."

Far from being cowed, Arthur only smiled. "I didn't think you'd seen it."

A world-weary expression of dutifully waiting to be informed of what "it" was infused Dominic's countenance.

"Why, the Place, of course."

"The Place?" echoed Dominic, bewildered.

"The Place," repeated Arthur. "You know, it's that little piece of land you've spent half of the last ten years trying to buy."

"But..." Dominic stopped. It came as a shock to realise that desire for the Place, an obsession nursed and fed for years, had simply been forgotten, displaced, rendered unimportant by his desire for Georgiana. In fact he hadn't thought of the Place with a view to gaining possession for weeks. Not since he had met Georgiana. He frowned.

Arthur sat back and watched his friend's face as the

pieces fell into place. It wasn't hard to work out the probabilities once the facts had been pointed out. And, despite Dominic's reputation with the ladies, Arthur, remembering the euphoric daydream that had possessed his own sharp wits in the days he had wooed Bella, found nothing odd in the notion that his brother-in-law had completely mislaid his obsession in the whirl of recent weeks.

Eventually Dominic's features relaxed slightly and he glanced up to meet Arthur's grey gaze. "So she thinks I'm marrying her to get my hands on the Place." It was a statement, not a question.

Arthur shrugged. "It's hardly an uncommon event, for men to marry for property. And I doubt she has any idea of the relative value of the Place and your own estates. But I'd go bail Bella's edified her with the tale of your desire for the land." He paused, but Dominic was frowning at the inkstand on the desk. "Has she given you any other reason for her refusal?"

Without looking up, Dominic shook his head slowly. "Not this time. The reason for her first refusal was quite different." He glanced up with a wry grin. "She'd heard the stories of Elaine Changley and had convinced herself I was in love with Elaine."

"And only wanted to marry her for her dowry?"

Dominic looked struck. "She didn't actually say so," he mused, "but I suppose that must have been in her mind. I didn't think further than disabusing her of the idea that I'd ever been truly enamoured of or considered marrying Elaine Changley."

Arthur said nothing.

Then Dominic shook his head. "No, it won't fit. I

started paying court to her at the Hattringhams' ball, before any of us knew she owned the Place.''

''The masked ball?'' said Arthur, tapping one finger against his lips. ''I assume she knew you knew who she was, that night.''

Dominic shifted in his chair. ''No. But I told her I did know later.''

''How later?''

Exasperated, Dominic frowned at his brother-in-law. ''At the Massinghams' rout.''

''*After* our little visit to Lincoln's Inn.''

With a long drawn sigh of frustration, Dominic stretched and crossed his arms behind his head. ''You're right.'' He considered the inkstand again. Then he said, as if talking to himself, ''So I'll just have to remove that little obstacle from my path.''

Perfectly satisfied with the effects of his interference, Arthur leant back in his chair and watched as his brother-in-law planned his next moves. Finally Dominic looked up.

''There are only two more days left to the Season. How long do you plan to remain in Green Street?''

Arthur smiled. ''For as long as it takes you to settle this business.''

A quick smile lit Dominic's face. ''You are coming to Candlewick, aren't you?''

Arthur nodded. ''I've already sent instructions for Jonathon and his nurse to travel direct to Candlewick. The weather's closing in and, as you know, I'm not one to take chances. They should be there by now. I'd thought to send Bella down as soon as she's free of her social activities. Mrs Landy can fuss over her more effectively than anyone else. I'll go to the Lodge and check through business there, then come across before Christmas.''

To all this, Dominic nodded. ''It'll take a day or two to deal with the Place. But once I've cleared that hurdle from my path, I don't expect any further impediment to our affairs.'' He paused, then added with a slightly grim smile, ''I would be obliged if you would inform Miss Hartley that I have some...pressing business to attend to, but will call on her in two days' time to continue our discussion of her future.'' He considered his words, then shrugged and rose. ''With luck, I'll be able to escort both Bella and Georgiana down a few days after that.''

''Good,'' said Arthur. ''The news from the country is that there'll be early snows. I'd feel happier once Bella's safely installed at Candlewick.'' He watched as Dominic crossed to the door, waiting until his fingers were on the handle to say, ''By the by, do let me know if you feel the need for any further assistance in this matter.''

Dominic smiled sweetly. ''My friend, I've often thought it was a good thing for England that you were born an Englishman. God only knows what might have happened if Napoleon and his generals had had you as a quartermaster.''

Arthur laughed.

With a neat bow, Dominic left, closing the door softly behind him.

To Georgiana's dismay, relief was not her predominant emotion on waking the next morning to no extravagant gifts, no note requesting her company on a drive, nothing. She sighed. She told herself sternly it was how she wanted things to be. He had at last accepted the fact she would not marry him.

Feeling at one with the gloomy morning, close and grey with drizzle, she dressed without interest and wended her way downstairs, wondering what she could do to fill in the bleak hours.

But she had barely left the breakfast-table to join Bella in the back parlour when Johnson came to summon her.

"A legal gentleman, miss. Name of Whitworth."

Brows rising, Georgiana stood and laid aside her embroidery. "In the drawing-room, Johnson?"

The butler bowed and escorted her to where Mr Whitworth the elder waited patiently, his bright eyes darting curiously about the white and gilt room.

As soon as he had bowed to her, Georgiana waved him to a chair. He looked alarmed when it creaked protestingly under his weight. But Georgiana was too puzzled to waste any time reassuring him. She hadn't sent for him. Why was he here?

Apparently agreeing his presence required immediate explanation, Mr Whitworth made haste to answer her unvoiced query. "My dear Miss Hartley, forgive my calling on you unheralded, but we have received a very generous offer for the Place. The buyer is most urgent to settle, so I took the liberty of calling in person."

Georgiana's immediate reaction was of immense relief. She would be rid of her albatross of an inheritance. If it hadn't been for the Place, she would not now be subject to the most deadening melancholy. And she would certainly never want to return there, as close as it was to Candlewick. But, hard on the heels of relief, came a swift understanding of what it would mean to Dominic—no! Lord Alton—if she sold the Place to another. A sharp stab of empathy brought an impulsive denial to her lips. But she bit the words back and forced herself to consider more carefully.

Dominic wanted the Place...wanted it so badly that he would even marry to get it. But, although she loved him, he didn't love her. She would not, could not, allow him to sacrifice either himself or her to the misery of a one-sided marriage. But she could give him what he wanted.

Mr Whitworth stirred uneasily, then cleared his throat.

Before he could launch into one of his long-winded discourses, Georgiana held up a small hand, commanding silence.

Only a moment's thought was required to convince her Dominic would not accept the Place as a gift from her. But there was nothing to stop her offering to sell it to him. He had tried to buy it from Charles, after all.

"What were the conditions offered by this buyer? And who is he?"

Mr Whitworth was only too happy to answer Georgiana's first question, naming a sum which meant nothing to her, but which, he assured her ponderously, was, "Very generous. Exceedingly so!"

After a moment, he went on, "But the thing that moved me to come here in this manner, my dear Miss

Hartley, is that the buyer wishes an answer by this afternoon.''

"This afternoon?'' echoed Georgiana. She looked at her solicitor. His excited urgency was apparent in the way he almost bobbed in his chair. "Surely, that's rather unusual?''

Mr Whitworth pursed his lips, and she feared she was about to be told every case of rapid sale he had ever heard of, chapter and verse. But instead his breath came out in a little whoosh. "Well, yes,'' he admitted. "But whoever has that sort of money to throw down can generally call the tune.''

"Who is this buyer?''

"Ah,'' said Mr Whitworth, eyeing her uneasily. "That's another thing. The man who contacted us is an agent, and he won't reveal the name of his principal.''

So she could be selling to anyone. Georgiana made up her mind. "I wish to consult with my friends on this matter. I will undertake to send my answer to you this afternoon.''

She rose, in a fever to get on with her latest impulsive start.

As if only too keen for her to put the wheels into motion, Mr Whitworth rose too, and rolled forward to take her hand. "Certainly, Miss Hartley. My brother and I will hold ourselves in readiness to act on your behalf as soon as you have communicated your wishes to us.''

With that solemn promise, he bowed low and took his leave.

For some moments Georgiana stood, head bowed,

eyes on the patterned rug. Then, resolutely straightening her spine, she crossed the room to the small escritoire. Seating herself before it, she pulled forward a pristine sheet of paper and, after examing the nib carefully, dipped it determinedly into the standish. This wasn't going to be easy, but there really was no alternative.

GEORGIANA'S missive brought Dominic to Green Street at noon. As her note had contained little beyond a summons, he used the time while Johnson went in search of her to pace the drawing-room, pondering the possibilities. Avoiding the little tables Bella seemed to have a peculiar penchant for strewing about her rooms, Dominic had arrived for the third time by the fireplace when he heard the door open.

Entering as calmly as she could, Georgiana wished for the tenth time that morning that she did not have to face Dominic—Lord Alton!—over this particular matter. The very thought of the Place rubbed a sore spot in her heart, aggravating its already fragile condition. Thoughts of Lord Alton brought even more pain. But she was determined to go through with it. Unconscious of the worried frown that marred her smooth brow, she pressed her hands together to still their trembling, only to find herself forced, by his outstretched hand, to surrender one into his clasp.

"My lord." Her greeting was little better than a whisper. Pulling herself together with an effort, Georgiana raised her head to look into his eyes, steeling herself for the battle to meet his gaze and remain lucid. To her relief, she found it easier than she had anticipated. He was looking at her with undisguised concern.

"Georgiana, my dear, what's the matter?"

And suddenly it was easy to tell him.

"I've received an offer for the Place. A mystery buyer." She paused, temporarily distracted by the sudden intentness in his gaze, and promptly lost her thread. Luckily her rehearsed phrases came to her rescue. "I remembered how keen you were to buy the property from Charles. I wondered if you still wished to purchase it."

Dominic watched as, gently withdrawing her hand from his, Georgiana subsided into one corner of the sofa, lilac skirts softly sighing, and fixed him with her candid hazel gaze. Outwardly he smiled, warmly, comfortingly. Inwardly he wondered where it was that he had left his usual facility for managing such *affaires de coeur*. He had certainly misplaced it. Ever since Georgiana Hartley had magically appeared in his life, his touch had deserted him. He had told his agent to purchase the Place without revealing his name, purely to spare her any undue embarrassment. Instead, having once again failed to predict her reactions to the events he caused to happen, he had forced her to face the very object he was endeavouring to remove from the relationship.

Capturing her eyes with his, he smiled again. "I'm afraid, my dear, I've a confession to make." He could see from her eyes that she had jumped to the right conclusion, but he confirmed it. "I'm the mystery buyer."

"Oh."

Georgiana's eyes fell. She felt decidedly deflated.

Acutely sensitive where she was concerned, Dominic moved to take her hands in his, and drew her to her feet before him. In his present mood he would not trust himself on the sofa beside her. Standing this close to her, holding her hands so he would not sweep her into his arms, was bad enough, feeling as he did. He looked down on her golden head, bent so he could not see her eyes.

"Georgiana?"

But she would not look up. Her eyes seemed to be fixed on her hands, clasped lightly in his. So, with the patience of one who knew all the moves, Dominic slowly raised her hands, first one, then the other, to his lips. Inevitably, her eyes followed...and were trapped when they met his. He smiled, incapable of entirely hiding his triumph. "Sweetheart, do you know why I want to buy the Place?"

With an effort Georgiana tore her gaze from those fascinating eyes. That blue gaze held untold power over her, giving tantalising glimpses of emotions she did not understand but of which she longed to learn more. But she was returning to Ravello. Forcing a tight smile to her lips, she nodded. "Yes. Bella explained."

"I sincerely doubt Bella could explain." He smiled as she turned to him, hope and uncertainty warring in her big eyes. "Oh, I know Bella told you I've always wanted the Place, to return Candlewick to completeness. That has, in the past, been something of an obsession with me. Recently that obsession has been eclipsed by a far greater desire. It had, in fact, completely slipped my mind. Until..." Dominic paused, then decided to leave Arthur out of his explanation. "Until I realised you might misconstrue my interest in you for an interest in your property."

If the matter hadn't been so intensely important, so vitally crucial to him, he would have been amused by the sheer intensity of her concentration. Her huge hazel eyes glowed with hope, tinged with disbelief. He had expected that and did not let it worry him. He would convince her he loved her if it was the last thing he did in life. Despite his firm intentions, he felt himself drowning in her honey-gold gaze, felt the inevitable effect of her nearness start to test his restraint.

"My love, I want to buy the Place so it can no longer stand as a point of confusion between us." Dominic dropped a kiss on her knuckles and decided he had better get out of the room with all speed. If he didn't, she would be in his arms and he had no idea where it would end. "If you agree, send a message to Whitworth and he'll settle it with my man of business." He paused, looking deep into the darkened centres of her wide eyes. Smiling, he released one of her hands, carrying the other to his lips in a parting salute. "Once the sale is finalised, I'll call on you and we can discuss our...mutual interest further."

His look dared her to deny him, but Georgiana was too dazed to do anything but stare.

With a gentle chuckle, Dominic lifted a finger to her cheek in a fleeting caress, then bowed elegantly and left her.

CHAPTER ELEVEN

THE SHARP CRACK as the wax seal broke beneath Dominic's long fingers echoed hollowly in the library of Alton House. Outside, Grosvenor Square lay somnolent under a blanket of fog. The weather had turned with a vengeance, and all who could were making hurried preparations to quit the capital before the roads became impassable. Hurriedly scanning his agent's letter, Dominic put it aside and spread the folded parchment the packet had contained. In the warmth and comfort of his library, in the glow of expensive wax candles, Dominic stared at the title-deed of the Place, which he had longed to hold for so long. It was his. Candlewick was whole once more.

Conscious of a mild elation on that score, Dominic grinned wryly. Far stronger was the relief that now Georgiana could have no more doubts of his love for her, no more excuses to deny his suit.

His eyes narrowed. The recollection that he had on more than one occasion underestimated her ability to misread his intentions surfaced. For some reason, she seemed unable to believe he truly loved her. Incomprehensible though that was, it would be unwise to ignore that particular foible. First his ex-mistress, then the Place—what would the next obstacle in this particular course be?

Unbidden, laughter bubbled up. He had never had the slightest trouble making offers before, although admittedly for less exalted positions. However, to date, his particular concern had always been to ensure the women involved never imagined him to be in love with them. He had never had to convince a woman of his love before. And here he was, getting his feet in a tangle at every step, no doubt providing Arthur with untold amusement. All in all, wooing an angel was proving the very devil of a task.

With a self-deprecatory smile, he put the title-deed in the top drawer of his desk, locking it with a small key from his watch chain.

There was only one way forward. His mind refused to entertain the thought of any outcome bar success. He did not doubt he would win her in the end. It was his patience he doubted. Still, at least this time he was forewarned. And if, instead, she fell into his arms without raising any more quibbles, he would be doubly grateful.

Imagining how he would express his gratitude to his beloved, he settled his shoulders more comfortably against the leather and fixed his gaze on the ceiling. A smile of anticipation curved his lips.

Ten minutes later his reverie was interrupted by sounds of altercation in his hall. The library door flew open.

Bella entered. Timms followed close behind, trying to retrieve the bonnet she still wore.

"Dominic! Thank God you're here! You'll have to

do something. I never imagined she'd do anything so rash!'' Succeeding in tugging her bonnet strings free, she paused only to hand her headgear to Timms before impetuously throwing herself at her brother, who had risen and come forward to meet her. Her small hands grasped his arms. "You must go after her!''

"Yes, of course,'' Dominic replied, gently detaching her before turning her towards the *chaise*. "And I undoubtedly shall, as soon as you have calmed sufficiently to tell me where and why.''

His calm, deliberate tones had the desired effect. Bella plumped down on the *chaise* with relief, her bearing losing the frenetic tenseness of a moment before.

"It's just so unexpected. I had no inkling she might do such a thing.''

Dominic forced himself to take the seat facing his sister, reminding himself that any attempt to drag stories out of Bella faster than she was prepared to tell them inevitably took longer than allowing her to proceed at her own pace. Relieved to see her colour improving, and assuming from her words that Georgiana was not in any mortal danger, he contented himself with a bland, "What's happened?''

"I didn't know anything about it until I came downstairs half an hour ago. We were at the Ranleighs' last night—such a crowd! The rooms were so stuffy, I was quite worn out, so I slept late.'' Bella opened her reticule, hunting through its contents. "I found this on the breakfast-table.''

Dominic took the single sheet of delicately tinted paper and smoothed it out. As he scanned its contents, his jaw hardened. Undoubtedly, it was past time some-one took Georgiana Hartley in hand. The note blithely informed Bella that its writer had decided to ask the tenants of her father's London property whether they had any idea where his missing pictures might be. As she had ascertained that the house was located in Jermyn Street, she did not imagine she would be away long.

"She told me that when she wrote to Mr Whitworth to instruct him to sell the Place she remembered to ask about the London house. Johnson says she received a letter this morning."

"Jermyn Street!" Dominic stood and paced the room, incapable of remaining still. The words, Doesn't she know better? rang in his brain, but he didn't utter them—he knew the answer. There were times when Georgiana Hartley was too much the impulsive inno-cent for her own good. Over the past ten or more years, Jermyn Street had become the popular address for the well-heeled bachelors of the *ton*, which number included a disproportionate percentage of the most dangerous rakes and roués in England. His gaze re-turned to Bella's anxious face. "Do you have any idea of the number?"

Bella blushed. Under cover of fossicking in her ret-icule once more, she explained, "In the circumstances, I thought I should see if I could find the letter from the Whitworths. It was on her dresser." She looked up to hand the plain white envelope to her brother.

Dominic received it with undisguised relief and a fleeting smile for Bella's notions of propriety. "Good girl.'' Then he was reading the fine legal script. ''Seventeen. Who lives at 17 Jermyn Street?''

Bella shook her head, her gaze on her brother's face. He was clearly going through his acquaintance. Then she saw his expression drain.

''Good God!''

Bella paled. ''Who is it?''

''Harry Edgcombe.''

''Oh, dear.'' Bella's wide blue gaze had not left her brother's face. Recognising from uncomfortable experience the emotions flaring in his eyes, she suddenly wondered whether she would have done better by Georgiana to have tried to find Arthur, instead of flying to Dominic.

Abruptly Dominic headed for the door. ''Wait here until I get back.''

Seriously alarmed now, Bella half rose. ''Don't you think I should come, too?''

Dominic paused, hand on the door-handle. ''It would be best if this was done with as little fuss as possible. I'll bring her back here.''

And with that grim promise he was gone, leaving Bella with nothing to do but sink back on the *chaise*, wondering if Georgiana was strong enough to weather both Harry Edgcombe's advances *and* Dominic's temper.

DOMINIC DIDN'T bother with his carriage. As the hackney he'd hired pulled up outside 17 Jermyn Street, he reflected that the anonymity of the hack was an added advantage, distinctly preferable to his carriage with his liveried coachman. Instructing the driver to wait for him, he ascended the three steps to the polished oak door and beat a resounding tattoo. Heaven help Harry if he'd gone too far.

The door was opened by a very correct gentleman's gentleman. Recognising the Viscount, he smiled politely. "I'm afraid his lordship is currently engaged, m'lord."

"I know that. I'm here to disengage him."

And with that the astonished retainer was set firmly aside. Dominic closed the door behind him. His gaze swept the hallway and found Cruickshank, seated in a stiff-backed chair in the shadows. Surprised, she came to her feet.

"Where's your mistress?"

Trained to respond to the voice of authority, Cruickshank immediately bobbed a curtsy. "In the drawing-room, m'lord." With a nod, she indicated the door opposite her chair.

Stripping off his gloves and handing them, together with his cane, to Lord Edgcombe's bemused valet, Dominic said, "I suggest you return to Winsmere House. I will be taking your mistress to meet Lady Winsmere. I would imagine they'll return home in a few hours. Should Lord Winsmere enquire, you may inform him they're in my charge."

Bright blue eyes met faded blue. Cruickshank hesitated, then bobbed again in acquiescence. "Very good, m'lord."

With Lord Edgcombe's valet distracted by Cruickshank's departure, Dominic strolled forward and, after a fractional hesitation, opened the drawing-room door.

The sight which met his eyes would have made him

laugh if he hadn't been so angry. Georgiana was seated in a chair by the hearth and had clearly been listening with her customary intentness to one of Harry's tales. He was leaning against the mantelpiece, negligently attired in a green smoking jacket, his pose calculated to impress the viewer with his particular brand of assured arrogance. Despite himself, Dominic's lips twitched. The door shut behind him with a sharp click. Both fair heads turned his way.

While most of his attention was centred on Georgiana, Dominic did not miss the relief which showed fleetingly in Harry's eyes. Relieved in turn of its most urgent worry, his mind went on to register the expression in Georgiana's hazel gaze. Total innocence. Then, as he watched, she blushed deliciously and, flustered, looked away.

Inwardly, Dominic smiled. He did not make the mistake of imagining her sudden consciousness was due to delayed guilt on being discovered in such a compromising situation. Oh, no—*he* was the cause of Georgiana's blushes, not Harry. Which fact compensated at least in part for his agony of the past ten minutes.

An interested spectator to Georgiana's reaction, Harry pushed away from the mantelpiece, a smile of real mirth lighting his face. "Ah, Dominic. I wondered how long you'd be."

Acknowledging this greeting, and the information it contained, by shaking Harry's offered hand, Dominic turned to find Georgiana rising to her feet.

"I had no idea... I wasn't expecting..."

"Me to arrive so soon?" suggested Dominic. He

advanced upon his love, capturing one delicate hand and raising it to his lips. "I finished my business rather earlier than I had hoped. I take it you've finished yours?"

Georgiana was completely bemused. The last person she had thought to meet this afternoon was Lord Alton. And none of his words, nor Lord Edgcombe's, seemed to make any sense. Entirely at sea, she simply stared into his lordship's blue eyes, traitorously hoping he would take charge.

"No sign of these paintings, I'm afraid," put in Lord Edgcombe, shaking his head. He added in explanation to Dominic, "Moscombe has been with me since I moved here, and he insists the place was completely empty. Even the attics."

Dominic nodded, and tucked Georgiana's hand into its accustomed place in the crook of his arm. "It was a long shot. Still," he added, blue eyes intent on Harry, "no harm done."

Harry's eyes widened in mock alarm. "None in the least, I assure you." Then a gleam of wicked amusement lit his grey eyes. "Mind you, it did occur to me that Miss Hartley might like to view my art collection."

Dominic's black brows rose. "Your etchings, perhaps?"

Harry grinned. "Just so."

"Etchings?" queried Georgiana.

"Never mind!" said Dominic in the voice of a man goaded. He gazed down into wide hazel eyes and wished they were in his drawing-room rather than

Harry's. "Come," he added in gentler tones. "I'll return you to Bella."

Walking beside him to the door, Georgiana struggled to free enough of her mind from its preoccupation with Lord Alton to make sense of what was going on. Emerging into the hall, she looked about for Cruickshank.

"I've sent your maid on." Dominic was beside her, holding her coat.

"Oh," said Georgiana, suddenly aware of a disturbing glint in his lordship's blue eyes. Did that mean she would be travelling in a closed carriage alone with him?

Settling Georgiana's coat over her shoulders, Dominic cast a sharp glance at their host, standing genially beside them. "Harry…?"

Lord Edgcombe's grey eyes met his over Georgiana's head. A slight frown and a shake of the head was all the immediate response Harry made as Georgiana turned to thank him for his trouble. He charmingly disclaimed all effort, bowing with easy grace over her hand. As he straightened, his eyes intercepted Dominic's blue gaze.

"Not a word, I assure you." The grey eyes glinted, amusement in their depths. "You have my heartfelt thanks. Can you doubt it? Any word from me would cook my own goose, after all."

Reassured but puzzled, Dominic raised his brows in question.

Harry grinned and waved an airy hand. "M'sisters are a mite pressed at the moment, it seems. Can you imagine their joy if they learned of—er—what so recently transpired? Why, it would spell the end to my distinguished career.'' He fixed Dominic with a winning smile. "No, no, m'lad. Rather you than me.''

Walking towards the door ahead of the two men, Georgiana, no longer subject to Viscount Alton's mesmerising gaze, tried to follow the gist of their conversation, to no avail. When she turned in the doorway to bid Lord Edgcombe goodbye, it was to see both men cordially shaking hands. Piqued, feeling that something was going on literally over her head, Georgiana tilted her chin a fraction higher and coolly responded to Lord Edgcombe's farewell.

Turning to the street, she majestically descended the steps, but had barely gained the pavement before Lord Alton's long fingers grasped her elbow. A spurt of anger urged her to shake off his hand, but the memory of that odd glint she had seen in his eye undermined her confidence. Before she had time to do more than register the fact that it was into a hackney rather than one of his own carriages he was helping her, she was inside. He followed her, taking the seat beside her. Immediately the driver whistled up his horse and they moved off.

Georgiana strove to quiet her nerves, aquiver with an unnameable emotion. She kept her eyes on the streetscape while she tried to make sense of events. Why had he come to fetch her? Bella? Impulsively, she turned.

"Is Bella all right?"

His face was a mask. At her question, one black brow rose. "As far as I am aware." After a moment he added, "She's waiting at Alton House."

Alerted by the chilled crispness of his tone, Georgiana eyed him warily. "Did she send you for me?"

Suddenly noticing the tension in his long frame, Georgiana tensed too. But his calmly enunciated, "Yes. She sent me," gave her no clue to the cause of what she suspected was his displeasure.

Irritated by his odd behaviour, Georgiana frowned and asked, "Why?"

"Because, having learned that you had taken yourself off to visit a house in Jermyn Street, which, to one who knows London, means almost certainly to call on a bachelor alone, she needed someone to rescue you."

"But I didn't need rescuing," declared Georgiana, turning to face him more fully. "There was nothing the least wrong."

At his strangled laugh she flushed and went on, "I admit it was a relief to find it was Lord Edgcombe who lives there, but that just made it easier. And I made sure I took Cruickshank with me so I wasn't alone."

"When I entered the house, Cruickshank was in the hall and you were most definitely alone with Harry." With an effort, Dominic kept his voice even.

Flushing at the censure in his tone, Georgiana swung her gaze to the street. "Yes, but there wasn't... I was in no danger of..." Georgiana broke off. Now she thought it over, she was no longer so sure she hadn't been in danger. There had been a rather disquieting gleam in Lord Edgcombe's grey eyes when she had first arrived. However, the more they had talked, the more she had become convinced he was merely slightly nervous over something. Maybe she had misread the signs. Still, he had done nothing to deserve Lord Alton's suspicions. "Lord Edgcombe was most truly the gentleman."

"I would imagine Harry would always act the gentleman he undoubtedly is," Dominic retorted, asperity colouring his words. "But that doesn't mean he isn't a rake and a gamester, and therefore totally unsuitable as private company for a young lady. Such as yourself."

There was no mistaking the anger in the clipped words. Amazed, her own temper flying, Georgiana turned an incredulous face to him. "But you're a rake and a gamester, too. Why is it safe for me to be alone with you but not with him?"

At her question Dominic closed his eyes in exasperation and thought determinedly about his old nurse, about climbing trees at Candlewick—anything to shut out the urge to sweep her on to his lap and kiss her witless. Safe? She was pushing her luck.

Anger growing at his refusal to answer, Georgiana continued, her long irritation with the oddities of English mores finding sudden outlet. "Why did you send Cruckers away? Surely it's not acceptable for me to be riding in a carriage alone with you?"

Forcibly keeping his eyes shut, Dominic answered, "The only reason it's acceptable for you to be alone with me is because we're soon to be married." He waited for her "Oh" of understanding. When no sound came, he slowly opened his eyes.

Georgiana was staring at him in total confusion.

Quickly Dominic closed his eyes. She was definitely not safe.

For long minutes Georgiana could do nothing but stare. But the fact that he had his eyes closed made it easier for her to think. He should have received the deed of the Place that morning. Dominic had said he would visit her once the sale was finalised, *to discuss their mutual interest.* She had no idea what he had meant by that. Now that he owned the Place, she could see no reason why he would still want to marry her.

In real perturbation, Georgiana stared at the handsome face, wishing she could read his motives in the even features. Then, like a beacon on a hill, she saw the light. He had gone too far, too publicly, to draw back now. And that old scandal, the one that had started his rakish career, hung like Damocles' sword, forcing him to offer for her or face the censure of the *ton.*

Which meant she would have to deny him again, one last time. And make it convincing.

She knew he did not love her, not as she understood love. He had shown no fiery passion, uttered no impassioned speeches nor indulged in any melodramatic gestures—all components of love as she knew it. The only time he had kissed her, it had been like a magic caress, so light that she could have dreamt it. But she was in love with him. And, because there seemed to be developing a strange conduit of communication between them, one that did not need words, or even gestures, a sensing that relied on something other than the physical, because of this, she would have to end it now. Or he would know.

And that would be even harder to bear.

Despite his wanting to marry her for her property, something she was honest enough to acknowledge was commonplace in his world, she had always felt safe with him. He had never intentionally done anything to cause her grief. If he ever learned she loved him—not gently, as a well bred young lady should, but to distraction—she doubted he would accept a denial of his suit. He would not cause her pain.

Could he be made to understand that loving him as she did, being married to him, knowing he did not love her in the same way, would cause her even greater pain that if she was never to see him again?

His eyes remained shut. Georgiana could not resist the temptation to study his face, memorising each detail, storing the vision in her heart to last her for a lifetime. She saw his eyelids flicker, then slowly rise. Ill prepared to meet his blue gaze, she straightened and turned slightly away, furiously blinking back the tears which suddenly threatened, pressing her hands tightly together to still their trembling.

Dominic took one look at his love, all but quivering with suppressed emotion, and his anger abruptly vanished.

"Georgiana?"

When she made no answer beyond a small wave of her hand, Dominic drew back, giving her the time she needed to compose herself, ruthlessly stilling the instinctive urge to wrap her in his arms and comfort her. He didn't dare touch her. Frustrated beyond measure, he felt an insane desire to laugh, to catch her to him and kiss her worries, whatever they were, away. Her silence screamed the fact that she was still labouring under some delusion sufficient to make her balk at the very mention of marriage. Her forlorn countenance showed he had his work very much ahead of him.

His eyes on her guinea-gold curls, Dominic sighed. He wanted her, and he was tired of the roundabout the prescribed methods of courtship had put them on.

He waited until her breathing became less laboured, until the pulse at the base of her throat beat less tumultuously. Then he tried again. "Georgiana, my dear, what is it?"

Georgiana put up one small hand in a gesture he found both imperious and, in her present state, endearing.

"Please, my lord. You must let me speak." Her voice was low, urgent and breathless.

"Of course, my dear." Dominic managed a politely attentive tone. He made no move to take her hand, but continued to sit beside her, the flounce of her skirt brushing his boots, his head inclined to watch her face. She did not look up at him, but fixed her gaze on her clasped hands, tensed in her lap.

Georgiana drew a shuddering breath at his easy acquiescence. If only he would remain so calm, she might manage to accomplish her task. But he was near, so near. Speak—she had to speak or her resolution would crumble. "My lord, you must believe that I most earnestly value your friendship, and the...the proper feeling that lies behind your wish to marry me." She paused, reaching deep to dredge the remainder of her strength, before continuing, "I am aware—have always been aware—that my ownership of the Place was fundamental to your interest in me. Now that you own the Place, there is no reason for any further talk of marriage between us." Resolutely she swallowed the sob that rose in her throat and hurried on. "I realise that, if I were of the *ton* and chose to continue living in London, our association these past weeks might give rise to awkward conjecture. However, as I intend returning to Ravello shortly, I beg you will not let such considerations sway you."

Beside her, Dominic allowed his brows to rise. A smile, soft and gentle, curved his lips.

Georgiana drew a deep breath. "My lord, I hope you will see that, in the circumstances, there is no reason for you to offer for me. Indeed," she said, struggling to subdue her treacherous tears, "I beg you will not renew your offer."

"Of course not."

The calm words brought Georgiana up short. One moment she was about to dissolve in tears, the next she had turned and her eyes met his. "I beg your pardon?" she asked weakly.

Smiling sympathetically, Dominic said, "My dear, if my offering for you will cause you distress, then of course I'll not do it. I would never knowingly distress you."

The look which accompanied his words warmed Georgiana through and through, despite the total depression which now hung like a cold black pall over her. He was convinced. He was going to make it easy for her. Tremulously, she smiled.

Seeing this evidence that she had pulled back from

the brink, Dominic smiled back and possessed himself of one small hand.

Georgiana was so relieved that she only just stopped herself from leaning against him, so close as he was. Her head was spinning. Was it possible to feel so cherished and yet know one was unloved? She wasn't sure. In fact she was no longer sure of any number of things. But thankfully he had taken charge. She was sure he wouldn't press her for further words.

Words, especially from his beloved, were very far from Dominic's mind. He had no intention of giving her the opportunity to refuse him again. It occurred to him that there were other routes to his desired goal. The time had come to consider alternatives—his patience was wearing wafer-thin. On impulse, he raised the hand he held and touched it to his lips, then, yielding to a need he was endeavouring to subdue, turned it and pressed a kiss to her palm. He heard the sharp intake of her breath, and glanced up to smile reassuringly at her.

"My dear, you're overset. I give you my word I'll press you to do nothing unless it is your wish, urge you to nothing beyond what is in your heart to do. Remember that."

Georgiana blushed. As a parting speech, it held a note of promise entirely out of place with its supposed intent.

Dominic watched her confusion grow, turning her eyes a deeper shade, like toffee. Repressing the all but overwhelming urge to kiss her, he reluctantly released her hand, adding in a conversational tone, "It's very likely I'll be out of town for the next few days, but

I'll see you before you leave town.'' It would take a day or two to organise his trap, but he had no intention of letting her escape.

The hack turned into a square and pulled up before an imposing mansion. Within minutes Georgiana was ushered inside to find Bella anxiously waiting.

''DUCKETT? What the devil are you doing here?''

Slouched in the armchair before the fireplace, Dominic frowned as his head butler, whom he had supposed still at Candlewick, entered the room. Unperturbed by his greeting, Duckett held a long taper to the fire and proceeded to circumnavigate the room, lighting candles as he went.

''Timms is ill, m'lord. You'd given orders to shut up this house, so the lad very properly sent for me.''

Dominic snorted. Lad? Timms was all of thirty-five if he was a day. But he was one of Duckett's protégés and, provided he obeyed Duckett's guidelines to the letter, would always be assured of the head butler's protection.

Turning the fragile glass balloon he held so that the candlelight caught and reflected from the golden liquid within, Dominic found himself staring at the glowing colour, the same colour as her eyes. With an effort, he withdrew his gaze and found his head butler engaged in the demeaning task of making up the fire.

''Duckett, I have a problem.''

''My lord?''

''A problem with a lady, you understand.''

''I understand perfectly, my lord.''

''I sincerely doubt it,'' replied Dominic. He eyed

his henchman appraisingly. It wasn't the first time he had unburdened himself to Duckett, and doubtless wouldn't be the last. Duckett had started service as a stableboy with his grandfather. He had rapidly progressed through the ranks, reaching his present position shortly after Dominic had attained his majority. They'd been firm friends forever, it seemed, despite a good ten years' difference in age.

"I'd value your opinion, Duckett."

"Very good, m'lord." With the fire blazing, Duckett rose and unobtrusively busied himself, straightening books and stacking magazines.

"The situation," said Dominic, "can only be described as delicate. The lady in question is both young and innocent. The crux of the problem is that she has great difficulty in believing herself to be loved."

Dominic waited for some response, but none came. He turned and saw Duckett flicking the dust from a book before replacing it on the shelf.

"Are you listening, Duckett?"

"Naturally, m'lord."

Dominic let his head fall back against the chair. "Very good." Taking a moment to gather his thoughts, he went on, "This being so, the said lady invents the most tortuous reasons to account for my wanting to marry her, and for refusing my suit. The first was that I was in love with a courtesan and intended marrying her. Having convinced her this was untrue, I then found she believed that I wished to marry her in order to gain title to the Place, which she owns. Owned, I should say, because today I bought it from her. The title-deed now resides in my strong-box and has lost all relevance to the proceedings. The last twist in the tale is that she now perceives that I feel I must marry her because, due to the public nature of my pursuit of her, not to do so would leave her open to the usual opprobrium.'' Dominic paused to take a swig of the fiery liquid in his glass. ''You now have the facts, Duckett. I am presently searching for ways and means of removing her to a suitably isolated locale, sufficiently private to allow me to convince her that I do in fact love her while at the same time rendering her opinion on the subject irrelevant.''

A slight frown marred Duckett's majestic countenance. ''I take it the young lady returns your affections, my lord?''

''The young lady is head over heels in love with me, if you must know.''

''Ah,'' said Duckett, nodding sagely. ''Just so.''

Dominic eyed his impeccable retainer through narrowed eyes. Duckett's gaze was fixed in the far distance. Then, quite suddenly, a smile quirked at the corners of his mouth.

''What are you thinking of, Duckett?''

The soft question brought Duckett to himself with a start. Then he smiled at his master. ''It just occurred to me, m'lord, that now that you own the Place you'd want Jennings and me to put our people through it— to tidy it up, as it were.''

Puzzled, Dominic nodded. ''Yes, but—''

Duckett held up a restraining hand. ''That being so, m'lord, I dare say there'll be personal belongings— things to do with the Hartleys—that we'd need to know what to do with. And, I should warn you, old

Ben says the snows are no more than a few days away.''

Dominic's eyes, vacant, remained trained on his butler's face as the grandfather clock in the corner ticked on. Then, to Duckett's relief, the blue gaze focused. Dominic smiled wickedly. ''Duckett, prince of butlers, you're a rascal. I'd be shocked, if I weren't so grateful. No wonder I pay you so well.'' Struggling upright, Dominic drained his glass and handed it to the waiting Duckett. ''We'll set out at first light.''

''Very good, m'lord,'' replied Duckett.

CHAPTER TWELVE

BEING TRULY ALONE again was worse than Georgiana had expected. Bella's brother had come to fill a void in her heart she hadn't even known existed. Until he was gone.

Idly plying her needle over the slippers she intended leaving as a parting gift to Arthur, Georgiana stifled a despondent sigh. The day outside was dull and grey, but no more dismal than the state of her heart. Bella, reclining on the *chaise* in the middle of the room, flicking through the latest *Ladies' Journal,* seemed almost as subdued as she. But, in her friend's case, there was a peacefulness in her quiet which Georgiana, in her tortured state, could only envy.

The Season had come to an end two days before. During the last ball, at Lady Matcham's, there had been much talk of country visits and plans for the annual festivities. Georgiana had listened and tried to summon an enthusiasm she could not feel. To her, the future looked cold and bleak. She waited for Arthur's decision on when they would leave Green Street, Bella and he bound for Candlewick, she for the Continent. He had asked her if she would stay until his business in London was completed, to keep Bella company.

Naturally, she could not possibly refuse such a request. Particularly now that Lord Alton had left London.

He had sent a short note to Bella, simply informing her he had business in the country and would welcome her to Candlewick whenever she chose to quit town.

There had been no word to Bella's protégée.

Casting another glance at Bella, Georgiana couldn't help feeling guilty that she had not been able to satisfy her friend's ambition, and, worse, would not be returning to London to continue their friendship. Arthur would have to find some other distraction for his wife next Season. Georgiana knew she would never return. She would never be able to face Lord Alton's bride. He would eventually marry—an inescapable fate for one such as he. Already she felt a potent jealousy for the beautiful woman who would be his wife. Feeling despair weigh heavily on her shoulders, she forced away her unhappy thoughts and bent over her embroidery.

The door opened.

"A note for you, miss."

Frowning, Georgiana reached for the white rectangle on Johnson's salver, images of Charles and Lord Ellsmere in her mind. But one glance at the strong script emblazoned across the white parchment dispelled those weaker images, replacing them with a handsome, dark-featured face with warm blue eyes.

With the unnerving sensation of having her heart in her throat, Georgiana nodded a dismissal to Johnson and broke open the seal.

"What is it?" asked Bella, struggling to sit up.

Slowly Georgiana scanned the single sheet. Then,

absent-mindedly, she said, "Your brother wants me to go down to the Place. His people want to know what to do with the furniture and so on."

Bella, now sitting, nodded. "Yes, of course. You must tell them whether you want anything set aside."

"But I don't think there could possibly be anything I would want—" Georgiana began.

"You can't tell that," said Bella seriously. "Who knows? They might even stumble across those paintings of your father's."

Bella put her head on one side, the better to view her friend. To her mind, something was not entirely right between Georgiana and Dominic. Why on earth Georgie should fall into such a lethargy just because Dominic repaired to the country for a few days she could not imagine. As she saw it, it was only to be expected that her brother would want to see his affairs at Candlewick organised before he took his intended bride down for a prolonged stay. Despite the fact Dominic had apparently not as yet proposed, Bella was quite sure he would and that Georgiana's plans for removal to Italy would never be realised. She knew her brother well enough to be certain he would view any interference with his schemes in a dim light. But, in this case, her confidence in the eventual outcome was supreme. Consequently, she was waiting with perfect equanimity for the time to come for them to leave for Candlewick.

"When are you to go?" Bella asked.

"He says he'll come and fetch me tomorrow," answered Georgiana, still struggling with conflicting emotions. The note was little more than a polite summons, its wording leaving no room for manoeuvre and even less for escape. Lord Alton would give himself the pleasure of fetching Miss Hartley at ten the next morning. He would undertake to return her to town that evening.

"Perhaps I should come down with you," Bella suggested. "There's nothing to keep me here, and I would like to see Jonathon."

Georgiana readily agreed. In her present state, spending two hours and more in a closed carriage alone with Lord Alton was an undertaking too unnerving even to contemplate.

But when the subject was broached with Arthur that evening he surprised them both by vetoing his wife's part in it.

"I'm afraid, my dear, that I would prefer you to remain in London for the next day or two. As Dominic plans to bring Georgiana back the same day, I really don't think you should leave Green Street just yet."

Put like that, it was impossible to argue the point.

Georgiana retired for the night, trying in vain to quell the entirely inappropriate leaping of her heart whenever she thought of the morrow. All was at an end between Lord Alton and herself. Why, then, did anticipation run in tantalising shivers down every nerve?

PRECISELY AT TEN the next morning, Lord Alton's travelling chaise pulled up outside Winsmere House. Strolling unannounced into his sister's back parlour, Dominic could not repress a smile at the picture that met his eyes. On the window-seat, his beloved sat, perfectly ready, fingers nervously twisting in the ribbons of her bonnet. Her gaze was fixed on the garden, a dull prospect beyond the glass.

His sister lay on the *chaise,* staring at the ceiling, a slight frown puckering her brows. It was she who first saw him.

"Oh!"

With that exclamation Bella sat up, putting up a hand to straighten the wisp of lace she had started experimenting with atop her dark curls. Dominic held out a hand to assist her to right herself, bending to drop an affectionate kiss on her cheek. Then he stood back and eyed her headgear.

Bella held her breath.

After a moment, Dominic's brows rose. "Has Arthur seen that yet?"

"No," said Bella.

"In that case, I suggest you burn it before he does."

"Oh!" Spots of colour flew in Bella's cheeks, eliciting a chuckle from her unrepentant brother. "If you've a mind to be disagreeable, I'll leave you," she replied haughtily.

But Dominic only smiled. "Don't trouble yourself. It's I who am about to leave you. If Miss Hartley is ready?"

Finding herself the object of his calm blue gaze, Georgiana nodded and rose. Within a matter of minutes her cloak had been gently placed about her shoulders and she was settled in the luxury of his carriage, a warm brick at her feet, a soft rug wrapped protectively about her knees.

Taking his seat beside her, and giving the order to

start, Dominic turned and smiled. "The journey should not be too tedious, I hope."

At his smile, all Georgiana's fears dissolved. She smiled back.

They preserved a comfortable silence as the coach wended its way through the crowded streets. Once the outskirts of town were reached, and the power of the four horses began to make itself felt, Dominic turned to Georgiana. "Have you heard of Prinny's latest start?"

She hadn't, of course. Without effort, he entertained her with stories of the *ton* and other suitable anecdotes, until she had relaxed enough to ask some questions of her own. These, not surprisingly, were focused on the Place. Perfectly content with the topic, Dominic described the actual land attached to the Place, and how it related to his own far-flung acres.

"So, you see, the Place all but cuts my holdings in two, at least in that area. It has meant that my people constantly have to route all their movements around the Place, often tripling distances. Aside from being purely a nuisance, it has in recent years become an eyesore—a blot on the landscape. It's been irritating to me, as much as to my farmers, to see good land go to ruin."

Georgiana nodded, the memory of the Place as she had last seen it vivid in her mind.

Dominic paused to glance once more out of the window. The one subject he was most assiduously avoiding was the weather. He had ensured that Georgiana was seated on the left on the carriage, so her gaze, should it wander, dwelt only on the relatively clear skies to the west. On his side the eastern horizon was obscured by slate-grey clouds of the peculiar quality which, to one country-bred, denoted but one outcome. Snow. By nightfall.

The temperature was starting to fall precipitate, even though it wanted half an hour to noon. He did not think Georgiana would notice, wrapped up as she was. Still, it wouldn't do to become too complacent on that score. With a wicked grin, he turned to her once more, his brain making a rapid inventory of the latest *on dits,* selecting those suitable for his purpose.

By his order, the coach took them direct to the Place. It was well after noon when he alighted and handed Georgiana down. His steward, Jennings, and Duckett were there to meet them.

"I'll leave you with Duckett, my dear," Dominic said. "I'll be with Jennings if you need me."

Recognising Duckett, Georgiana was relieved to have his comforting presence beside her as she walked the old rooms of the Place. There was no piece of furniture she remembered with any particular affection. When appealed to, Duckett suggested the vicar's wife, who managed the local charity, and promised to convey the furniture to her.

"There's just one more matter, miss," said Duckett, pausing at the top of the stairs.

Dominic, having finished his instructions to Jennings, approving the steward's suggestion that the Place be made over as a single unit into a farm, came to stand at the foot of the stairs. Spying Georgiana and Duckett in the shadows at their head, he ran lightly up to join them.

"I was just telling Miss Hartley, m'lord, that when our people went through the attics they found one of them sealed up. An old cupboard had been moved across the door. Took three men to shift it. Then it was a struggle to force the door—looked to have been left locked for years. The room inside seems to have been used for painting—bits of rag and dabs of paint all over. There were lots of old paintings stacked by the walls. We didn't know what to do with them, so we left it until you came. Would you care to take a look, miss?"

Her father's paintings? His studio at the Place? Georgiana simply stared at Duckett.

Correctly gauging his love's reaction, Dominic took her hand and drew it through his arm. "Lead the way, Duckett."

Escorted in Duckett's wake, Georgiana drew a deep breath. "Oh, Dominic! If only…"

He glanced down, smiling, inordinately pleased to hear his name on her lips. "Patience. A moment and we'll see."

He helped her up the narrow stairs to the low-ceilinged attics. A white patch on one wall of the first room showed where the old cupboard had been. Now the concealed door stood ajar.

Duckett pushed it open and stood aside to allow Georgiana to enter. Dominic released her and, when she hesitated, gave her an encouraging nudge.

Dazed, she stepped over the threshold, lifting her skirts free of the dusty floor. There was little doubt this had been her father's eyrie. Long windows all but filled the outer wall. Now half covered with creeper, clear, they would have allowed light to flood the large room. An easel stood in the middle of the floor, empty; a paint-stained rag hung on a nail at one corner. Georgiana gazed about. The odd smell of old paints was still detectable, wafting like a ghost about the room.

For one instant, reminded so vividly of the life that had been, she felt the past threaten to engulf her. She struggled to keep back the tears. Then she heard a soft movement behind her and Dominic was there, his hands closing gently on her upper arms, comforting by his touch, by his solid warmth so close behind her. Like an anchor, he held her in the present, defying the past to claim her.

Georgiana drew a deep breath. Calm once more, she put up a hand to touch one of his. Her gaze fell on the canvases, stacked against the side-wall. She moved to touch them and he released her immediately, following her across the floor.

Without words, they set about the task of examining her father's last legacy.

Most of the portraits were of adolescent youths. After a pensive moment, staring at one of a gentle-eyed young man with reddish tints in his hair, Dominic grinned. "Ah! Now I understand."

Patiently Georgiana waited to be educated.

Dominic's smile warned her. "Your father was clearly an astute man. He wanted to leave you something which was sure to retain its value, regardless of the vacillations of fashion. So he left you these." Still Georgiana waited. Displaying the canvas in his hand, Dominic said, "This one's William Grenville as a young man." When Georgiana still looked blank he explained, "Grenville was one of our recent Prime Ministers. His family will pay a small fortune for this. And," he continued, replacing the portrait and picking up another, "unless I miss my guess, this one is Spencer Perceval, another Prime Minister. That one," he said, pointing to another study of an earnest young man, "could be Castlereagh, though I'm not certain." He bent again to flick through the portraits.

There were sixteen in the series, and Dominic could put a name to nine and guess at the others. But the three portraits at the bottom of the pile, once they were uncovered, claimed his and Georgiana's complete attention.

The first was of a young woman, with a sweet face crowned by masses of brown hair. Her eyes, startlingly clear hazel, shone out of the canvas, bright and clear. It was the portrait of Georgiana's mother.

Leaving Georgiana to gaze on her mother's face, Dominic pulled the next from the pile. A young baby rolled playfully on the grass beside the same woman. A gentle smile, full of love, curved the woman's fine lips.

Wordlessly offering this picture to Georgiana, Dominic reached for the last. This showed a young girl, of six or so summers, long golden hair hanging in plaits down her back, honey-gold eyes alight with mischief. A dusting of freckles was scattered across the bridge of her pert nose. Dominic smiled. Turning to Georgiana, he put one finger under her chin and turned her face towards him. After a careful examination, which ignored her brimming eyes, he stated, "You've lost your freckles."

Georgiana smiled tremulously, recognising his attempt to lighten her mood and grateful for it.

Dominic smiled back and released her, gently flicking her cheek with his finger. He glanced about them. "Now that this room has been opened again, I rather think these pictures should be removed from here."

Georgiana looked blank.

"Shall I get Duckett to pack them up and take them to Candlewick? You can decide what to do with them later."

Still dazed by their discoveries, Georgiana nodded her agreement. Duckett began to move about her, carefully stacking the paintings into smaller piles to be carried downstairs by his minions.

"And now," Dominic said, coming once more to stand beside her, "you must be famished. I'll take you to Candlewick, and Mrs Landy can feed us."

Quite forgetting the long trip back to London, Georgiana, happiness filling her heart, and enjoying the novelty of having someone to share it with, allowed herself to be escorted downstairs and into the carriage.

Mrs Landy had a meal waiting. She scolded Dominic for keeping Georgiana so long in the cold, causing Georgiana's brow to rise. But Dominic only laughed.

When they had eaten, he left her in Mrs Landy's care while he went out to talk with his bailiff.

It wasn't until, over tea and scones in the housekeeper's rooms, she noticed the day drawing in that Georgiana started to become uneasy. As the hour dragged by and Dominic did not return, her sense of premonition grew.

The light had faded to a premature dusk when he

finally appeared. He came into the drawing-room, where she had retreated, stamping his feet to restore the circulation. He crossed to the fire and bent to warm his hands. Straightening, he smiled at her reassuringly, but his words dispelled the effect. "I'm afraid, my dear, that we won't be able to return to town tonight. The weather's turned nasty and the roads are freezing. There's snow on the way, and I doubt we'd make the Great North Road before we were stuck in a drift."

At the sight of his satisfied smile, Georgiana's eyes grew round. He'd planned this, she was sure. But why, for heaven's sake?

But her host gave her no opportunity to ponder that vital question. He challenged her to a game of chess, to which she had admitted fair knowledge, and, by the time Georgiana had conceded her king, Mrs Landy was at the door, smiling and waiting to take her to her room to freshen up before dinner. The clouds of worried questions that flitted through Georgiana's mind seemed ridiculous when faced with the solid respectability of that worthy dame.

A sense of unreality hung over her during dinner, eaten in the large dining-room. The huge table, which Mrs Landy had informed her could seat fifty, had thankfully had all its leaves taken out, rendering it a suitable size for household dining. She was seated on Dominic's right, and so attentive was her host that she had no time to question the propriety of the proceedings. The food was delicious, and the wine Dominic allowed Duckett to supply her with was cool and sweet. A discussion of the portraits her father had left her occupied much of their time, until, with the removal of the last course, Dominic pushed back his chair and rose, waving Duckett aside and coming to assist her to her feet. "Come. We'll be more comfortable in the drawing-room."

The presence of Duckett behind her chair had soothed her troublesome conscience, pricking with half-understood suspicion. Now, as the drawing-room door closed and she realised he was no longer in the room with them, her jitters woke afresh. Her nervousness spiralling upwards, she crossed the room towards the *chaise* angled before the big fireplace, conscious that he followed close behind.

"Georgiana."

The single word, uttered in the most compelling of tones, stopped her before the marble hearth. Recognising the futility of attempting evasion, Georgiana turned slowly to meet him. He was closer than she had realised. She found herself enfolded in his arms, like delicate porcelain. Looking up, she felt her eyelids automatically drop as his head lowered to hers and he kissed her, so gently that the caress captivated her senses. This time, the kiss did not end, but went on to steal her breath, and her wits. Her nervousness disappeared, chased away by the warm glow of desire which spread insidiously through her veins. In response to some inner prompting, she slipped her arms free of his hold and twined them about his neck. His lips firmed against hers, until she parted her lips in welcome and, by imperceptible degrees, the kiss deepened.

Suddenly her mind, all alive to every incoming sensation, registered the restraint in his body, the tightness in the muscles holding her so gently, the iron control which stopped him from crushing her to him. She moved closer, letting her body press, soft but firm, against his.

Dominic stiffened with the effort to hold his passions in check. He raised his head to look down into her face. In surprise, he viewed hazel eyes smoky with desire, lips parted slightly in flagrant temptation. The siren he had glimpsed in the Massinghams' library stood within the circle of his arms, her body pliant against his. And it was all he could do to draw breath and, his voice husky, demand, "Marry me, Georgiana."

His words slowly penetrated the fog of desire which swirled through Georgiana's mind. They made no sense. Nothing made any sense any more. He had the Place. This wasn't supposed to be happening. Georgiana ignored his talk and, instead, tightened her hold on him, forcing his lips back to hers.

With a groan, Dominic recognised her state. But he was powerless to resist her blatant demands. His lips closed on hers and he tried very hard to think of other things—anything other than the slim form snuggling so invitingly against him. His plan of gentle wooing had not taken into account the possibility of such responses on her part. In the dim hope that her mind would return presently if he kept their lovemaking in a frustratingly light vein, he rained gentle kisses on her lips and face, ignoring her attempts to ensnare him in a deeper caress. Gradually her flaring passion abated somewhat—enough, at least, for him to try again.

"Georgiana?"

"Mmm." She moved seductively against him, and he caught his breath.

"Marry me, love. Say yes. Now."

"Y... What?" Abruptly Georgiana's eyes focused. Slowly her mind followed. Then, still dazed, she shook her head.

To her amazement, she found herself looking up into eyes darkened with desire but lit by underlying sparks of anger.

"I do hope, my love, that you are not going to tell me you won't marry me."

The clipped accents sobered her. The warmth of his arms still surrounded her, making it difficult to think. Her hands on his shoulders, Georgiana tried to ease from his embrace, only to find the arms holding her so gently were, in fact, made of steel. "I can't think," she murmured protestingly.

"Don't think," came his voice, so close that his breath caressed her cheek. "Just say yes."

Again she shook her head, not daring to meet his eyes. Unequal to this battle, she leant her forehead against his shoulder. She felt his arms come up to draw her closer against him, his solid warmth comforting rather than threatening. Ridiculous, she thought, to feel so wholly at peace in the arms of a man who did not love her.

"Why?"

The question drifted softly, a murmur in her mind.

"Because you don't love me." She answered aloud without realising it.

"*What?*"

Abruptly he held her from him, staring at her in

stunned disbelief. His eyes searched her face, then his lips twitched. Closing his eyes in exasperation, Dominic drew her head back until it was once again pillowed on his shoulder.

Georgiana snuggled against him, still dazed from his kisses, still wanting more, but not, at this juncture, daring to tempt him further. His insistence on marriage baffled her. Her own responses confused her even more. How wanton she became, with him.

Dominic waited until he had regained some measure of control over his reeling senses before asking, in a perfectly amiable tone, "Do you think, my love, you could explain to me why you think I don't love you?"

The effort required to return their interaction to an acceptable footing was entirely beyond Georgiana. She contemplated attempting to retreat without explaining herself, but doubted she had the strength to win free of his arms, let alone his presence. So when his lips found her ear and nuzzled gently, inviting her confidence, she sighed and said, "You don't really love me, you only say you do. I saw you kiss Lady Changley once. You never kiss me like that."

Put into words, it did not sound particularly rational, but it was the best she could do, with him so close.

Silence greeted her revelation. After a moment she glanced up to find him regarding her, an odd expression in his eyes.

"Do you mean to say that *that* is why you've held me off for so long? Because I *didn't* kiss you the way I did Lady Changley?"

His voice sounded strangled. Georgiana looked up

at him in concern. When she neglected to answer, he shook her slightly. She nodded.

A groan rewarded her honesty. "Georgiana!"

Then she was swept into his arms and ruthlessly kissed, passionately kissed, until her legs collapsed under her and she had to cling to him for support. And still the kiss went on, demanding, commanding and utterly devastating. When at long last she was allowed to emerge, she was shaken to the very depths of her being.

"Oh!"

It was all she could say. She looked up at him, love, joy and wonder dancing in the golden flames of her eyes.

With a wordless groan, Dominic crushed her to him once more, burying his face in her silken curls.

"But why?" asked a dazzled Georgiana. "Dominic, why didn't you kiss me like that before?"

To her amazement, she felt his shoulders shake.

Dominic could contain his laughter no longer. And, although his love struggled in his embrace, he held her tightly until he felt rather less crazed and more capable of answering her sanely. Only then did he ease his hold enough to allow her to look up into his face.

Reassured at seeing her own love reflected in his blue eyes—eyes which held warmth and gentle affection as well as the passion she had not recognised before—Georgiana smiled and waited patiently.

Drawing a deep breath, Dominic sought for words to explain how her innocence had tripped him up yet again. "I was most careful, I'll have you know, not to expose you to my desire, because my sweetest love, it

is generally held that innocent young ladies are not—
er—sufficiently robust to withstand such raw passions.''

The incredulous widening of his love's innocent
stare nearly had him in stitches again.

''Aren't I supposed to like...? No, that can't be
true.''

Dominic was nuzzling her ear again. ''I assure you
it is,'' he murmured. ''If I'd kissed any of the gentle
debs as I've just kissed you, seven out of ten would
faint dead away and the other three would have had
the vapours.''

Georgiana giggled.

Then she felt the arms around her shift slightly and
one strong hand found her chin, tilting it up so that he
could gaze into her eyes, his own burning again with
the dark lights she now understood. A sensuous shiver
ran through her.

A slow and infinitely wicked smile curved Dominic's lips. When he spoke, his voice was husky and
deep. ''Enough of the rest of this crazy world. Come,
let me see if I can convince you of just how irrevo-
cably I love you.''

His lips closed over hers, and Georgiana, swept
away on a tide of passion, gave herself up wholeheart-
edly to that enterprise.

''Ahem!''

The discreet cough from the doorway brought Dominic's head up. ''What the devil?'' Frowning direfully,
he turned his head and located the intruder. ''Duckett?''

At the door, Duckett stood correctly to attention, his

gaze fixed on the far wall. "I'm sorry to interrupt, m'lord, but I thought you'd want to know that Lady Winsmere has just arrived."

"Bella?" Dominic's incredulous question hung quivering in the air, but Duckett had already gone, leaving the door ajar.

Brows flying in disbelief, Dominic looked down at the woman still held securely in his arms. "I suppose we'd better go and see what your chaperon has to say."

Georgiana smiled. "I wonder why she's come."

"Precisely my question. We'd better ask her." Keeping Georgiana within the circle of his arm, Dominic strolled to the door.

In the doorway, they paused to take in the scene. Only one of the large double doors was open, with one of the footmen standing in its protection with a branch of candles, trying to cast some light on to the steps outside. Blasts of cold air hurled into the hall, bringing swirls of snowflakes to flutter and melt on the tiles. On the porch a carpet of snow, already some inches thick, bore witness to the intensity of the storm outside. As Georgiana and Dominic watched, two footmen emerged from the darkness, bearing Bella between them. Duckett followed immediately behind, the shoulders of his dark coat already dusted with snow.

As soon as everyone was inside, the footmen slammed the door shut against the elemental fury ravaging the night.

Immediately her feet hit the floor, Bella glanced about. Her eyes found Georgiana and Dominic, side by side in the drawing-room doorway. "There you are! Really, Georgie, you're going to have to be more careful!'' She bustled up and embraced Georgiana before turning a censorious look on her brother. ''And you, of all people, should have known better!''

Intrigued, Dominic allowed one brow to quirk upward. Holding the door wide, he bowed slightly, ushering both Bella and Georgiana into the drawing-room. He closed the door firmly.

''Now, Bella, cut line. What on earth made you leave Green Street in this hoydenish fashion?''

In response to her brother's crisp question, Bella simply stared.

''*Hoydenish?* Dominic Ridgeley! To call me hoydenish when you've all but compromised Georgiana by unthinkingly bringing her here when you might have guessed the snows were coming on. Why, if I hadn't set out as soon as the first snowflake fell, she'd have had to spend the night here with you unchaperoned. I would have thought with all your experience you would have seen the danger as well as I.''

''Precisely.''

The exasperated tone brought Bella's eyes to his face. Her confidence faltered. ''You knew...'' Bewildered, she glanced from Dominic's face to Georgiana's, then back again. ''I don't understand.''

Dominic sighed. ''Before your arrival interrupted us, Georgiana and I were examining a number of the reasons for our impending marriage. As my affianced wife, she most definitely does not need the services of a chaperon when with me.''

''Oh.'' Bella looked at Georgiana, but her protégée was watching Dominic, a strange little smile on her lips.

Dominic, meanwhile, had crossed to the bell-pull. "Yes. *Oh!* And, what's more, you'll have brought your husband out in these foul conditions—"

"But Arthur doesn't know," Bella interrupted to assure him.

"Most assuredly Arthur didn't know when you left Green Street. However, he will certainly have found out long since and be close behind you. Talking about people who should know better, dear sister, in your condition you have no business to go gallivanting around the country in snowstorms."

Bella gasped. "My condition? Whatever do you—?"

"My lord?"

Dominic turned to the door. "Ah, Mrs Landy."

But before he could give any orders, there came again the sound of the great front doors opening. Voices, all masculine, were heard in the hall.

Bella put a hand to her lips.

Dominic glanced at her but said nothing, his attention returning to the door.

Arthur walked in. One glance was sufficient for everyone to see he was displeased. He nodded a wordless greeting to his brother-in-law, then fixed his wife with a stern eye. "Bella, what's the meaning of this?"

Small hands fluttering, Bella went quickly to his side. "Arthur, you're frozen." When her husband's gaze did not waver, she hurriedly explained, "But really, you must see. If I hadn't come, Georgiana would have been alone here with Dominic."

"My dear, your brother is perfectly capable of managing his own affairs. You're my affair, and I cannot condone your careering across the countryside in this fashion. Not in your condition."

For the second time that evening, Bella was struck dumb.

Before she could recover her wits, Dominic smoothly intervened. "I suggest you let Mrs Landy take you upstairs, Bella. You should get to bed immediately."

"Quite so," agreed Arthur, turning to nod to Mrs Landy, still standing by the door. "My lady is expecting and needs to rest."

Abruptly Bella found her voice. "Whatever do you mean? I'm not—"

"Yes, you are!" said two male voices in emphatic unison.

Bella blinked. Then, as the truth dawned, she smiled beatifically. "Oh," she said.

"Arthur," pleaded Dominic, in a tone of desperation, "take her away. Please?"

Arthur smiled.

Mrs Landy took her cue and bustled forward. "Now if you'll just come along, Miss Bella, we'll get you nicely settled..."

Within a minute, an unresisting Bella had been borne away.

"I'm sure Duckett can organise some dinner for you," said Dominic to Arthur.

Arthur nodded. "If you don't mind, I'll take a tray upstairs with Bella. But first I think I'll go and find some of that excellent brandy you keep in your library.'' The shrewd grey gaze came to rest on Georgiana's face. ''I'm glad to see you've come to your senses, Georgiana. You belong here, my dear.'' With a smile and a nod to each of them, he left.

''Now where were we?'' asked Dominic, as he came to stand once more in front of Georgiana and drew her back into his arms.

Georgiana stared up into his face, her eyes alight with love and laughter. ''Did you really plan to compromise me?''

From under heavy lids, Dominic's blue eyes watched her. He smiled, slowly, knowing what it did to her. ''Mm-hm,'' he assented, nodding solemnly. ''After all, you did beg me not to offer for you. If I couldn't get you to agree any other way, then I was quite prepared to compromise you shamelessly.''

Returning the smile, his golden angel turned into a golden siren and wound her arms about his neck. ''Shamelessly?''

It was the last word Georgiana uttered for quite some time. A log crashing into the stillness of the room finally broke the spell that held them. Dominic raised his head and glanced around to make sure the log had not rolled from the hearth. Turning back, he surprised an impish smile on his love's face. One dark brow rose in question.

Georgiana saw it. She hesitated, then, her smile broadening, she explained, ''I was remembering the first time I saw the Fragonard.'' She inclined her head in the direction of the masterpiece above the fireplace. ''I wondered then what sort of man would hang such a painting in such a place.''

A rakish smile lit his face. "The same sort of man who has two other Fragonards."

Her golden eyes begged the invitation.

"Would you like to see the other two?"

"Mm-hm," Georgiana murmured, one tiny fingertip tracing the line of his jaw. "Where are they?"

"Upstairs," Dominic said, in between dropping tantalising little kisses along her lips. "In the master bedroom."

"Ah," said Georgiana, far more interested in his kisses than in any painting. After a moment she moved closer and asked, "Does that matter?"

With mock-seriousness, Dominic considered the point. One brow rose sternly. "It occurs to me, my love, that, as you have yet to formally accept my offer, such an excursion would be highly improper."

Georgiana smiled, letting her fingertip wander to trace the line of his lips. She glanced up at him through her lashes. "And if I were to accept your offer?"

The blue eyes gleamed. "That, of course, would cast an entirely different light on the matter."

Their gazes locked. For one moment, all was still. Then a slow smile twisted Dominic's lips.

"Georgiana, my love, will you marry me?"

Her face alight, Georgiana squealed as his arms tightened about her. "Yes!" she said, laughing. Then, as his head bent to hers, "Oh, yes."

Much later, curled on his lap, warm and secure and pleasantly intoxicated, Georgiana recalled the paintings. She looked into his face. His eyes were closed,

If you enjoyed what you just read,
then we've got an offer you can't resist!

Take 2 bestselling novels FREE!
Plus get a FREE surprise gift!

Clip this page and mail it to The Best of the Best™

IN U.S.A.
3010 Walden Ave.
P.O. Box 1867
Buffalo, N.Y. 14240-1867

IN CANADA
P.O. Box 609
Fort Erie, Ontario
L2A 5X3

YES! Please send me 2 free Best of the Best™ novels and my free surprise gift. After receiving them, if I don't wish to receive anymore, I can return the shipping statement marked cancel. If I don't cancel, I will receive 4 brand-new novels every month, before they're available in stores! In the U.S.A., bill me at the bargain price of $4.74 plus 25¢ shipping and handling per book and applicable sales tax, if any*. In Canada, bill me at the bargain price of $5.24 plus 25¢ shipping and handling per book and applicable taxes**. That's the complete price and a savings of over 20% off the cover prices—what a great deal! I understand that accepting the 2 free books and gift places me under no obligation ever to buy any books. I can always return a shipment and cancel at any time. Even if I never buy another The Best of the Best™ book, the 2 free books and gift are mine to keep forever.

185 MDN DNWF
385 MDN DNWG

Name	(PLEASE PRINT)	
Address	Apt.#	
City	State/Prov.	Zip/Postal Code

* Terms and prices subject to change without notice. Sales tax applicable in N.Y.
** Canadian residents will be charged applicable provincial taxes and GST.
All orders subject to approval. Offer limited to one per household and not valid to current The Best of the Best™ subscribers.
® are registered trademarks of Harlequin Enterprises Limited.

BOB02-R   ©1998 Harlequin Enterprises Limited

MIRABooks.com

We've got the lowdown on your favorite author!

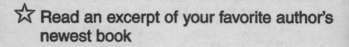

☆ Read an excerpt of your favorite author's newest book

☆ Check out her bio

☆ Talk to her in our Discussion Forums

☆ Read interviews, diaries, and more

☆ Find her current besteller, and even her backlist titles

All this and more available at

www.MiraBooks.com

MEAUT1R2